Stephen Crane (November 1, 1871 – June 5, 1900) was an American poet, novelist, and short story writer. Prolific throughout his short life, he wrote notable works in the Realist tradition as well as early examples of American Naturalism and Impressionism. He is recognized by modern critics as one of the most innovative writers of his generation. The ninth surviving child of Methodist parents, Crane began writing at the age of four and had published several articles by the age of 16. Having little interest in university studies though he was active in a fraternity, he left Syracuse University in 1891 to work as a reporter and writer. Crane's first novel was the 1893 Bowery tale Maggie: A Girl of the Streets, generally considered by critics to be the first work of American literary Naturalism. He won international acclaim in 1895 for his Civil War novel The Red Badge of Courage, which he wrote without having any battle experience. (Source: Wikipedia)

Literary works:
Maggie: A Girl of the Streets (1893)
The Red Badge of Courage (1895)
The Black Riders and Other Lines (1895)
George's Mother (1896)
The Third Violet (1897)
The Open Boat and Other Tales of Adventure (1898)
War is Kind (1899)
Active Service (1899)
The Monster and Other Stories (1899)
Wounds in the Rain (1900)
Great Battles of the World
The O'Ruddy (1903)
The Monster. London
Last Words. London
Whilomville Stories

PRINCE CLASSICS

WHILOMVILLE
STORIES
(ILLUSTRATED)
&
MAGGIE

STEPHEN CRANE

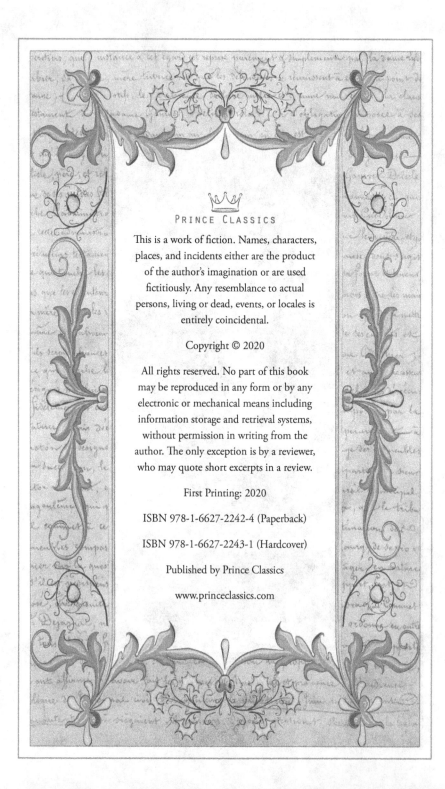

PRINCE CLASSICS

This is a work of fiction. Names, characters, places, and incidents either are the product of the author's imagination or are used fictitiously. Any resemblance to actual persons, living or dead, events, or locales is entirely coincidental.

First Printing: 2020

ISBN 978-1-6627-2242-4 (Paperback)

ISBN 978-1-6627-2243-1 (Hardcover)

Published by Prince Classics

www.princeclassics.com

Contents

WHILOMVILLE
STORIES
(ILLUSTRATED)
&
MAGGIE

WHILOMVILLE STORIES
(ILLUSTRATED)

I. THE ANGEL CHILD

I

ALTHOUGH Whilomville was in no sense a summer resort, the advent of the warm season meant much to it, for then came visitors from the city— people of considerable confidence—alighting upon their country cousins. Moreover, many citizens who could afford to do so escaped at this time to the sea-side. The town, with the commercial life quite taken out of it, drawled and drowsed through long months, during which nothing was worse than the white dust which arose behind every vehicle at blinding noon, and nothing was finer than the cool sheen of the hose sprays over the cropped lawns under the many maples in the twilight.

One summer the Trescotts had a visitation. Mrs. Trescott owned a cousin who was a painter of high degree. I had almost said that he was of national reputation, but, come to think of it, it is better to say that almost everybody in the United States who knew about art and its travail knew about him. He had picked out a wife, and naturally, looking at him, one wondered how he had done it. She was quick, beautiful, imperious, while he was quiet, slow, and misty. She was a veritable queen of health, while he, apparently, was of a most brittle constitution. When he played tennis, particularly, he looked every minute as if he were going to break.

They lived in New York, in awesome apartments wherein Japan and Persia, and indeed all the world, confounded the observer. At the end was a cathedral-like studio. They had one child. Perhaps it would be better to say that they had one CHILD. It was a girl. When she came to Whilomville with her parents, it was patent that she had an inexhaustible store of white frocks, and that her voice was high and commanding. These things the town knew quickly. Other things it was doomed to discover by a process.

Her effect upon the children of the Trescott neighborhood was singular. They at first feared, then admired, then embraced. In two days she was a Begum. All day long her voice could be heard directing, drilling, and compelling those free-born children; and to say that they felt oppression would be wrong, for they really fought for records of loyal obedience.

All went well until one day was her birthday.

On the morning of this day she walked out into the Trescott garden and said to her father, confidently, "Papa, give me some money, because this is my birthday."

He looked dreamily up from his easel. "Your birthday?" he murmured. Her envisioned father was never energetic enough to be irritable unless some one broke through into that place where he lived with the desires of his life. But neither wife nor child ever heeded or even understood the temperamental values, and so some part of him had grown hardened to their inroads. "Money?" he said. "Here." He handed her a five-dollar bill. It was that he did not at all understand the nature of a five-dollar bill. He was deaf to it. He had it; he gave it; that was all.

She sallied forth to a waiting people—Jimmie Trescott, Dan Earl, Ella Earl, the Margate twins, the three Phelps children, and others. "I've got some pennies now," she cried, waving the bill, "and I am going to buy some candy." They were deeply stirred by this announcement. Most children are penniless three hundred days in the year, and to another possessing five pennies they pay deference. To little Cora waving a bright green note these children paid heathenish homage. In some disorder they thronged after her to a small shop on Bridge Street hill. First of all came ice-cream. Seated in the comic little back parlor, they clamored shrilly over plates of various flavors, and the shopkeeper marvelled that cream could vanish so quickly down throats that seemed wide open, always, for the making of excited screams.

These children represented the families of most excellent people. They were all born in whatever purple there was to be had in the vicinity of Whilomville. The Margate twins, for example, were out-and-out prizewinners. With their long golden curls and their countenances of similar vacuity, they shone upon the front bench of all Sunday-school functions, hand in hand, while their uplifted mother felt about her the envy of a hundred other parents, and less heavenly children scoffed from near the door.

Then there was little Dan Earl, probably the nicest boy in the world, gentle, fine-grained, obedient to the point where he obeyed anybody. Jimmie Trescott himself was, indeed, the only child who was at all versed in villany, but in these particular days he was on his very good behavior. As a matter of fact, he was in love. The beauty of his regal little cousin had stolen his manly heart.

Yes, they were all most excellent children, but, loosened upon this candy-shop with five dollars, they resembled, in a tiny way, drunken revelling soldiers within the walls of a stormed city. Upon the heels of ice-cream and cake came chocolate mice, butter-scotch, "everlastings," chocolate cigars, taffy-on-a-stick, taffy-on-a-slate-pencil, and many semi-transparent devices resembling lions, tigers, elephants, horses, cats, dogs, cows, sheep, tables, chairs, engines (both railway and for the fighting of fire), soldiers, fine ladies, odd-looking men, clocks, watches, revolvers, rabbits, and bedsteads. A cent was the price of a single wonder.

Some of the children, going quite daft, soon had thought to make fight over the spoils, but their queen ruled with an iron grip. Her first inspiration was to satisfy her own fancies, but as soon as that was done she mingled prodigality with a fine justice, dividing, balancing, bestowing, and sometimes taking away from somebody even that which he had.

It was an orgy. In thirty-five minutes those respectable children looked as if they had been dragged at the tail of a chariot. The sacred Margate twins, blinking and grunting, wished to take seat upon the floor, and even the most durable Jimmie Trescott found occasion to lean against the counter, wearing at the time a solemn and abstracted air, as if he expected something to happen to him shortly.

Of course their belief had been in an unlimited capacity, but they found there was an end. The shopkeeper handed the queen her change.

"Two seventy-three from five leaves two twenty-seven, Miss Cora," he said, looking upon her with admiration.

She turned swiftly to her clan. "O-oh!" she cried, in amazement. "Look how much I have left!" They gazed at the coins in her palm. They knew then that it was not their capacities which were endless; it was the five dollars.

The queen led the way to the street. "We must think up some way of spending more money," she said, frowning. They stood in silence, awaiting her further speech.

Suddenly she clapped her hands and screamed with delight. "Come on!" she cried. "I know what let's do." Now behold, she had discovered the red and white pole in front of the shop of one William Neeltje, a barber by trade.

It becomes necessary to say a few words concerning Neeltje. He was new to the town. He had come and opened a dusty little shop on dusty Bridge Street hill, and although the neighborhood knew from the courier winds that his diet was mainly cabbage, they were satisfied with that meagre data. Of course Riefsnyder came to investigate him for the local Barbers' Union, but he found in him only sweetness and light, with a willingness to charge any price at all for a shave or a haircut. In fact, the advent of Neeltje would have made barely a ripple upon the placid bosom of Whilomville if it were not that his name was Neeltje.

At first the people looked at his sign-board out of the eye corner, and wondered lazily why any one should bear the name of Neeltje; but as time went on, men spoke to other men, saying, "How do you pronounce the name of that barber up there on Bridge Street hill?" And then, before any could prevent it, the best minds of the town were splintering their lances against William Neeltje's sign-board. If a man had a mental superior, he guided him seductively to this name, and watched with glee his wrecking. The clergy of the town even entered the lists. There was one among them who had taken a collegiate prize in Syriac, as well as in several less opaque languages, and the other clergymen—at one of their weekly meetings—sought to betray him into this ambush. He pronounced the name correctly, but that mattered

16

little, since none of them knew whether he did or did not; and so they took triumph according to their ignorance. Under these arduous circumstances it was certain that the town should look for a nickname, and at this time the nickname was in process of formation. So William Neeltje lived on with his secret, smiling foolishly towards the world.

"Come on," cried little Cora. "Let's all get our hair cut. That's what let's do. Let's all get our hair cut! Come on! Come on! Come on!" The others were carried off their feet by the fury of this assault. To get their hair cut! What joy! Little did they know if this were fun; they only knew that their small leader said it was fun. Chocolate-stained but confident, the band marched into William Neeltje's barber shop.

"We wish to get our hair cut," said little Cora, haughtily.

Neeltje, in his shirt-sleeves, stood looking at them with his half-idiot smile.

"Hurry, now!" commanded the queen. A dray-horse toiled step by step, step by step, up Bridge Street hill; a far woman's voice arose; there could be heard the ceaseless hammers of shingling carpenters; all was summer peace. "Come on, now. Who's goin' first? Come on, Ella; you go first. Gettin' our hair cut! Oh what fun!"

Little Ella Earl would not, however, be first in the chair. She was drawn towards it by a singular fascination, but at the same time she was afraid of it, and so she hung back, saying: "No! You go first! No! You go first!" The question was precipitated by the twins and one of the Phelps children. They made simultaneous rush for the chair, and screamed and kicked, each pair preventing the third child. The queen entered this mêlée, and decided in favor of the Phelps boy. He ascended the chair. Thereat an awed silence fell upon the band. And always William Neeltje smiled fatuously.

He tucked a cloth in the neck of the Phelps boy, and taking scissors, began to cut his hair. The group of children came closer and closer. Even the queen was deeply moved. "Does it hurt any?" she asked, in a wee voice.

"Naw," said the Phelps boy, with dignity. "Anyhow, I've had m' hair cut afore."

When he appeared to them looking very soldierly with his cropped little head, there was a tumult over the chair. The Margate twins howled; Jimmie Trescott was kicking them on the shins. It was a fight.

But the twins could not prevail, being the smallest of all the children. The queen herself took the chair, and ordered Neeltje as if he were a lady's-maid. To the floor there fell proud ringlets, blazing even there in their humiliation with a full fine bronze light. Then Jimmie Trescott, then Ella Earl (two long ash-colored plaits), then a Phelps girl, then another Phelps girl; and so on from head to head. The ceremony received unexpected check when the turn came to Dan Earl. This lad, usually docile to any rein, had suddenly grown mulishly obstinate. No, he would not, he would not. He himself did not seem to know why he refused to have his hair cut, but, despite the shrill derision of the company, he remained obdurate. Anyhow, the twins, long held in check, and now feverishly eager, were already struggling for the chair.

"THE QUEEN HERSELF TOOK THE CHAIR"

And so to the floor at last came the golden Margate curls, the heart treasure and glory of a mother, three aunts, and some feminine cousins.

All having been finished, the children, highly elate, thronged out into the street. They crowed and cackled with pride and joy, anon turning to scorn the cowardly Dan Earl.

Ella Earl was an exception. She had been pensive for some time, and now the shorn little maiden began vaguely to weep. In the door of his shop William Neeltje stood watching them, upon his face a grin of almost inhuman idiocy.

II

It now becomes the duty of the unfortunate writer to exhibit these children to their fond parents. "Come on, Jimmie," cried little Cora, "let's go show mamma." And they hurried off, these happy children, to show mamma.

The Trescotts and their guests were assembled indolently awaiting the luncheon-bell. Jimmie and the angel child burst in upon them. "Oh, mamma," shrieked little Cora, "see how fine I am! I've had my hair cut! Isn't it splendid? And Jimmie too!"

The wretched mother took one sight, emitted one yell, and fell into a chair. Mrs. Trescott dropped a large lady's journal and made a nerveless mechanical clutch at it. The painter gripped the arms of his chair and leaned forward, staring until his eyes were like two little clock faces. Dr. Trescott did not move or speak.

To the children the next moments were chaotic. There was a loudly wailing mother, and a pale-faced, aghast mother; a stammering father, and a grim and terrible father. The angel child did not understand anything of it save the voice of calamity, and in a moment all her little imperialism went to the winds. She ran sobbing to her mother. "Oh, mamma! mamma! mamma!"

The desolate Jimmie heard out of this inexplicable situation a voice which he knew well, a sort of colonel's voice, and he obeyed like any good soldier. "Jimmie!"

He stepped three paces to the front. "Yes, sir."

"How did this—how did this happen?" said Trescott.

Now Jimmie could have explained how had happened anything which had happened, but he did not know what had happened, so he said, "I—I—nothin'."

"'LOOK!' SHE DECLAIMED"

The words turned the mind of the mother of the angel child. She looked up, her eyes blazing. "Frock!" she repeated. "Frock! What do I care for her frock? Frock!" she choked out again from the depths of her bitterness. Then she arose suddenly, and whirled tragically upon her husband. "Look!" she declaimed. "All—her lovely—hair—all her lovely hair—gone—gone!" The painter was apparently in a fit; his jaw was set, his eyes were glazed, his body was stiff and straight. "All gone—all—her lovely hair—all gone—my poor little darlin'—my—poor—little—darlin'!" And the angel child added her heart-broken voice to her mother's wail as they fled into each other's arms.

In the mean time Trescott was patiently unravelling some skeins of Jimmie's tangled intellect. "And then you went to this barber's on the hill. Yes. And where did you get the money? Yes. I see. And who besides you and Cora had their hair cut? The Margate twi—Oh, lord!"

Over at the Margate place old Eldridge Margate, the grandfather of the twins, was in the back garden picking pease and smoking ruminatively to himself. Suddenly he heard from the house great noises. Doors slammed, women rushed up-stairs and down-stairs calling to each other in voices of agony. And then full and mellow upon the still air arose the roar of the twins in pain.

Old Eldridge stepped out of the pea-patch and moved towards the house, puzzled, staring, not yet having decided that it was his duty to rush forward. Then around the corner of the house shot his daughter Mollie, her face pale with horror.

"What's the matter?" he cried.

"Oh, father," she gasped, "the children! They—"

Then around the corner of the house came the twins, howling at the top of their power, their faces flowing with tears. They were still hand in hand, the ruling passion being strong even in this suffering. At sight of them old Eldridge took his pipe hastily out of his mouth. "Good God!" he said.

And now what befell one William Neeltje, a barber by trade? And what was said by angry parents of the mother of such an angel child? And what was the fate of the angel child herself?

There was surely a tempest. With the exception of the Margate twins, the boys could well be eliminated from the affair. Of course it didn't matter if their hair was cut. Also the two little Phelps girls had had very short hair, anyhow, and their parents were not too greatly incensed. In the case of Ella Earl, it was mainly the pathos of the little girl's own grieving; but her mother played a most generous part, and called upon Mrs. Trescott, and condoled with the mother of the angel child over their equivalent losses. But the Margate contingent! They simply screeched.

"AROUND THE CORNER OF THE HOUSE CAME THE TWINS"

Trescott, composed and cool-blooded, was in the middle of a giddy whirl. He was not going to allow the mobbing of his wife's cousins, nor was he going to pretend that the spoliation of the Margate twins was a virtuous and beautiful act. He was elected, gratuitously, to the position of a buffer.

But, curiously enough, the one who achieved the bulk of the misery was old Eldridge Margate, who had been picking pease at the time. The feminine Margates stormed his position as individuals, in pairs, in teams, and *en masse*. In two days they may have aged him seven years. He must destroy the utter Neeltje. He must midnightly massacre the angel child and her mother. He must dip his arms in blood to the elbows.

Trescott took the first opportunity to express to him his concern over the affair, but when the subject of the disaster was mentioned, old Eldridge, to the doctor's great surprise, actually chuckled long and deeply. "Oh, well, look-a-here," he said. "I never was so much in love with them there damn curls. The curls was purty—yes—but then I'd a darn sight rather see boys look more like boys than like two little wax figgers. An', ye know, the little cusses like it themselves. *They* never took no stock in all this washin' an' combin' an' fixin' an' goin' to church an' paradin' an' showin' off. They stood it because they were told to. That's all. Of course this here Neel-te-gee, er whatever his name is, is a plumb dumb ijit, but I don't see what's to be done, now that the kids is full well cropped. I might go and burn his shop over his head, but that wouldn't bring no hair back onto the kids. They're even kicking on sashes now, and that's all right, 'cause what fer does a boy want a sash?"

Whereupon Trescott perceived that the old man wore his brains above his shoulders, and Trescott departed from him rejoicing greatly that it was only women who could not know that there was finality to most disasters, and that when a thing was fully done, no amount of door-slammings, rushing up-stairs and down-stairs, calls, lamentations, tears, could bring back a single hair to the heads of twins.

But the rains came and the winds blew in the most biblical way when a certain fact came to light in the Trescott household. Little Cora, corroborated by Jimmie, innocently remarked that five dollars had been given her by her father on her birthday, and with this money the evil had been wrought.

Trescott had known it, but he—thoughtful man—had said nothing. For her part, the mother of the angel child had up to that moment never reflected that the consummation of the wickedness must have cost a small sum of money. But now it was all clear to her. He was the guilty one—he! "My angel child!"

AT THE RAILWAY STATION

The scene which ensued was inspiriting. A few days later, loungers at the railway station saw a lady leading a shorn and still undaunted lamb. Attached to them was a husband and father, who was plainly bewildered, but still more plainly vexed, as if he would be saying: "Damn 'em! Why can't they leave me alone?"

II. LYNX-HUNTING

JIMMIE lounged about the dining-room and watched his mother with large, serious eyes. Suddenly he said, "Ma—now—can I borrow pa's gun?"

She was overcome with the feminine horror which is able to mistake preliminary words for the full accomplishment of the dread thing. "Why, Jimmie!" she cried. "Of al-l wonders! Your father's gun! No indeed you can't!"

He was fairly well crushed, but he managed to mutter, sullenly, "Well, Willie Dalzel, he's got a gun." In reality his heart had previously been beating with such tumult—he had himself been so impressed with the daring and sin of his request—that he was glad that all was over now, and his mother could do very little further harm to his sensibilities. He had been influenced into the venture by the larger boys.

"'MA—NOW—CAN I BORROW PA'S GUN?'"

"Huh!" the Dalzel urchin had said; "your father's got a gun, hasn't he? Well, why don't you bring that?"

Puffing himself, Jimmie had replied, "Well, I can, if I want to." It was a black lie, but really the Dalzel boy was too outrageous with his eternal bill-posting about the gun which a beaming uncle had intrusted to him. Its possession made him superior in manfulness to most boys in the neighborhood—or at least they enviously conceded him such position—but he was so overbearing, and stuffed the fact of his treasure so relentlessly down their throats, that on this occasion the miserable Jimmie had lied as naturally as most animals swim.

Willie Dalzel had not been checkmated, for he had instantly retorted, "Why don't you get it, then?"

"Well, I can, if I want to."

"Well, get it, then!"

"Well, I can, if I want to."

Thereupon Jimmie had paced away with great airs of surety as far as the door of his home, where his manner changed to one of tremulous misgiving as it came upon him to address his mother in the dining-room. There had happened that which had happened.

When Jimmie returned to his two distinguished companions he was blown out with a singular pomposity. He spoke these noble words: "Oh, well, I guess I don't want to take the gun out to-day."

They had been watching him with gleaming ferret eyes, and they detected his falsity at once. They challenged him with shouted gibes, but it was not in the rules for the conduct of boys that one should admit anything whatsoever, and so Jimmie, backed into an ethical corner, lied as stupidly, as desperately, as hopelessly as ever lone savage fights when surrounded at last in his jungle.

Such accusations were never known to come to any point, for the reason that the number and kind of denials always equalled or exceeded the number of accusations, and no boy was ever brought really to book for these misdeeds.

In the end they went off together, Willie Dalzel with his gun being a trifle in advance and discoursing upon his various works. They passed along a maple-lined avenue, a highway common to boys bound for that free land of hills and woods in which they lived in some part their romance of the moment, whether it was of Indians, miners, smugglers, soldiers, or outlaws. The paths were their paths, and much was known to them of the secrets of the dark green hemlock thickets, the wastes of sweet-fern and huckleberry, the cliffs of gaunt bluestone with the sumach burning red at their feet. Each boy had, I am sure, a conviction that some day the wilderness was to give forth to him a marvellous secret. They felt that the hills and the forest knew much, and they heard a voice of it in the silence. It was vague, thrilling, fearful, and altogether fabulous. The grown folk seemed to regard these wastes merely as so much distance between one place and another place, or as a rabbit-cover, or as a district to be judged according to the value of the timber; but to the boys it spoke some great inspiring word, which they knew even as those who pace the shore know the enigmatic speech of the surf. In the mean time they lived there, in season, lives of ringing adventure—by dint of imagination.

The boys left the avenue, skirted hastily through some private grounds, climbed a fence, and entered the thickets. It happened that at school the previous day Willie Dalzel had been forced to read and acquire in some part a solemn description of a lynx. The meagre information thrust upon him had caused him grimaces of suffering, but now he said, suddenly, "I'm goin' to shoot a lynx."

The other boys admired this statement, but they were silent for a time. Finally Jimmie said, meekly, "What's a lynx?" He had endured his ignorance as long as he was able.

The Dalzel boy mocked him. "Why, don't you know what a lynx is? A lynx? Why, a lynx is a animal somethin' like a cat, an' it's got great big green eyes, and it sits on the limb of a tree an' jus' glares at you. It's a pretty bad animal, I tell you. Why, when I—"

"Huh!" said the third boy. "Where'd you ever see a lynx?"

"Oh, I've seen 'em—plenty of 'em. I bet you'd be scared if you seen one once."

Jimmie and the other boy each demanded, "How do you know I would?"

They penetrated deeper into the wood. They climbed a rocky zigzag path which led them at times where with their hands they could almost touch the tops of giant pines. The gray cliffs sprang sheer towards the sky. Willie Dalzel babbled about his impossible lynx, and they stalked the mountain-side like chamois-hunters, although no noise of bird or beast broke the stillness of the hills. Below them Whilomville was spread out somewhat like the cheap green and black lithograph of the time—"A Bird's-eye View of Whilomville, N. Y."

THE DALZEL BOY TAKING THE PART OF A BANDIT CHIEF

In the end the boys reached the top of the mountain and scouted off among wild and desolate ridges. They were burning with the desire to slay large animals. They thought continually of elephants, lions, tigers, crocodiles. They discoursed upon their immaculate conduct in case such monsters confronted them, and they all lied carefully about their courage.

The breeze was heavy with the smell of sweet-fern. The pines and hemlocks sighed as they waved their branches. In the hollows the leaves of the laurels were lacquered where the sunlight found them. No matter the weather, it would be impossible to long continue an expedition of this kind without a fire, and presently they built one, snapping down for fuel the brittle under-branches of the pines. About this fire they were willed to conduct a sort of play, the Dalzel boy taking the part of a bandit chief, and the other boys being his trusty lieutenants. They stalked to and fro, long-strided, stern yet devil-may-care, three terrible little figures.

Jimmie had an uncle who made game of him whenever he caught him in this kind of play, and often this uncle quoted derisively the following classic: "Once aboard the lugger, Bill, and the girl is mine. Now to burn the château and destroy all evidence of our crime. But, hark'e, Bill, no wiolence." Wheeling abruptly, he addressed these dramatic words to his comrades. They were impressed; they decided at once to be smugglers, and in the most ribald fashion they talked about carrying off young women.

At last they continued their march through the woods. The smuggling *motif* was now grafted fantastically upon the original lynx idea, which Willie Dalzel refused to abandon at any price.

Once they came upon an innocent bird who happened to be looking another way at the time. After a great deal of manœvering and big words, Willie Dalzel reared his fowling-piece and blew this poor thing into a mere rag of wet feathers, of which he was proud.

Afterwards the other big boy had a turn at another bird. Then it was plainly Jimmie's chance. The two others had, of course, some thought of cheating him out of this chance, but of a truth he was timid to explode such a thunderous weapon, and as soon as they detected this fear they simply overbore him, and made it clearly understood that if he refused to shoot he would lose his caste, his scalp-lock, his girdle, his honor.

They had reached the old death-colored snake-fence which marked the limits of the upper pasture of the Fleming farm. Under some hickory-trees the path ran parallel to the fence. Behold! a small priestly chipmonk came to a rail, and folding his hands on his abdomen, addressed them in his own tongue. It was Jimmie's shot. Adjured by the others, he took the gun. His face was stiff with apprehension. The Dalzel boy was giving forth fine words. "Go ahead. Aw, don't be afraid. It's nothin' to do. Why, I've done it a million times. Don't shut both your eyes, now. Jus' keep one open and shut the other one. He'll get away if you don't watch out. Now you're all right. Why don't you let 'er go? Go ahead."

"THERE WAS A FRIGHTFUL ROAR"

Jimmie, with his legs braced apart, was in the centre of the path. His back was greatly bent, owing to the mechanics of supporting the heavy gun. His companions were screeching in the rear. There was a wait.

Then he pulled trigger. To him there was a frightful roar, his cheek and his shoulder took a stunning blow, his face felt a hot flush of fire, and opening his two eyes, he found that he was still alive. He was not too dazed to instantly adopt a becoming egotism. It had been the first shot of his life.

But directly after the well-mannered celebration of this victory a certain cow, which had been grazing in the line of fire, was seen to break wildly across the pasture, bellowing and bucking. The three smugglers and lynx-hunters looked at each other out of blanched faces. Jimmie had hit the cow. The first evidence of his comprehension of this fact was in the celerity with which he returned the discharged gun to Willie Dalzel.

They turned to flee. The land was black, as if it had been overshadowed suddenly with thick storm-clouds, and even as they fled in their horror a gigantic Swedish farm-hand came from the heavens and fell upon them, shrieking in eerie triumph. In a twinkle they were clouted prostrate. The Swede was elate and ferocious in a foreign and fulsome way. He continued to beat them and yell.

From the ground they raised their dismal appeal. "Oh, please, mister, we didn't do it! He did it! I didn't do it! We didn't do it! We didn't mean to do it! Oh, please, mister!"

In these moments of childish terror little lads go half-blind, and it is possible that few moments of their after-life made them suffer as they did when the Swede flung them over the fence and marched them towards the farm-house. They begged like cowards on the scaffold, and each one was for himself. "Oh, please let me go, mister! I didn't do it, mister! He did it! Oh, p-l-ease let me go, mister!"

The boyish view belongs to boys alone, and if this tall and knotted laborer was needlessly without charity, none of the three lads questioned it.

Usually when they were punished they decided that they deserved it, and the more they were punished the more they were convinced that they were criminals of a most subterranean type. As to the hitting of the cow being a pure accident, and therefore not of necessity a criminal matter, such reading never entered their heads. When things happened and they were caught, they commonly paid dire consequences, and they were accustomed to measure the probabilities of woe utterly by the damage done, and not in any way by the culpability. The shooting of the cow was plainly heinous, and undoubtedly their dungeons would be knee-deep in water.

"'I THOUGHT SHE WAS A LYNX'"

"He did it, mister!" This was a general outcry. Jimmie used it as often as did the others. As for them, it is certain that they had no direct thought of betraying their comrade for their own salvation. They thought themselves guilty because they were caught; when boys were not caught they might possibly be innocent. But captured boys were guilty. When they cried out that Jimmie was the culprit, it was principally a simple expression of terror.

Old Henry Fleming, the owner of the farm, strode across the pasture towards them. He had in his hand a most cruel whip. This whip he flourished. At his approach the boys suffered the agonies of the fire regions. And yet anybody with half an eye could see that the whip in his hand was a mere accident, and that he was a kind old man—when he cared.

When he had come near he spoke crisply. "What you boys ben doin' to my cow?" The tone had deep threat in it. They all answered by saying that none of them had shot the cow. Their denials were tearful and clamorous, and they crawled knee by knee. The vision of it was like three martyrs being dragged towards the stake. Old Fleming stood there, grim, tight-lipped. After a time he said, "Which boy done it?"

There was some confusion, and then Jimmie spake. "I done it, mister."

Fleming looked at him. Then he asked, "Well, what did you shoot 'er fer?"

Jimmie thought, hesitated, decided, faltered, and then formulated this: "I thought she was a lynx."

Old Fleming and his Swede at once lay down in the grass and laughed themselves helpless.

III. THE LOVER AND THE TELLTALE

WHEN the angel child returned with her parents to New York, the fond heart of Jimmie Trescott felt its bruise greatly. For two days he simply moped, becoming a stranger to all former joys. When his old comrades yelled invitation, as they swept off on some interesting quest, he replied with mournful gestures of disillusion.

He thought often of writing to her, but of course the shame of it made him pause. Write a letter to a girl? The mere enormity of the idea caused him shudders. Persons of his quality never wrote letters to girls. Such was the occupation of mollycoddles and snivellers. He knew that if his acquaintances and friends found in him evidences of such weakness and general milkiness, they would fling themselves upon him like so many wolves, and bait him beyond the borders of sanity.

However, one day at school, in that time of the morning session when children of his age were allowed fifteen minutes of play in the school-grounds, he did not as usual rush forth ferociously to his games. Commonly he was of the worst hoodlums, preying upon his weaker brethren with all the cruel disregard of a grown man. On this particular morning he stayed in the school-room, and with his tongue stuck from the corner of his mouth, and his head twisting in a painful way, he wrote to little Cora, pouring out to her all the poetry of his hungry soul, as follows: "My dear Cora I love thee with all my hart oh come bac again, bac, bac gain for I love thee best of all oh come bac again When the spring come again we'l fly and we'l fly like a brid."

As for the last word, he knew under normal circumstances perfectly well how to spell "bird," but in this case he had transposed two of the letters through excitement, supreme agitation.

Nor had this letter been composed without fear and furtive glancing. There was always a number of children who, for the time, cared more for the quiet of the school-room than for the tempest of the play-ground, and there was always that dismal company who were being forcibly deprived of their recess—who were being "kept in." More than one curious eye was turned upon the desperate and lawless Jimmie Trescott suddenly taken to ways of peace, and as he felt these eyes he flushed guiltily, with felonious glances from side to side.

It happened that a certain vigilant little girl had a seat directly across the aisle from Jimmie's seat, and she had remained in the room during the intermission, because of her interest in some absurd domestic details concerning her desk. Parenthetically it might be stated that she was in the habit of imagining this desk to be a house, and at this time, with an important little frown, indicative of a proper matron, she was engaged in dramatizing her ideas of a household.

But this small Rose Goldege happened to be of a family which numbered few males. It was, in fact, one of those curious middle-class families that hold much of their ground, retain most of their position, after all their visible means of support have been dropped in the grave. It contained now only a collection of women who existed submissively, defiantly, securely, mysteriously, in a pretentious and often exasperating virtue. It was often too triumphantly clear that they were free of bad habits. However, bad habits is a term here used in a commoner meaning, because it is certainly true that the principal and indeed solitary joy which entered their lonely lives was the joy of talking wickedly and busily about their neighbors. It was all done without dream of its being of the vulgarity of the alleys. Indeed it was simply a constitutional but not incredible chastity and honesty expressing itself in its ordinary superior way of the whirling circles of life, and the vehemence of the criticism was not lessened by a further infusion of an acid of worldly defeat, worldly suffering, and worldly hopelessness.

Out of this family circle had sprung the typical little girl who discovered Jimmie Trescott agonizingly writing a letter to his sweetheart. Of course all the children were the most abandoned gossips, but she was peculiarly adapted to the purpose of making Jimmie miserable over this particular point. It was her life to sit of evenings about the stove and hearken to her mother and a lot of spinsters talk of many things. During these evenings she was never licensed to utter an opinion either one way or the other way. She was then simply a very little girl sitting open-eyed in the gloom, and listening to many things which she often interpreted wrongly. They on their part kept up a kind of a smug-faced pretence of concealing from her information in detail of the widespread crime, which pretence may have been more elaborately dangerous than no pretence at all. Thus all her home-teaching fitted her to recognize at once in Jimmie Trescott's manner that he was concealing something that would properly interest the world. She set up a scream. "Oh! Oh! Oh! Jimmie Trescott's writing to his girl! Oh! Oh!"

Jimmie cast a miserable glance upon her—a glance in which hatred mingled with despair. Through the open window he could hear the boisterous cries of his friends—his hoodlum friends—who would no more understand the utter poetry of his position than they would understand an ancient tribal sign-language. His face was set in a truer expression of horror than any of the romances describe upon the features of a man flung into a moat, a man shot in the breast with an arrow, a man cleft in the neck with a battle-axe. He was suppedaneous of the fullest power of childish pain. His one course was to rush upon her and attempt, by an impossible means of strangulation, to keep her important news from the public.

The teacher, a thoughtful young woman at her desk upon the platform, saw a little scuffle which informed her that two of her scholars were larking. She called out sharply. The command penetrated to the middle of an early world struggle. In Jimmie's age there was no particular scruple in the minds of the male sex against laying warrior hands upon their weaker sisters. But, of course, this voice from the throne hindered Jimmie in what might have been a berserk attack.

Even the little girl was retarded by the voice, but, without being unlawful, she managed soon to shy through the door and out upon the play-ground, yelling, "Oh, Jimmie Trescott's been writing to his girl!"

The unhappy Jimmie was following as closely as he was allowed by his knowledge of the decencies to be preserved under the eye of the teacher.

37

Jimmie himself was mainly responsible for the scene which ensued on the play-ground. It is possible that the little girl might have run, shrieking his infamy, without exciting more than a general but unmilitant interest. These barbarians were excited only by the actual appearance of human woe; in that event they cheered and danced. Jimmie made the strategic mistake of pursuing little Rose, and thus exposed his thin skin to the whole school. He had in his cowering mind a vision of a hundred children turning from their play under the maple-trees and speeding towards him over the gravel with sudden wild taunts. Upon him drove a yelping demoniac mob, to which his words were futile. He saw in this mob boys that he dimly knew, and his deadly enemies, and his retainers, and his most intimate friends. The virulence of his deadly enemy was no greater than the virulence of his intimate friend. From the outskirts the little informer could be heard still screaming the news, like a toy parrot with clock-work inside of it. It broke up all sorts of games, not so much because of the mere fact of the letter-writing, as because the children knew that some sufferer was at the last point, and, like little blood-fanged wolves, they thronged to the scene of his destruction. They galloped about him shrilly chanting insults. He turned from one to another, only to meet with howls. He was baited.

Then, in one instant, he changed all this with a blow. Bang! The most pitiless of the boys near him received a punch, fairly and skilfully, which made him bellow out like a walrus, and then Jimmie laid desperately into the whole world, striking out frenziedly in all directions. Boys who could handily whip him, and knew it, backed away from this onslaught. Here was intention—serious intention. They themselves were not in frenzy, and their cooler judgment respected Jimmie's efforts when he ran amuck. They saw that it really was none of their affair. In the mean time the wretched little girl who had caused the bloody riot was away, by the fence, weeping because boys were fighting.

Jimmie several times hit the wrong boy—that is to say, he several times hit a wrong boy hard enough to arouse also in him a spirit of strife. Jimmie wore a little shirt-waist. It was passing now rapidly into oblivion. He was sobbing, and there was one blood stain upon his cheek. The school-ground sounded like a pinetree when a hundred crows roost in it at night.

"THEY GALLOPED ABOUT HIM, SHRILLY CHANTING INSULTS."

Then upon the situation there pealed a brazen bell. It was a bell that these children obeyed, even as older nations obey the formal law which is printed in calf-skin. It smote them into some sort of inaction; even Jimmie was influenced by its potency, although, as a finale, he kicked out lustily into the legs of an intimate friend who had been one of the foremost in the torture.

When they came to form into line for the march into the school-room it was curious that Jimmie had many admirers. It was not his prowess; it was the soul he had infused into his gymnastics; and he, still panting, looked about him with a stern and challenging glare.

And yet when the long tramping line had entered the school-room his status had again changed. The other children then began to regard him as a boy in disrepair, and boys in disrepair were always accosted ominously from the throne. Jimmie's march towards his seat was a feat. It was composed partly of a most slinking attempt to dodge the perception of the teacher and partly of pure braggadocio erected for the benefit of his observant fellow-men.

The teacher looked carefully down at him. "Jimmie Trescott," she said.

"Yes'm," he answered, with businesslike briskness, which really spelled out falsity in all its letters.

"Come up to the desk."

He rose amid the awe of the entire school-room. When he arrived she said,

"Jimmie, you've been fighting."

"Yes'm," he answered. This was not so much an admission of the fact as it was a concessional answer to anything she might say.

"Who have you been fighting?" she asked.

"I dunno', 'm."

Whereupon the empress blazed out in wrath. "You don't know who you've been fighting?"

Jimmie looked at her gloomily. "No, 'm."

She seemed about to disintegrate to mere flaming fagots of anger. "You don't know who you've been fighting?" she demanded, blazing. "Well, you stay in after school until you find out."

As he returned to his place all the children knew by his vanquished air that sorrow had fallen upon the house of Trescott. When he took his seat he saw gloating upon him the satanic black eyes of the little Goldege girl.

IV. "SHOWIN' OFF"

JIMMIE TRESCOTT'S new velocipede had the largest front wheel of any velocipede in Whilomville. When it first arrived from New York he wished to sacrifice school, food, and sleep to it. Evidently he wished to become a sort of a perpetual velocipede-rider. But the powers of the family laid a number of judicious embargoes upon him, and he was prevented from becoming a fanatic. Of course this caused him to retain a fondness for the three-wheeled thing much longer than if he had been allowed to debauch himself for a span of days. But in the end it was an immaterial machine to him. For long periods he left it idle in the stable.

One day he loitered from school towards home by a very circuitous route. He was accompanied by only one of his retainers. The object of this détour was the wooing of a little girl in a red hood. He had been in love with her for some three weeks. His desk was near her desk in school, but he had never spoken to her. He had been afraid to take such a radical step. It was not customary to speak to girls. Even boys who had school-going sisters seldom addressed them during that part of a day which was devoted to education.

The reasons for this conduct were very plain. First, the more robust boys considered talking with girls an unmanly occupation; second, the greater part of the boys were afraid; third, they had no idea of what to say, because they esteemed the proper sentences should be supernaturally incisive and eloquent. In consequence, a small contingent of blue-eyed weaklings were the sole intimates of the frail sex, and for it they were boisterously and disdainfully called "girl-boys."

But this situation did not prevent serious and ardent wooing. For instance, Jimmie and the little girl who wore the red hood must have exchanged glances at least two hundred times in every school-hour, and this exchange of glances accomplished everything. In them the two children renewed their curious inarticulate vows.

Jimmie had developed a devotion to school which was the admiration of his father and mother. In the mornings he was so impatient to have it made known to him that no misfortune had befallen his romance during the night that he was actually detected at times feverishly listening for the "first bell." Dr. Trescott was exceedingly complacent of the change, and as for Mrs. Trescott, she had ecstatic visions of a white-haired Jimmie leading the nations in knowledge, comprehending all from bugs to comets. It was merely the doing of the little girl in the red hood.

When Jimmie made up his mind to follow his sweetheart home from school, the project seemed such an arbitrary and shameless innovation that he hastily lied to himself about it. No, he was not following Abbie. He was merely making his way homeward through the new and rather longer route of Bryant Street and Oakland Park. It had nothing at all to do with a girl. It was a mere eccentric notion.

"Come on," said Jimmie, gruffly, to his retainer. "Let's go home this way."

"What fer?" demanded the retainer.

"Oh, b'cause."

"Huh?"

"Oh, it's more fun—goin' this way."

The retainer was bored and loath, but that mattered very little. He did not know how to disobey his chief. Together they followed the trail of red-hooded Abbie and another small girl. These latter at once understood the object of the chase, and looking back giggling, they pretended to quicken their pace. But they were always looking back. Jimmie now began his courtship in earnest. The first thing to do was to prove his strength in battle. This was transacted by means of the retainer. He took that devoted boy and flung him heavily to the ground, meanwhile mouthing a preposterous ferocity.

The retainer accepted this behavior with a sort of bland resignation. After his overthrow he raised himself, coolly brushed some dust and dead leaves from his clothes, and then seemed to forget the incident.

"I can jump farther'n you can," said Jimmie, in a loud voice.

"I know it," responded the retainer, simply.

But this would not do. There must be a contest.

"Come on," shouted Jimmie, imperiously. "Let's see you jump."

The retainer selected a footing on the curb, balanced and calculated a moment, and jumped without enthusiasm. Jimmie's leap of course was longer.

"There!" he cried, blowing out his lips. "I beat you, didn't I? Easy. I beat you." He made a great hubbub, as if the affair was unprecedented.

"Yes," admitted the other, emotionless.

Later, Jimmie forced his retainer to run a race with him, held more jumping matches, flung him twice to earth, and generally behaved as if a retainer was indestructible. If the retainer had been in the plot, it is conceivable that he would have endured this treatment with mere whispered, half-laughing protests. But he was not in the plot at all, and so he became enigmatic. One cannot often sound the profound well in which lie the meanings of boyhood.

Following the two little girls, Jimmie eventually passed into that suburb of Whilomville which is called Oakland Park. At his heels came a badly battered retainer. Oakland Park was a somewhat strange country to the boys. They were dubious of the manners and customs, and of course they would have to meet the local chieftains, who might look askance upon this invasion.

Jimmie's girl departed into her home with a last backward glance that almost blinded the thrilling boy. On this pretext and that pretext, he kept his retainer in play before the house. He had hopes that she would emerge as soon as she had deposited her school-bag.

A boy came along the walk. Jimmie knew him at school. He was Tommie Semple, one of the weaklings who made friends with the fair sex. "Hello, Tom," said Jimmie. "You live round here?"

"Yeh," said Tom, with composed pride. At school he was afraid of Jimmie, but he did not evince any of this fear as he strolled well inside his own frontiers. Jimmie and his retainer had not expected this boy to display the manners of a minor chief, and they contemplated him attentively. There was a silence. Finally Jimmie said:

"I can put you down." He moved forward briskly. "Can't I?" he demanded.

The challenged boy backed away. "I know you can," he declared, frankly and promptly.

The little girl in the red hood had come out with a hoop. She looked at Jimmie with an air of insolent surprise in the fact that he still existed, and began to trundle her hoop off towards some other little girls who were shrilly playing near a nurse-maid and a perambulator.

Jimmie adroitly shifted his position until he too was playing near the perambulator, pretentiously making mince-meat out of his retainer and Tommie Semple.

Of course little Abbie had defined the meaning of Jimmie's appearance in Oakland Park. Despite this nonchalance and grand air of accident, nothing could have been more plain. Whereupon she of course became insufferably vain in manner, and whenever Jimmie came near her she tossed her head and turned away her face, and daintily swished her skirts as if he were contagion itself. But Jimmie was happy. His soul was satisfied with the mere presence of the beloved object so long as he could feel that she furtively gazed upon him from time to time and noted his extraordinary prowess, which he was proving upon the persons of his retainer and Tommie Semple. And he was making an impression. There could be no doubt of it. He had many times caught her eye fixed admiringly upon him as he mauled the retainer. Indeed, all the little girls gave attention to his deeds, and he was the hero of the hour.

Presently a boy on a velocipede was seen to be tooling down towards them. "Who's this comin'?" said Jimmie, bluntly, to the Semple boy.

"That's Horace Glenn," said Tommie, "an' he's got a new velocipede, an' he can ride it like anything."

"Can you lick him?" asked Jimmie.

"I don't—I never fought with 'im," answered the other. He bravely tried to appear as a man of respectable achievement, but with Horace coming towards them the risk was too great. However, he added, *"Maybe* I could."

The advent of Horace on his new velocipede created a sensation which he haughtily accepted as a familiar thing. Only Jimmie and his retainer remained silent and impassive. Horace eyed the two invaders.

"Hello, Jimmie!"

"Hello, Horace!"

After the typical silence Jimmie said, pompously, "I got a velocipede."

"Have you?" asked Horace, anxiously. He did not wish anybody in the world but himself to possess a velocipede.

"Yes," sang Jimmie. "An' it's a bigger one than that, too! A good deal bigger! An' it's a better one, too!"

"Huh!" retorted Horace, sceptically.

"'Ain't I, Clarence? 'Ain't I? 'Ain't I got one bigger'n that?"

The retainer answered with alacrity:

"Yes, he has! A good deal bigger! An' it's a dindy, too!"

This corroboration rather disconcerted Horace, but he continued to scoff at any statement that Jimmie also owned a velocipede. As for the contention that this supposed velocipede could be larger than his own, he simply wouldn't hear of it.

Jimmie had been a very gallant figure before the coming of Horace, but the new velocipede had relegated him to a squalid secondary position. So he affected to look with contempt upon it. Voluminously he bragged of the velocipede in the stable at home. He painted its virtues and beauty in loud and extravagant words, flaming words. And the retainer stood by, glibly endorsing everything.

The little company heeded him, and he passed on vociferously from extravagance to utter impossibility. Horace was very sick of it. His defence was reduced to a mere mechanical grumbling: "Don't believe you got one 'tall. Don't believe you got one 'tall."

Jimmie turned upon him suddenly. "How fast can you go? How fast can you go?" he demanded. "Let's see. I bet you can't go fast."

Horace lifted his spirits and answered with proper defiance. "Can't I?" he mocked. "Can't I?"

"No, you can't," said Jimmie. "You can't go fast."

Horace cried: "Well, you see me now! I'll show you! I'll show you if I can't go fast!" Taking a firm seat on his vermilion machine, he pedalled furiously up the walk, turned, and pedalled back again. "There, now!" he shouted, triumphantly. "Ain't that fast? There, now!" There was a low murmur of appreciation from the little girls. Jimmie saw with pain that even his divinity was smiling upon his rival. "There! Ain't that fast? Ain't that fast?" He strove to pin Jimmie down to an admission. He was exuberant with victory.

Notwithstanding a feeling of discomfiture, Jimmie did not lose a moment of time. "Why," he yelled, "that ain't goin' fast 'tall! That ain't goin' fast 'tall! Why, I can go almost *twice* as fast as that! Almost twice as fast! Can't I, Clarence?"

The royal retainer nodded solemnly at the wide-eyed group. "Course you can!"

"Why," spouted Jimmie, "you just ought to see me ride once! You just ought to see me! Why, I can go like the wind! Can't I, Clarence? And I can ride far, too—oh, awful far! Can't I, Clarence? Why, I wouldn't have that one! 'Tain't any good! You just ought to see mine once!"

The overwhelmed Horace attempted to reconstruct his battered glories. "I can ride right over the curb-stone—at some of the crossin's," he announced, brightly.

Jimmie's derision was a splendid sight. "'*Right over the curb-stone!*' Why, that wouldn't be *nothin'* for me to do! I've rode mine down Bridge Street hill. Yessir! 'Ain't I, Clarence? Why, it ain't nothin' to ride over a curb-stone—not for *me*! Is it, Clarence?"

"Down Bridge Street hill? You never!" said Horace, hopelessly.

"Well, didn't I, Clarence? Didn't I, now?"

The faithful retainer again nodded solemnly at the assemblage.

At last Horace, having fallen as low as was possible, began to display a spirit for climbing up again. "Oh, you can do wonders!" he said, laughing. "You can do wonders! I s'pose you could ride down that bank there?" he asked, with art. He had indicated a grassy terrace some six feet in height which bounded one side of the walk. At the bottom was a small ravine in which the reckless had flung ashes and tins. "I s'pose you could ride down that bank?"

All eyes now turned upon Jimmie to detect a sign of his weakening, but he instantly and sublimely arose to the occasion. "That bank?" he asked, scornfully. "Why, I've ridden down banks like that many a time. 'Ain't I, Clarence?"

This was too much for the company. A sound like the wind in the leaves arose; it was the song of incredulity and ridicule. "O—o—o—o—o!" And on the outskirts a little girl suddenly shrieked out, "Story-teller!"

Horace had certainly won a skirmish. He was gleeful. "Oh, you can do wonders!" he gurgled. "You can do wonders!" The neighborhood's superficial hostility to foreigners arose like magic under the influence of his sudden success, and Horace had the delight of seeing Jimmie persecuted in that manner known only to children and insects.

"'I—' HE BEGAN. THEN HE VANISHED FROM THE EDGE OF THE WALK."

Jimmie called angrily to the boy on the velocipede, "If you'll lend me yours, I'll show you whether I can or not."

Horace turned his superior nose in the air. "Oh no! I don't ever lend it." Then he thought of a blow which would make Jimmie's humiliation complete. "Besides," he said, airily, "'tain't really anything hard to do. I could do it—easy—if I wanted to."

But his supposed adherents, instead of receiving this boast with cheers, looked upon him in a sudden blank silence. Jimmie and his retainer pounced like cats upon their advantage.

"Oh," they yelled, "you *could*, eh? Well, let's see you do it, then! Let's see you do it! Let's see you do it! Now!" In a moment the crew of little spectators were gibing at Horace.

The blow that would make Jimmie's humiliation complete! Instead, it had boomeranged Horace into the mud. He kept up a sullen muttering:

"'Tain't really anything! I could if I wanted to!"

"Dare you to!" screeched Jimmie and his partisans. "Dare you to! Dare you to! Dare you to!"

There were two things to be done—to make gallant effort or to retreat. Somewhat to their amazement, the children at last found Horace moving through their clamor to the edge of the bank. Sitting on the velocipede, he looked at the ravine, and then, with gloomy pride, at the other children. A hush came upon them, for it was seen that he was intending to make some kind of an ante-mortem statement.

"I—" he began. Then he vanished from the edge of the walk. The start had been unintentional—an accident.

The stupefied Jimmie saw the calamity through a haze. His first clear vision was when Horace, with a face as red as a red flag, arose bawling from his tangled velocipede. He and his retainer exchanged a glance of horror and fled the neighborhood. They did not look back until they had reached the top of the hill near the lake. They could see Horace walking slowly under the maples towards his home, pushing his shattered velocipede before him. His chin was thrown high, and the breeze bore them the sound of his howls.

V. MAKING AN ORATOR

IN the school at Whilomville it was the habit, when children had progressed to a certain class, to have them devote Friday afternoon to what was called elocution. This was in the piteously ignorant belief that orators were thus made. By process of school law, unfortunate boys and girls were dragged up to address their fellow-scholars in the literature of the mid-century. Probably the children who were most capable of expressing themselves, the children who were most sensitive to the power of speech, suffered the most wrong. Little blockheads who could learn eight lines of conventional poetry, and could get up and spin it rapidly at their classmates, did not undergo a single pang. The plan operated mainly to agonize many children permanently against arising to speak their thought to fellow-creatures.

Jimmie Trescott had an idea that by exhibition of undue ignorance he could escape from being promoted into the first class room which exacted such penalty from its inmates. He preferred to dwell in a less classic shade rather than venture into a domain where he was obliged to perform a certain duty which struck him as being worse than death. However, willy-nilly, he was somehow sent ahead into the place of torture.

Every Friday at least ten of the little children had to mount the stage beside the teacher's desk and babble something which none of them understood. This was to make them orators. If it had been ordered that they should croak like frogs, it would have advanced most of them just as far towards oratory.

Alphabetically Jimmie Trescott was near the end of the list of victims, but his time was none the less inevitable. "Tanner, Timmens, Trass, Trescott—" He saw his downfall approaching.

He was passive to the teacher while she drove into his mind the incomprehensible lines of "The Charge of the Light Brigade":

Half a league, half a league,

Half a league onward—

He had no conception of a league. If in the ordinary course of life somebody had told him that he was half a league from home, he might have been frightened that half a league was fifty miles; but he struggled manfully with the valley of death and a mystic six hundred, who were performing something there which was very fine, he had been told. He learned all the verses.

But as his own Friday afternoon approached he was moved to make known to his family that a dreadful disease was upon him, and was likely at any time to prevent him from going to his beloved school.

On the great Friday when the children of his initials were to speak their pieces Dr. Trescott was away from home, and the mother of the boy was alarmed beyond measure at Jimmie's curious illness, which caused him to lie on the rug in front of the fire and groan cavernously.

She bathed his feet in hot mustard water until they were lobster-red. She also placed a mustard plaster on his chest.

He announced that these remedies did him no good at all—no good at all. With an air of martyrdom he endured a perfect downpour of motherly attention all that day. Thus the first Friday was passed in safety.

With singular patience he sat before the fire in the dining-room and looked at picture-books, only complaining of pain when he suspected his mother of thinking that he was getting better.

The next day being Saturday and a holiday, he was miraculously delivered from the arms of disease, and went forth to play, a blatantly healthy boy.

He had no further attack until Thursday night of the next week, when he announced that he felt very, very poorly. The mother was already chronically alarmed over the condition of her son, but Dr. Trescott asked him questions which denoted some incredulity. On the third Friday Jimmie was dropped at the door of the school from the doctor's buggy. The other children, notably those who had already passed over the mountain of distress, looked at him with glee, seeing in him another lamb brought to butchery. Seated at his desk in the school-room, Jimmie sometimes remembered with dreadful distinctness every line of "The Charge of the Light Brigade," and at other times his mind was utterly empty of it. Geography, arithmetic, and spelling—usually great tasks—quite rolled off him. His mind was dwelling with terror upon the time when his name should be called and he was obliged to go up to the platform, turn, bow, and recite his message to his fellow-men.

Desperate expedients for delay came to him. If he could have engaged the services of a real pain, he would have been glad. But steadily, inexorably, the minutes marched on towards his great crisis, and all his plans for escape blended into a mere panic fear.

The maples outside were defeating the weakening rays of the afternoon sun, and in the shadowed school-room had come a stillness, in which, nevertheless, one could feel the complacence of the little pupils who had already passed through the flames. They were calmly prepared to recognize as a spectacle the torture of others.

Little Johnnie Tanner opened the ceremony. He stamped heavily up to the platform, and bowed in such a manner that he almost fell down. He blurted out that it would ill befit him to sit silent while the name of his fair Ireland was being reproached, and he appealed to the gallant soldier before him if every British battle-field was not sown with the bones of sons of the Emerald Isle. He was also heard to say that he had listened with deepening surprise and scorn to the insinuation of the honorable member from North Glenmorganshire that the loyalty of the Irish regiments in her Majesty's service could be questioned. To what purpose, then, he asked, had the blood of Irishmen flowed on a hundred fields? To what purpose had Irishmen gone to their death with bravery and devotion in every part of the world where the victorious flag of England had been carried? If the honorable member for North Glenmorganshire insisted upon construing a mere pothouse row between soldiers in Dublin into a grand treachery to the colors and to her Majesty's uniform, then it was time for Ireland to think bitterly of her dead sons, whose graves now marked every step of England's progress, and yet who could have their honors stripped from them so easily by the honorable member for North Glenmorganshire. Furthermore, the honorable member for North Glenmorganshire—

It is needless to say that little Johnnie Tanner's language made it exceedingly hot for the honorable member for North Glenmorganshire. But Johnnie was not angry. He was only in haste. He finished the honorable member for North Glenmorganshire in what might be called a gallop.

Susie Timmens then went to the platform, and with a face as pale as death whisperingly reiterated that she would be Queen of the May. The child represented there a perfect picture of unnecessary suffering. Her small lips were quite blue, and her eyes, opened wide, stared with a look of horror at nothing.

The phlegmatic Trass boy, with his moon face only expressing peasant parentage, calmly spoke some undeniably true words concerning destiny.

In his seat Jimmie Trescott was going half blind with fear of his approaching doom. He wished that the Trass boy would talk forever about destiny. If the school-house had taken fire he thought that he would have felt simply relief. Anything was better. Death amid the flames was preferable to a recital of "The Charge of the Light Brigade."

But the Trass boy finished his remarks about destiny in a very short time. Jimmie heard the teacher call his name, and he felt the whole world look at him. He did not know how he made his way to the stage. Parts of him seemed to be of lead, and at the same time parts of him seemed to be light as air, detached. His face had gone as pale as had been the face of Susie Timmens. He was simply a child in torment; that is all there is to be said specifically about it; and to intelligent people the exhibition would have been not more edifying than a dog-fight.

He bowed precariously, choked, made an inarticulate sound, and then he suddenly said,

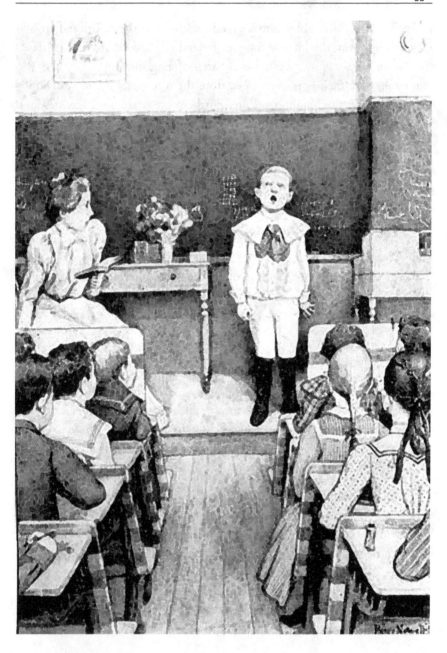

"AND THEN HE SUDDENLY SAID, 'HALF A LEG—'"

"Half a leg—"

"*League*," said the teacher, coolly.

"Half a leg—"

"*League*," said the teacher.

"*League*," repeated Jimmie, wildly.

"Half a league, half a league, half a league onward."

He paused here and looked wretchedly at the teacher.

"Half a league," he muttered—"half a league—"

He seemed likely to keep continuing this phrase indefinitely, so after a time the teacher said, "Well, go on."

"Half a league," responded Jimmie.

The teacher had the opened book before her, and she read from it:

"'All in the valley of Death
Rode the—'

Go on," she concluded.

Jimmie said,

"All in the valley of Death

Rode the—the—the—"

He cast a glance of supreme appeal upon the teacher, and breathlessly whispered, "Rode the what?"

The young woman flushed with indignation to the roots of her hair.

"Rode the six hundred,"

she snapped at him.

The class was arustle with delight at this cruel display. They were no better than a Roman populace in Nero's time.

Jimmie started off again:

"Half a leg—league, half a league, half a league onward.

All in the valley of death rode the six hundred.

Forward—forward—forward—"

"The Light Brigade," suggested the teacher, sharply.

"The Light Brigade," said Jimmie. He was about to die of the ignoble pain of his position.

As for Tennyson's lines, they had all gone grandly out of his mind, leaving it a whited wall.

The teacher's indignation was still rampant. She looked at the miserable wretch before her with an angry stare.

"You stay in after school and learn that all over again," she commanded. "And be prepared to speak it next Friday. I am astonished at you, Jimmie. Go to your seat."

If she had suddenly and magically made a spirit of him and left him free to soar high above all the travail of our earthly lives she could not have overjoyed him more. He fled back to his seat without hearing the low-toned gibes of his schoolmates. He gave no thought to the terrors of the next Friday. The evils of the day had been sufficient, and to a childish mind a week is a great space of time.

With the delightful inconsistency of his age he sat in blissful calm, and watched the sufferings of an unfortunate boy named Zimmerman, who was the next victim of education. Jimmie, of course, did not know that on this day there had been laid for him the foundation of a finished incapacity for public speaking which would be his until he died.

VI. SHAME

DON'T come in here botherin' me," said the cook, intolerantly. "What with your mother bein' away on a visit, an' your father comin' home soon to lunch, I have enough on my mind—and that without bein' bothered with *you*. The kitchen is no place for little boys, anyhow. Run away, and don't be interferin' with my work." She frowned and made a grand pretence of being deep in herculean labors; but Jimmie did not run away.

"Now—they're goin' to have a picnic," he said, half audibly.

"What?"

"Now—they're goin' to have a picnic."

"Who's goin' to have a picnic?" demanded the cook, loudly. Her accent could have led one to suppose that if the projectors did not turn out to be the proper parties, she immediately would forbid this picnic.

Jimmie looked at her with more hopefulness. After twenty minutes of futile skirmishing, he had at least succeeded in introducing the subject. To her question he answered, eagerly:

"Oh, everybody! Lots and lots of boys and girls. Everybody."

"Who's everybody?"

According to custom, Jimmie began to singsong through his nose in a quite indescribable fashion an enumeration of the prospective picnickers: "Willie Dalzel an' Dan Earl an' Ella Earl an' Wolcott Margate an' Reeves Margate an' Walter Phelps an' Homer Phelps an' Minnie Phelps an'—oh— lots more girls an'—everybody. An' their mothers an' big sisters too." Then he announced a new bit of information: "They're goin' to have a picnic."

"Well, let them," said the cook, blandly.

Jimmie fidgeted for a time in silence. At last he murmured, "I—now—I thought maybe you'd let me go."

The cook turned from her work with an air of irritation and amazement that Jimmie should still be in the kitchen. "Who's stoppin' you?" she asked, sharply. "I ain't stoppin' you, am I?"

"No," admitted Jimmie, in a low voice.

"Well, why don't you go, then? Nobody's stoppin' you."

"But," said Jimmie, "I—you—now—each fellow has got to take somethin' to eat with 'm."

"Oh ho!" cried the cook, triumphantly. "So that's it, is it? So that's what you've been shyin' round here fer, eh? Well, you may as well take yourself off without more words. What with your mother bein' away on a visit, an' your father comin' home soon to his lunch, I have enough on my mind—an' that without being bothered with *you*!"

Jimmie made no reply, but moved in grief towards the door. The cook continued: "Some people in this house seem to think there's 'bout a thousand cooks in this kitchen. Where I used to work b'fore, there was some reason in 'em. I ain't a horse. A picnic!"

Jimmie said nothing, but he loitered.

"Seems as if I had enough to do, without havin' you come round talkin' about picnics. Nobody ever seems to think of the work I have to do. Nobody ever seems to think of it. Then they come and talk to me about picnics! What do I care about picnics?"

Jimmie loitered.

"Where I used to work b'fore, there was some reason in 'em. I never heard tell of no picnics right on top of your mother bein' away on a visit an' your father comin' home soon to his lunch. It's all foolishness."

Little Jimmie leaned his head flat against the wall and began to weep. She stared at him scornfully. "Cryin', eh? Cryin'? What are you cryin' fer?"

"N-n-nothin'," sobbed Jimmie.

There was a silence, save for Jimmie's convulsive breathing. At length the cook said: "Stop that blubberin', now. Stop it! This kitchen ain't no place fer it. Stop it!... Very well! If you don't stop, I won't give you nothin' to go to the picnic with—there!"

For the moment he could not end his tears. "You never said," he sputtered—"you never said you'd give me anything."

"An' why would I?" she cried, angrily. "Why would I—with you in here a-cryin' an' a-blubberin' an' a-bleatin' round? Enough to drive a woman crazy! I don't see how you could expect me to! The idea!"

Suddenly Jimmie announced: "I've stopped cryin'. I ain't goin' to cry no more 'tall."

"Well, then," grumbled the cook—"well, then, stop it. I've got enough on my mind." It chanced that she was making for luncheon some salmon croquettes. A tin still half full of pinky prepared fish was beside her on the table. Still grumbling, she seized a loaf of bread and, wielding a knife, she cut from this loaf four slices, each of which was as big as a six-shilling novel. She profligately spread them with butter, and jabbing the point of her knife into the salmon-tin, she brought up bits of salmon, which she flung and flattened upon the bread. Then she crashed the pieces of bread together in pairs, much as one would clash cymbals. There was no doubt in her own mind but that she had created two sandwiches.

"There," she cried. "That'll do you all right. Lemme see. What 'll I put 'em in? There—I've got it." She thrust the sandwiches into a small pail and jammed on the lid. Jimmie was ready for the picnic. "Oh, thank you, Mary!" he cried, joyfully, and in a moment he was off, running swiftly.

The picnickers had started nearly half an hour earlier, owing to his inability to quickly attack and subdue the cook, but he knew that the rendezvous was in the grove of tall, pillarlike hemlocks and pines that grew on a rocky knoll at the lake shore. His heart was very light as he sped, swinging his pail. But a few minutes previously his soul had been gloomed in despair; now he was happy. He was going to the picnic, where privilege of participation was to be bought by the contents of the little tin pail.

When he arrived in the outskirts of the grove he heard a merry clamor, and when he reached the top of the knoll he looked down the slope upon a scene which almost made his little breast burst with joy. They actually had two camp-fires! Two camp-fires! At one of them Mrs. Earl was making something—chocolate, no doubt—and at the other a young lady in white duck and a sailor hat was dropping eggs into boiling water. Other grown-up people had spread a white cloth and were laying upon it things from baskets. In the deep cool shadow of the trees the children scurried, laughing. Jimmie hastened forward to join his friends.

Homer Phelps caught first sight of him. "Ho!" he shouted; "here comes Jimmie Trescott! Come on, Jimmie; you be on our side!" The children had divided themselves into two bands for some purpose of play. The others of Homer Phelps's party loudly endorsed his plan. "Yes, Jimmie, you be on our side." Then arose the usual dispute. "Well, we got the weakest side."

"'Tain't any weaker'n ours."

Homer Phelps suddenly started, and looking hard, said, "What you got in the pail, Jim?"

Jimmie answered, somewhat uneasily, "Got m' lunch in it."

Instantly that brat of a Minnie Phelps simply tore down the sky with her shrieks of derision. "Got his *lunch* in it! In a *pail*!" She ran screaming to her mother. "Oh, mamma! Oh, mamma! Jimmie Trescott's got his picnic in a pail!"

Now there was nothing in the nature of this fact to particularly move the others—notably the boys, who were not competent to care if he had brought his luncheon in a coal-bin; but such is the instinct of childish society that they all immediately moved away from him. In a moment he had been made a social leper. All old intimacies were flung into the lake, so to speak. They dared not compromise themselves. At safe distances the boys shouted, scornfully: "Huh! Got his picnic in a pail!" Never again during that picnic did the little girls speak of him as Jimmie Trescott. His name now was Him.

His mind was dark with pain as he stood, the hangdog, kicking the gravel, and muttering as defiantly as he was able, "Well, I can have it in a pail if I want to." This statement of freedom was of no importance, and he knew it, but it was the only idea in his head.

"'JIMMY TRESCOTT'S GOT HIS PICNIC IN A PAIL!'"

He had been baited at school for being detected in writing a letter to little Cora, the angel child, and he had known how to defend himself, but this situation was in no way similar. This was a social affair, with grown people on all sides. It would be sweet to catch the Margate twins, for instance, and hammer them into a state of bleating respect for his pail; but that was a matter for the jungles of childhood, where grown folk seldom penetrated. He could only glower.

The amiable voice of Mrs. Earl suddenly called: "Come, children! Everything's ready!" They scampered away, glancing back for one last gloat at Jimmie standing there with his pail.

He did not know what to do. He knew that the grown folk expected him at the spread, but if he approached he would be greeted by a shameful chorus from the children—more especially from some of those damnable little girls. Still, luxuries beyond all dreaming were heaped on that cloth. One could not forget them. Perhaps if he crept up modestly, and was very gentle and very nice to the little girls, they would allow him peace. Of course it had been dreadful to come with a pail to such a grand picnic, but they might forgive him.

Oh no, they would not! He knew them better. And then suddenly he remembered with what delightful expectations he had raced to this grove, and self-pity overwhelmed him, and he thought he wanted to die and make every one feel sorry.

The young lady in white duck and a sailor hat looked at him, and then spoke to her sister, Mrs. Earl. "Who's that hovering in the distance, Emily?"

Mrs. Earl peered. "Why, it's Jimmie Trescott! Jimmie, come to the picnic! Why don't you come to the picnic, Jimmie?" He began to sidle towards the cloth.

But at Mrs. Earl's call there was another outburst from many of the children. "He's got his picnic in a pail! In a *pail*! Got it in a pail!"

Minnie Phelps was a shrill fiend. "Oh, mamma, he's got it in that pail! See! Isn't it funny? Isn't it dreadful funny?"

"What ghastly prigs children are, Emily!" said the young lady. "They are spoiling that boy's whole day, breaking his heart, the little cats! I think I'll go over and talk to him."

"Maybe you had better not," answered Mrs. Earl, dubiously. "Somehow these things arrange themselves. If you interfere, you are likely to prolong everything."

"Well, I'll try, at least," said the young lady.

At the second outburst against him Jimmie had crouched down by a tree, half hiding behind it, half pretending that he was not hiding behind it. He turned his sad gaze towards the lake. The bit of water seen through the shadows seemed perpendicular, a slate-colored wall. He heard a noise near him, and turning, he perceived the young lady looking down at him. In her hand she held plates. "May I sit near you?" she asked, coolly.

Jimmie could hardly believe his ears. After disposing herself and the plates upon the pine needles, she made brief explanation. "They're rather crowded, you see, over there. I don't like to be crowded at a picnic, so I thought I'd come here. I hope you don't mind."

Jimmie made haste to find his tongue. "Oh, I don't mind! I *like* to have you here." The ingenuous emphasis made it appear that the fact of his liking to have her there was in the nature of a law-dispelling phenomenon, but she did not smile.

"How large is that lake?" she asked.

Jimmie, falling into the snare, at once began to talk in the manner of a proprietor of the lake. "Oh, it's almost twenty miles long, an' in one place it's almost four miles wide! an' it's *deep* too—awful deep—an' it's got real steamboats on it, an'—oh—lots of other boats, an'—an'—an'—"

"Do you go out on it sometimes?"

"Oh, lots of times! My father's got a boat," he said, eying her to note the effect of his words.

She was correctly pleased and struck with wonder. "Oh, has he?" she cried, as if she never before had heard of a man owning a boat.

Jimmie continued: "Yes, an' it's a grea' big boat, too, with sails, real sails; an' sometimes he takes me out in her, too; an' once he took me fishin', an' we had sandwiches, plenty of 'em, an' my father he drank beer right out of the bottle—*right out of the bottle!*"

The young lady was properly overwhelmed by this amazing intelligence. Jimmie saw the impression he had created, and he enthusiastically resumed his narrative: "An' after, he let me throw the bottles in the water, and I throwed 'em 'way, 'way, 'way out. An' they sank, an'—never comed up," he concluded, dramatically.

His face was glorified; he had forgotten all about the pail; he was absorbed in this communion with a beautiful lady who was so interested in what he had to say.

She indicated one of the plates, and said, indifferently: "Perhaps you would like some of those sandwiches. I made them. Do you like olives? And there's a deviled egg. I made that also."

"Did you really?" said Jimmie, politely. His face gloomed for a moment because the pail was recalled to his mind, but he timidly possessed himself of a sandwich.

"Hope you are not going to scorn my deviled egg," said his goddess. "I am very proud of it." He did not; he scorned little that was on the plate.

Their gentle intimacy was ineffable to the boy. He thought he had a friend, a beautiful lady, who liked him more than she did anybody at the picnic, to say the least. This was proved by the fact that she had flung aside the luxuries of the spread cloth to sit with him, the exile. Thus early did he fall a victim to woman's wiles.

"Where do you live?" he asked, suddenly.

"Oh, a long way from here! In New York."

His next question was put very bluntly. "Are you married?"

"Oh no!" she answered, gravely.

Jimmie was silent for a time, during which he glanced shyly and furtively up at her face. It was evident that he was somewhat embarrassed. Finally he said, "When I grow up to be a man—"

"Oh, that is some time yet!" said the beautiful lady.

"But when I *do,* I—I should like to marry you."

"Well, I will remember it," she answered; "but don't talk of it now, because it's such a long time; and—I wouldn't wish you to consider yourself bound." She smiled at him.

He began to brag. "When I grow up to be a man, I'm goin' to have lots an' lots of money, an' I'm goin' to have a grea' big house, an' a horse an' a shot-gun, an' lots an' lots of books 'bout elephants an' tigers, an' lots an' lots of ice-cream an' pie an'—caramels." As before, she was impressed; he could see it. "An' I'm goin' to have lots an' lots of children—'bout three hundred, I guess—an' there won't none of 'em be girls. They'll all be boys—like me."

"Oh, my!" she said.

His garment of shame was gone from him. The pail was dead and well buried. It seemed to him that months elapsed as he dwelt in happiness near the beautiful lady and trumpeted his vanity.

At last there was a shout. "Come on! we're going home." The picnickers trooped out of the grove. The children wished to resume their jeering, for Jimmie still gripped his pail, but they were restrained by the circumstances. He was walking at the side of the beautiful lady.

During this journey he abandoned many of his habits. For instance, he never travelled without skipping gracefully from crack to crack between the stones, or without pretending that he was a train of cars, or without some mumming device of childhood. But now he behaved with dignity. He made no more noise than a little mouse. He escorted the beautiful lady to the gate of the Earl home, where he awkwardly, solemnly, and wistfully shook hands in good-by. He watched her go up the walk; the door clanged.

On his way home he dreamed. One of these dreams was fascinating. Supposing the beautiful lady was his teacher in school! Oh, my! wouldn't he be a good boy, sitting like a statuette all day long, and knowing every lesson to perfection, and—everything. And then supposing that a boy should sass her. Jimmie painted himself waylaying that boy on the homeward road, and the fate of the boy was a thing to make strong men cover their eyes with their hands. And she would like him more and more—more and more. And he— he would be a little god.

But as he was entering his father's grounds an appalling recollection came to him. He was returning with the bread-and-butter and the salmon untouched in the pail! He could imagine the cook, nine feet tall, waving her fist. "An' so that's what I took trouble for, is it? So's you could bring it back? So's you could bring it back?" He skulked towards the house like a marauding bushranger. When he neared the kitchen door he made a desperate rush past it, aiming to gain the stables and there secrete his guilt. He was nearing them, when a thunderous voice hailed him from the rear:

"Jimmie Trescott, where you goin' with that pail?"

It was the cook. He made no reply, but plunged into the shelter of the stables. He whirled the lid from the pail and dashed its contents beneath a heap of blankets. Then he stood panting, his eyes on the door. The cook did not pursue, but she was bawling:

"Jimmie Trescott, what you doin' with that pail?"

He came forth, swinging it. "Nothin'," he said, in virtuous protest.

"I know better," she said, sharply, as she relieved him of his curse.

In the morning Jimmie was playing near the stable, when he heard a shout from Peter Washington, who attended Dr. Trescott's horse:

"Jim! Oh, Jim!"

"What?"

"Come yah."

Jimmie went reluctantly to the door of the stable, and Peter Washington asked:

"Wut's dish yere fish an' brade doin' unner dese yer blankups?"

"I don't know. I didn't have nothin' to do with it," answered Jimmie, indignantly.

"Don' tell *me*!" cried Peter Washington, as he flung it all away—"don' tell *me*! When I fin' fish an' brade unner dese yer blankups, I don' go an' think dese yer ho'ses er yer pop's put 'em. I *know*. An' if I caitch enny more dish yer fish an' brade in dish yer stable, I'*ll* tell yer pop."

VII. THE CARRIAGE-LAMPS

IT was the fault of a small nickel-plated revolver, a most incompetent weapon, which, wherever one aimed, would fling the bullet as the devil willed, and no man, when about to use it, could tell exactly what was in store for the surrounding country. This treasure had been acquired by Jimmie Trescott after arduous bargaining with another small boy. Jimmie wended homeward, patting his hip pocket at every three paces.

Peter Washington, working in the carriage-house, looked out upon him with a shrewd eye. "Oh, Jim," he called, "wut you got in yer hind pocket?"

"Nothin'," said Jimmie, feeling carefully under his jacket to make sure that the revolver wouldn't fall out.

Peter chuckled. "S'more foolishness, I raikon. You gwine be hung one day, Jim, you keep up all dish yer nonsense."

Jimmie made no reply, but went into the back garden, where he hid the revolver in a box under a lilac-bush. Then he returned to the vicinity of Peter, and began to cruise to and fro in the offing, showing all the signals of one wishing to open treaty. "Pete," he said, "how much does a box of cartridges cost?"

Peter raised himself violently, holding in one hand a piece of harness, and in the other an old rag. "Ca'tridgers! *Ca'tridgers!* Lan'sake! wut the kid want with ca'tridgers? Knew it! Knew it! Come home er-holdin' on to his hind pocket like he got money in it. An' now he want ca'tridgers."

Jimmie, after viewing with dismay the excitement caused by his question, began to move warily out of the reach of a possible hostile movement.

"Ca'tridgers!" continued Peter, in scorn and horror. "Kid like you! No bigger'n er minute! Look yah, Jim, you done been swappin' round, an' you done got hol' of er pistol!" The charge was dramatic.

The wind was almost knocked out of Jimmie by this display of Peter's terrible miraculous power, and as he backed away his feeble denials were more convincing than a confession.

"I'll tell yer pop!" cried Peter, in virtuous grandeur. "I'll tell yer pop!"

In the distance Jimmie stood appalled. He knew not what to do. The dread adult wisdom of Peter Washington had laid bare the sin, and disgrace stared at Jimmie.

There was a whirl of wheels, and a high, lean trotting-mare spun Doctor Trescott's buggy towards Peter, who ran forward busily. As the doctor climbed out, Peter, holding the mare's head, began his denunciation:

"Docteh, I gwine tell on Jim. He come home er-holdin' on to his hind pocket, an' proud like he won a tuhkey-raffle, an' I sure know what he been up to, an' I done challenge him, an' he nev' say he didn't."

"Why, what do you mean?" said the doctor. "What's this, Jimmie?"

The boy came forward, glaring wrathfully at Peter. In fact, he suddenly was so filled with rage at Peter that he forgot all precautions. "It's about a pistol," he said, bluntly. "I've got a pistol. I swapped for it."

"I done tol' 'im his pop wouldn' stand no fiah-awms, an' him a kid like he is. I done tol' 'im. Lan' sake! he strut like he was a soldier! Come in yere proud, an' er-holdin' on to his hind pocket. He think he was Jesse James, I raikon. But I done tol' 'im his pop stan' no sech foolishness. First thing—*blam*—he shoot his haid off. No, seh, he too tinety t' come in yere er-struttin' like he jest bought Main Street. I tol' 'im. I done tol' 'im—shawp. I don' wanter be loafin' round dis yer stable if Jim he gwine go shootin' round an' shootin' round—*blim—blam—blim—blam*! No, seh. I retiahs. I retiahs. It's all right if er grown man got er gun, but ain't no kids come foolishin' round *me* with fiah-awms. No, seh. I retiahs."

"Oh, be quiet, Peter!" said the doctor. "Where is this thing, Jimmie?"

The boy went sulkily to the box under the lilac-bush and returned with the revolver. "Here 'tis," he said, with a glare over his shoulder at Peter. The doctor looked at the silly weapon in critical contempt.

"It's not much of a thing, Jimmie, but I don't think you are quite old enough for it yet. I'll keep it for you in one of the drawers of my desk."

Peter Washington burst out proudly: "I done tol' 'im th' docteh wouldn' stan' no traffickin' round yere with fiah-awms. I done tol' 'im."

Jimmie and his father went together into the house, and as Peter unharnessed the mare he continued his comments on the boy and the revolver. He was not cast down by the absence of hearers. In fact, he usually talked better when there was no one to listen save the horses. But now his observations bore small resemblance to his earlier and public statements. Admiration and the keen family pride of a Southern negro who has been long in one place were now in his tone.

"That boy! He's er devil! When he get to be er man—wow! He'll jes take an' make things whirl round yere. Raikon we'll all take er back seat when he come erlong er-raisin' Cain."

He had unharnessed the mare, and with his back bent was pushing the buggy into the carriage-house.

"Er pistol! An' him no bigger than er minute!"

A small stone whizzed past Peter's head and clattered on the stable. He hastily dropped all occupation and struck a curious attitude. His right knee was almost up to his chin, and his arms were wreathed protectingly about his head. He had not looked in the direction from which the stone had come, but he had begun immediately to yell:

"You Jim! Quit! Quit, I tell yer, Jim! Watch out! You gwine break somethin', Jim!"

"Yah!" taunted the boy, as with the speed and ease of a light-cavalryman he manœuvred in the distance. "Yah! Told on me, did you! Told on me, hey! There! How do you like that?" The missiles resounded against the stable.

"'YOU JIM! QUIT! QUIT, I TELL YER!'"

"Watch out, Jim! You gwine break something, Jim, I tell yer! Quit yer foolishness, Jim! Ow! Watch out, boy! I—"

There was a crash. With diabolic ingenuity, one of Jimmie's pebbles had entered the carriage-house and had landed among a row of carriage-lamps on a shelf, creating havoc which was apparently beyond all reason of physical law. It seemed to Jimmie that the racket of falling glass could have been heard in an adjacent county.

Peter was a prophet who after persecution was suffered to recall everything to the mind of the persecutor. "*There!* Knew it! Knew it! *Now* I raikon you'll quit. Hi! jes look ut dese yer lamps! Fer lan' sake! Oh, now yer pop jes break ev'ry bone in yer body!"

In the doorway of the kitchen the cook appeared with a startled face. Jimmie's father and mother came suddenly out on the front veranda. "What was that noise?" called the the doctor.

Peter went forward to explain. "Jim he was er-heavin' rocks at me, docteh, an' erlong come one rock an' go *blam* inter all th' lamps an' jes skitter 'em t' bits. I declayah—"

Jimmie, half blinded with emotion, was nevertheless aware of a lightning glance from his father, a glance which cowed and frightened him to the ends of his toes. He heard the steady but deadly tones of his father in a fury: "Go into the house and wait until I come."

Bowed in anguish, the boy moved across the lawn and up the steps. His mother was standing on the veranda still gazing towards the stable. He loitered in the faint hope that she might take some small pity on his state. But she could have heeded him no less if he had been invisible. He entered the house.

When the doctor returned from his investigation of the harm done by Jimmie's hand, Mrs. Trescott looked at him anxiously, for she knew that he was concealing some volcanic impulses. "Well?" she asked.

"It isn't the lamps," he said at first. He seated himself on the rail. "I don't know what we are going to do with that boy. It isn't so much the lamps as it is the other thing. He was throwing stones at Peter because Peter told me about the revolver. What are we going to do with him?"

"I'm sure I don't know," replied the mother. "We've tried almost everything. Of course much of it is pure animal spirits. Jimmie is not naturally vicious—"

"Oh, I know," interrupted the doctor, impatiently. "Do you suppose, when the stones were singing about Peter's ears, he cared whether they were flung by a boy who was naturally vicious or a boy who was not? The question might interest him afterward, but at the time he was mainly occupied in dodging these effects of pure animal spirits."

"Don't be too hard on the boy, Ned. There's lots of time yet. He's so young yet, and—I believe he gets most of his naughtiness from that wretched Dalzel boy. That Dalzel boy—well, he's simply awful!" Then, with true motherly instinct to shift blame from her own boy's shoulders, she proceeded to sketch the character of the Dalzel boy in lines that would have made that talented young vagabond stare. It was not admittedly her feeling that the doctor's attention should be diverted from the main issue and his indignation divided among the camps, but presently the doctor felt himself burn with wrath for the Dalzel boy.

"Why don't you keep Jimmie away from him?" he demanded. "Jimmie has no business consorting with abandoned little predestined jail-birds like him. If I catch him on the place I'll box his ears."

"It is simply impossible, unless we kept Jimmie shut up all the time," said Mrs. Trescott. "I can't watch him every minute of the day, and the moment my back is turned, he's off."

"I should think those Dalzel people would hire somebody to bring up their child for them," said the doctor. "They don't seem to know how to do it themselves."

Presently you would have thought from the talk that one Willie Dalzel had been throwing stones at Peter Washington because Peter Washington had told Doctor Trescott that Willie Dalzel had come into possession of a revolver.

In the mean time Jimmie had gone into the house to await the coming of his father. He was in a rebellious mood. He had not intended to destroy the carriage-lamps. He had been merely hurling stones at a creature whose perfidy deserved such action, and the hitting of the lamps had been merely another move of the great conspirator Fate to force one Jimmie Trescott into dark and troublous ways. The boy was beginning to find the world a bitter place. He couldn't win appreciation for a single virtue; he could only achieve quick, rigorous punishment for his misdemeanors. Everything was an enemy. Now there were those silly old lamps—what were they doing up on that shelf, anyhow? It would have been just as easy for them at the time to have been in some other place. But no; there they had been, like the crowd that is passing under the wall when the mason for the first time in twenty years lets fall a brick. Furthermore, the flight of that stone had been perfectly unreasonable. It had been a sort of freak in physical law. Jimmie understood that he might have thrown stones from the same fatal spot for an hour without hurting a single lamp. He was a victim—that was it. Fate had conspired with the detail of his environment to simply hound him into a grave or into a cell.

But who would understand? Who would understand? And here the boy turned his mental glance in every direction, and found nothing but what was to him the black of cruel ignorance. Very well; some day they would—

From somewhere out in the street he heard a peculiar whistle of two notes. It was the common signal of the boys in the neighborhood, and judging from the direction of the sound, it was apparently intended to summon him. He moved immediately to one of the windows of the sitting-room. It opened upon a part of the grounds remote from the stables and cut off from the veranda by a wing. He perceived Willie Dalzel loitering in the street. Jimmie whistled the signal after having pushed up the window-sash some inches. He saw the Dalzel boy turn and regard him, and then call several other boys. They stood in a group and gestured. These gestures plainly said: "Come out. We've got something on hand." Jimmie sadly shook his head.

But they did not go away. They held a long consultation. Presently Jimmie saw the intrepid Dalzel boy climb the fence and begin to creep among the shrubbery, in elaborate imitation of an Indian scout. In time he arrived under Jimmie's window, and raised his face to whisper: "Come on out! We're going on a bear-hunt."

A bear-hunt! Of course Jimmie knew that it would not be a real bear-hunt, but would be a sort of carouse of pretension and big talking and preposterous lying and valor, wherein each boy would strive to have himself called Kit Carson by the others. He was profoundly affected. However, the parental word was upon him, and he could not move. "No," he answered, "I can't. I've got to stay in."

"Are you a prisoner?" demanded the Dalzel boy, eagerly.

"No-o—yes—I s'pose I am."

The other lad became much excited, but he did not lose his wariness. "Don't you want to be rescued?"

"Why—no—I dun'no'," replied Jimmie, dubiously.

Willie Dalzel was indignant. "Why, of course you want to be rescued! We'll rescue you. I'll go and get my men." And thinking this a good sentence, he repeated, pompously, "I'll go and get my men." He began to crawl away, but when he was distant some ten paces he turned to say: "Keep up a stout heart. Remember that you have friends who will be faithful unto death. The time is not now far off when you will again view the blessed sunlight."

The poetry of these remarks filled Jimmie with ecstasy, and he watched eagerly for the coming of the friends who would be faithful unto death. They delayed some time, for the reason that Willie Dalzel was making a speech.

"Now, men," he said, "our comrade is a prisoner in yon—in yond—in that there fortress. We must to the rescue. Who volunteers to go with me?" He fixed them with a stern eye.

There was a silence, and then one of the smaller boys remarked,

"If Doc Trescott ketches us trackin' over his lawn—"

Willie Dalzel pounced upon the speaker and took him by the throat. The two presented a sort of a burlesque of the wood-cut on the cover of a dime novel which Willie had just been reading—*The Red Captain: A Tale of the Pirates of the Spanish Main.*

"You are a coward!" said Willie, through his clinched teeth.

"No, I ain't, Willie," piped the other, as best he could.

"I say you are," cried the great chieftain, indignantly. "Don't tell me I'm a liar." He relinquished his hold upon the coward and resumed his speech. "You know me, men. Many of you have been my followers for long years. You saw me slay Six-handed Dick with my own hand. You know I never falter. Our comrade is a prisoner in the cruel hands of our enemies. Aw, Pete Washington? He dassent. My pa says if Pete ever troubles me he'll brain 'im. Come on! To the rescue! Who will go with me to the rescue? Aw, come on! What are you afraid of?"

"HE TURNED TO SAY: 'KEEP UP A STOUT HEART'"

It was another instance of the power of eloquence upon the human mind. There was only one boy who was not thrilled by this oration, and he was a boy whose favorite reading had been of the road-agents and gun-fighters of the great West, and he thought the whole thing should be conducted in the Deadwood Dick manner. This talk of a "comrade" was silly; "pard" was the proper word. He resolved that he would make a show of being a pirate, and keep secret the fact that he really was Hold-up Harry, the Terror of the Sierras.

But the others were knit close in piratical bonds. One by one they climbed the fence at a point hidden from the house by tall shrubs. With many a low-breathed caution they went upon their perilous adventure.

Jimmie was grown tired of waiting for his friends who would be faithful unto death. Finally he decided that he would rescue himself. It would be a gross breach of rule, but he couldn't sit there all the rest of the day waiting for his faithful-unto-death friends. The window was only five feet from the ground. He softly raised the sash and threw one leg over the sill. But at the same time he perceived his friends snaking among the bushes. He withdrew his leg and waited, seeing that he was now to be rescued in an orthodox way. The brave pirates came nearer and nearer.

Jimmie heard a noise of a closing door, and turning, he saw his father in the room looking at him and the open window in angry surprise. Boys never faint, but Jimmie probably came as near to it as may the average boy.

"What's all this?" asked the doctor, staring. Involuntarily Jimmie glanced over his shoulder through the window. His father saw the creeping figures. "What are those boys doing?" he said, sharply, and he knit his brows.

"Nothin'."

"Nothing! Don't tell me that. Are they coming here to the window?"

"Y-e-s, sir."

"What for?"

"To—to see me."

"What about?"

"About—about nothin'."

"What about?"

Jimmie knew that he could conceal nothing.

"THE BOY TURNED AGAIN TO HIS FRIEND"

He said, "They're comin' to—to—to rescue me." He began to whimper.

The doctor sat down heavily.

"What? To rescue you?" he gasped.

"Y-yes, sir."

The doctor's eyes began to twinkle. "Very well," he said presently. "I will sit here and observe this rescue. And on no account do you warn them that I am here. Understand?"

Of course Jimmie understood. He had been mad to warn his friends, but his father's mere presence had frightened him from doing it. He stood trembling at the window, while the doctor stretched in an easy-chair near at hand. They waited. The doctor could tell by his son's increasing agitation that the great moment was near. Suddenly he heard Willie Dalzel's voice hiss out a word: "S-s-silence!" Then the same voice addressed Jimmie at the window: "Good cheer, my comrade. The time is now at hand. I have come. Never did the Red Captain turn his back on a friend. One minute more and you will be free. Once aboard my gallant craft and you can bid defiance to your haughty enemies. Why don't you hurry up? What are you standin' there lookin' like a cow for?"

"I—er—now—you—" stammered Jimmie.

Here Hold-up Harry, the Terror of the Sierras, evidently concluded that Willie Dalzel had had enough of the premier part, so he said:

"Brace up, pard. Don't ye turn white-livered now, fer ye know that Hold-up Harry, the Terrar of the Sarahs, ain't the man ter—"

"Oh, stop it!" said Willie Dalzel. "He won't understand that, you know. He's a pirate. Now, Jimmie, come on. Be of light heart, my comrade. Soon you—"

"I 'low arter all this here long time in jail ye thought ye had no friends mebbe, but I tell ye Hold-up Harry, the Terrar of the Sarahs—"

"A boat is waitin'—"

"I have ready a trusty horse—"

Willie Dalzel could endure his rival no longer.

"Look here, Henry, you're spoilin' the whole thing. We're all pirates, don't you see, and you're a pirate too."

"I ain't a pirate. I'm Hold-up Harry, the Terrar of the Sarahs."

"You ain't, I say," said Willie, in despair. "You're spoilin' everything, you are. All right, now. You wait. I'll fix you for this, see if I don't! Oh, come on, Jimmie. A boat awaits us at the foot of the rocks. In one short hour you'll be free forever from your ex—exewable enemies, and their vile plots. Hasten, for the dawn approaches."

"THEY WHIRLED AND SCAMPERED AWAY LIKE DEER"

The suffering Jimmie looked at his father, and was surprised at what he saw. The doctor was doubled up like a man with the colic. He was breathing heavily. The boy turned again to his friends. "I—now—look here," he began, stumbling among the words. "You—I—I don't think I'll be rescued to-day."

The pirates were scandalized. "What?" they whispered, angrily. "Ain't you goin' to be rescued? Well, all right for you, Jimmie Trescott. That's a nice way to act, that is!" Their upturned eyes glowered at Jimmie.

Suddenly Doctor Trescott appeared at the window with Jimmie. "Oh, go home, boys!" he gasped, but they did not hear him. Upon the instant they had whirled and scampered away like deer. The first lad to reach the fence was the Red Captain, but Hold-up Harry, the Terror of the Sierras, was so close that there was little to choose between them.

Doctor Trescott lowered the window, and then spoke to his son in his usual quiet way. "Jimmie, I wish you would go and tell Peter to have the buggy ready at seven o'clock."

"Yes, sir," said Jimmie, and he swaggered

out to the stables. "Pete, father wants the buggy ready at seven o'clock."

Peter paid no heed to this order, but with the tender sympathy of a true friend he inquired, "Hu't?"

"Hurt? Did what hurt?"

"Yer trouncin'."

"Trouncin'!" said Jimmie, contemptuously. "I didn't get any trouncin'."

"No?" said Peter. He gave Jimmie a quick shrewd glance, and saw that he was telling the truth. He began to mutter and mumble over his work. "Ump! Ump! Dese yer white folks act like they think er boy's made er glass. No trouncin'! Ump!" He was consumed with curiosity to learn why Jimmie had not felt a heavy parental hand, but he did not care to lower his dignity by asking questions about it. At last, however, he reached the limits of his endurance, and in a voice pretentiously careless he asked, "Didn' yer pop take on like mad er-bout dese yer cay'ge-lamps?"

"Carriage-lamps?" inquired Jimmie.

"Ump."

"No, he didn't say anything about carriage-lamps—not that I remember. Maybe he did, though. Lemme see.... No, he never mentioned 'em."

VIII. THE KNIFE

I

SI BRYANT'S place was on the shore of the lake, and his garden-patch, shielded from the north by a bold little promontory and a higher ridge inland, was accounted the most successful and surprising in all Whilomville township. One afternoon Si was working in the garden-patch, when Doctor Trescott's man, Peter Washington, came trudging slowly along the road, observing nature. He scanned the white man's fine agricultural results. "Take your eye off them there mellons, you rascal," said Si, placidly.

The negro's face widened in a grin of delight. "Well, Mist' Bryant, I raikon I ain't on'y make m'se'f covertous er-lookin' at dem yere mellums, sure 'nough. Dey suhtainly is grand."

"That's all right," responded Si, with affected bitterness of spirit. "That's all right. Just don't you admire 'em too much, that's all." Peter chuckled and chuckled. "Ma Lode! Mist' Bryant, y-y-you don' think I'm gwine come prowlin' in dish yer gawden?"

"No, I know you hain't," said Si, with solemnity. "B'cause, if you did, I'd shoot you so full of holes you couldn't tell yourself from a sponge."

"Um—no, seh! No, seh! I don' raikon you'll get chance at Pete, Mist' Bryant. No, seh. I'll take an' run 'long an' rob er bank 'fore I'll come foolishin' 'round *your* gawden, Mist' Bryant."

Bryant, gnarled and strong as an old tree, leaned on his hoe, and laughed a Yankee laugh. His mouth remained tightly closed, but the sinister lines which ran from the sides of his nose to the meetings of his lips developed to form a comic oval, and he emitted a series of grunts, while his eyes gleamed merrily and his shoulders shook. Pete, on the contrary, threw back his head and guffawed thunderously. The effete joke in regard to an American negro's fondness for watermelons was still an admirable pleasantry to them, and this was not the first time they had engaged in badinage over it. In fact, this venerable survival had formed between them a friendship of casual roadside quality.

Afterwards Peter went on up the road. He continued to chuckle until he was far away. He was going to pay a visit to old Alek Williams, a negro who lived with a large family in a hut clinging to the side of a mountain. The scattered colony of negroes which hovered near Whilomville was of interesting origin, being the result of some contrabands who had drifted as far north as Whilomville during the great civil war. The descendants of these adventurers were mainly conspicuous for their bewildering number, and the facility which they possessed for adding even to this number. Speaking, for example, of the Jacksons—one couldn't hurl a stone into the hills about Whilomville without having it land on the roof of a hut full of Jacksons. The town reaped little in labor from these curious suburbs. There were a few men who came in regularly to work in gardens, to drive teams, to care for horses, and there were a few women who came in to cook or to wash. These latter had usually drunken husbands. In the main the colony loafed in high spirits, and the industrious minority gained no direct honor from their fellows, unless they spent their earnings on raiment, in which case they were naturally treated with distinction. On the whole, the hardships of these people were the wind, the rain, the snow, and any other physical difficulties which they could cultivate. About twice a year the lady philanthropists of Whilomville went up against them, and came away poorer in goods but rich in complacence. After one of these attacks the colony would preserve a comic air of rectitude for two days, and then relapse again to the genial irresponsibility of a crew of monkeys.

Peter Washington was one of the industrious class who occupied a position of distinction, for he surely spent his money on personal decoration. On occasion he could dress better than the Mayor of Whilomville himself, or at least in more colors, which was the main thing to the minds of his admirers. His ideal had been the late gallant Henry Johnson, whose conquests in Watermelon Alley, as well as in the hill shanties, had proved him the equal if not the superior of any Pullman-car porter in the country. Perhaps Peter had too much Virginia laziness and humor in him to be a wholly adequate successor to the fastidious Henry Johnson, but, at any rate, he admired his memory so attentively as to be openly termed a dude by envious people.

"HE HEAVED ONE OF HIS EIGHT-OUNCE ROCKS"

On this afternoon he was going to call on old Alek Williams because Alek's eldest girl was just turned seventeen, and, to Peter's mind, was a triumph of beauty. He was not wearing his best clothes, because on his last visit Alek's half-breed hound Susie had taken occasion to forcefully extract a quite large and valuable part of the visitor's trousers. When Peter arrived at the end of the rocky field which contained old Alek's shanty he stooped and provided himself with several large stones, weighing them carefully in his hand, and finally continuing his journey with three stones of about eight ounces each. When he was near the house, three gaunt hounds, Rover and Carlo and Susie, came sweeping down upon him. His impression was that they were going to climb him as if he were a tree, but at the critical moment they swerved and went growling and snapping around him, their heads low, their eyes malignant. The afternoon caller waited until Susie presented her side to him, then he heaved one of his eight-ounce rocks. When it landed, her hollow ribs gave forth a drumlike sound, and she was knocked sprawling, her legs in the air. The other hounds at once fled in horror, and she followed as soon as she was able, yelping at the top of her lungs. The afternoon caller resumed his march.

At the wild expressions of Susie's anguish old Alek had flung open the door and come hastily into the sunshine. "Yah, you Suse, come erlong outa dat now. What fer you—Oh, how do, how do, Mist' Wash'ton—how do?"

"How do, Mist' Willums? I done foun' it necessa'y fer ter damnearkill dish yer dawg a yourn, Mist' Willums."

"Come in, come in, Mist' Wash'ton. Dawg no 'count, Mist' Wash'ton." Then he turned to address the unfortunate animal. "Hu't, did it? Hu't? 'Pears like you gwine dun some saince by time somebody brek yer back. 'Pears like I gwine club yer inter er frazzle 'fore you fin' out some saince. Gw'on 'way f'm yah!"

As the old man and his guest entered the shanty a body of black children spread out in crescent-shape formation and observed Peter with awe. Fat old Mrs. Williams greeted him turbulently, while the eldest girl, Mollie, lurked in a corner and giggled with finished imbecility, gazing at the visitor with eyes that were shy and bold by turns. She seemed at times absurdly over-confident, at times foolishly afraid; but her giggle consistently endured. It was a giggle on which an irascible but right-minded judge would have ordered her forthwith to be buried alive.

Amid a great deal of hospitable gabbling, Peter was conducted to the best chair out of the three that the house contained. Enthroned therein, he made himself charming in talk to the old people, who beamed upon him joyously. As for Mollie, he affected to be unaware of her existence. This may have been a method for entrapping the sentimental interest of that young gazelle, or it may be that the giggle had worked upon him.

He was absolutely fascinating to the old people. They could talk like rotary snow-ploughs, and he gave them every chance, while his face was illumined with appreciation. They pressed him to stay for supper, and he consented, after a glance at the pot on the stove which was too furtive to be noted.

During the meal old Alek recounted the high state of Judge Oglethorpe's kitchen-garden, which Alek said was due to his unremitting industry and fine intelligence. Alek was a gardener, whenever impending starvation forced him to cease temporarily from being a lily of the field.

"Mist' Bryant he suhtainly got er grand gawden," observed Peter.

"Dat so, dat so, Mist' Wash'ton," assented Alek. "He got fine gawden."

"Seems like I nev' *did* see sech mellums, big as er bar'l, layin' dere. I don't raikon an'body in dish yer county kin hol' it with Mist' Bryant when comes ter mellums."

"Dat so, Mist' Wash'ton."

They did not talk of watermelons until their heads held nothing else, as the phrase goes. But they talked of watermelons until, when Peter started for home that night over a lonely road, they held a certain dominant position in his mind. Alek had come with him as far as the fence, in order to protect him from a possible attack by the mongrels. There they had cheerfully parted, two honest men.

The night was dark, and heavy with moisture. Peter found it uncomfortable to walk rapidly. He merely loitered on the road. When opposite Si Bryant's place he paused and looked over the fence into the garden. He imagined he could see the form of a huge melon lying in dim stateliness not ten yards away. He looked at the Bryant house. Two windows, down-stairs, were lighted. The Bryants kept no dog, old Si's favorite child having once been bitten by a dog, and having since died, within that year, of pneumonia.

Peering over the fence, Peter fancied that if any low-minded night-prowler should happen to note the melon, he would not find it difficult to possess himself of it. This person would merely wait until the lights were out in the house, and the people presumably asleep. Then he would climb the fence, reach the melon in a few strides, sever the stem with his ready knife, and in a trice be back in the road with his prize. There need be no noise, and, after all, the house was some distance.

Selecting a smooth bit of turf, Peter took a seat by the road-side. From time to time he glanced at the lighted window.

II

When Peter and Alek had said good-bye, the old man turned back in the rocky field and shaped a slow course towards that high dim light which marked the little window of his shanty. It would be incorrect to say that Alek could think of nothing but watermelons. But it was true that Si Bryant's watermelon-patch occupied a certain conspicuous position in his thoughts.

He sighed; he almost wished that he was again a conscienceless pickaninny, instead of being one of the most ornate, solemn, and look-at-me-sinner deacons that ever graced the handle of a collection-basket. At this time it made him quite sad to reflect upon his granite integrity. A weaker man might perhaps bow his moral head to the temptation, but for him such a fall was impossible. He was a prince of the church, and if he had been nine princes of the church he could not have been more proud. In fact, religion was to the old man a sort of personal dignity. And he was on Sundays so obtrusively good that you could see his sanctity through a door. He forced it on you until you would have felt its influence even in a forecastle.

It was clear in his mind that he must put watermelon thoughts from him, and after a moment he told himself, with much ostentation, that he had done so. But it was cooler under the sky than in the shanty, and as he was not sleepy, he decided to take a stroll down to Si Bryant's place and look at the melons from a pinnacle of spotless innocence. Reaching the road, he paused to listen. It would not do to let Peter hear him, because that graceless rapscallion would probably misunderstand him. But, assuring himself that

91

Peter was well on his way, he set out, walking briskly until he was within four hundred yards of Bryant's place. Here he went to the side of the road, and walked thereafter on the damp, yielding turf. He made no sound.

He did not go on to that point in the main road which was directly opposite the water-melon-patch. He did not wish to have his ascetic contemplation disturbed by some chance wayfarer. He turned off along a short lane which led to Si Bryant's barn. Here he reached a place where he could see, over the fence, the faint shapes of the melons.

Alek was affected. The house was some distance away, there was no dog, and doubtless the Bryants would soon extinguish their lights and go to bed. Then some poor lost lamb of sin might come and scale the fence, reach a melon in a moment, sever the stem with his ready knife, and in a trice be back in the road with his prize. And this poor lost lamb of sin might even be a bishop, but no one would ever know it. Alek singled out with his eye a very large melon, and thought that the lamb would prove his judgment if he took that one.

He found a soft place in the grass, and arranged himself comfortably. He watched the lights in the windows.

III

It seemed to Peter Washington that the Bryants absolutely consulted their own wishes in regard to the time for retiring; but at last he saw the lighted windows fade briskly from left to right, and after a moment a window on the second floor blazed out against the darkness. Si was going to bed. In five minutes this window abruptly vanished, and all the world was night.

Peter spent the ensuing quarter-hour in no mental debate. His mind was fixed. He was here, and the melon was there. He would have it. But an idea of being caught appalled him. He thought of his position. He was the beau of his community, honored right and left. He pictured the consternation of his friends and the cheers of his enemies if the hands of the redoubtable Si Bryant should grip him in his shame.

He arose, and going to the fence, listened. No sound broke the stillness, save the rhythmical incessant clicking of myriad insects, and the guttural chanting of the frogs in the reeds at the lake-side. Moved by sudden decision, he climbed the fence and crept silently and swiftly down upon the melon. His open knife was in his hand. There was the melon, cool, fair to see, as pompous in its fatness as the cook in a monastery.

Peter put out a hand to steady it while he cut the stem. But at the instant he was aware that a black form had dropped over the fence lining the lane in front of him and was coming stealthily towards him. In a palsy of terror he dropped flat upon the ground, not having strength enough to run away. The next moment he was looking into the amazed and agonized face of old Alek Williams.

There was a moment of loaded silence, and then Peter was overcome by a mad inspiration. He suddenly dropped his knife and leaped upon Alek. "I got che!" he hissed. "I got che! I got che!" The old man sank down as limp as rags. "I got che! I got che! Steal Mist' Bryant's mellums, hey?"

Alek, in a low voice, began to beg. "Oh, Mist' Peter Wash'ton, don' go fer ter be too ha'd on er ole man! I nev' come yere fer ter steal 'em. 'Deed I didn't, Mist' Wash'ton! I come yere jes fer ter *feel* 'em. Oh, please, Mist' Wash'ton—"

"Come erlong outa yere, you ol' rip," said Peter, "an' don' trumple on dese yer baids. I gwine put you wah you won' ketch col'."

Without difficulty he tumbled the whining Alek over the fence to the roadway, and followed him with sheriff-like expedition! He took him by the scruff. "Come erlong, deacon. I raikon I gwine put you wah you kin pray, deacon. Come erlong, deacon."

The emphasis and reiteration of his layman's title in the church produced a deadly effect upon Alek. He felt to his marrow the heinous crime into which this treacherous night had betrayed him. As Peter marched his prisoner up the road towards the mouth of the lane, he continued his remarks: "Come erlong, deacon. Nev' see er man so anxious like erbout er mellum-paitch, deacon.

Seem like you jes must see'em er-growin' an' *feel* 'em, deacon. Mist' Bryant he'll be s'prised, deacon, findin' out you come fer ter *feel* his mellums. Come erlong, deacon. Mist' Bryant he expectin' some ole rip like you come soon."

They had almost reached the lane when Alek's cur Susie, who had followed her master, approached in the silence which attends dangerous dogs; and seeing indications of what she took to be war, she appended herself swiftly but firmly to the calf of Peter's left leg. The mêlée was short, but spirited. Alek had no wish to have his dog complicate his already serious misfortunes, and went manfully to the defence of his captor. He procured a large stone, and by beating this with both hands down upon the resounding skull of the animal, he induced her to quit her grip. Breathing heavily, Peter dropped into the long grass at the road-side. He said nothing.

"THE NEXT MOMENT HE WAS LOOKING INTO THE AMAZED AND AGONIZED FACE OF OLD ALEK"

"Mist' Wash'ton," said Alek at last, in a quavering voice, "I raikon I gwine wait yere see what you gwine do ter me."

Whereupon Peter passed into a spasmodic state, in which he rolled to and fro and shook.

"Mist' Wash'ton, I hope dish yer dog 'ain't gone an' give you fitses?"

Peter sat up suddenly. "No, she 'ain't," he answered; "but she gin me er big skeer; an' fer yer 'sistance with er cobblestone, Mist' Willums, I tell you what I gwine do—I tell you what I gwine do." He waited an impressive moment. "I gwine 'lease you!"

Old Alek trembled like a little bush in a wind. "Mist' Wash'ton?"

Quoth Peter, deliberately, "I gwine 'lease you."

The old man was filled with a desire to negotiate this statement at once, but he felt the necessity of carrying off the event without an appearance of haste. "Yes, seh; thank 'e, seh; thank 'e, Mist' Wash'ton. I raikon I ramble home pressenly." He waited an interval, and then dubiously said, "Good-evenin', Mist' Wash'ton."

"Good-evenin', deacon. Don' come foolin' roun' *feelin'* no mellums, and I say troof. Good-evenin', deacon."

Alek took off his hat and made three profound bows. "Thank 'e, seh. Thank 'e, seh. Thank 'e, seh."

Peter underwent another severe spasm, but the old man walked off towards his home with a humble and contrite heart.

IV

The next morning Alek proceeded from his shanty under the complete but customary illusion that he was going to work. He trudged manfully along until he reached the vicinity of Si Bryant's place. Then, by stages, he relapsed into a slink. He was passing the garden-patch under full steam, when, at some distance ahead of him, he saw Si Bryant leaning casually on the garden fence.

"Good-mornin', Alek."

"Good-mawnin', Mist' Bryant," answered Alek, with a new deference. He was marching on, when he was halted by a word—"Alek!"

He stopped. "Yes, seh."

"I found a knife this mornin' in th' road," drawled Si, "an' I thought maybe it was yourn."

Improved in mind by this divergence from the direct line of attack, Alek stepped up easily to look at the knife. "No, seh," he said, scanning it as it lay in Si's palm, while the cold steel-blue eyes of the white man looked down into his stomach, "'tain't no knife er mine." But he knew the knife. He knew it as if it had been his mother. And at the same moment a spark flashed through his head and made wise his understanding. He knew everything. "'Tain't much of er knife, Mist' Bryant," he said, deprecatingly.

"'Tain't much of a knife, I know that," cried Si, in sudden heat, "but I found it this mornin' in my watermelon-patch—hear?"

"Watahmellum-paitch?" yelled Alek, not astounded.

"Yes, in my watermelon-patch," sneered Si, "an' I think you know something about it, too!"

"Me?" cried Alek. "Me?"

"Yes—you!" said Si, with icy ferocity. "Yes—you!" He had become convinced that Alek was not in any way guilty, but he was certain that the old man knew the owner of the knife, and so he pressed him at first on criminal lines. "Alek, you might as well own up now. You've been meddlin' with my watermelons!"

"Me?" cried Alek again. "Yah's *ma* knife. I done cah'e it foh yeahs."

Bryant changed his ways. "Look here, Alek," he said, confidentially: "I know you and you know me, and there ain't no use in any more skirmishin'. *I* know that *you* know whose knife that is. Now whose is it?"

This challenge was so formidable in character that Alek temporarily quailed and began to stammer. "Er—now—Mist' Bryant—you—you—frien' er mine—"

"I know I'm a friend of yours, but," said Bryant, inexorably, "who owns this knife?"

Alek gathered unto himself some remnants of dignity and spoke with reproach: "Mist' Bryant, dish yer knife ain' mine."

"No," said Bryant, "it ain't. But you know who it belongs to, an' I want you to tell me—quick."

"Well, Mist' Bryant," answered Alek, scratching his wool, "I won't say 's I *do* know who b'longs ter dish yer knife, an' I won't say 's I *don't*."

Bryant again laughed his Yankee laugh, but this time there was little humor in it. It was dangerous.

Alek, seeing that he had gotten himself into hot water by the fine diplomacy of his last sentence, immediately began to flounder and totally submerge himself. "No, Mist' Bryant," he repeated, "I won't say 's I *do* know who b'longs ter dish yer knife, an' I won't say 's I *don't*." And he began to parrot this fatal sentence again and again. It seemed wound about his tongue. He could not rid himself of it. Its very power to make trouble for him seemed to originate the mysterious Afric reason for its repetition.

"Is he a very close friend of yourn?" said Bryant, softly.

"F-frien'?" stuttered Alek. He appeared to weigh this question with much care. "Well, seems like he *was* er frien', an' then agin, it seems like he—"

"It seems like he *wasn't*?" asked Bryant.

"Yes, seh, jest so, jest so," cried Alek. "Sometimes it seems like he wasn't. Then agin—" He stopped for profound meditation.

The patience of the white man seemed inexhaustible. At length his low and oily voice broke the stillness. "Oh, well, of course if he's a friend of yourn, Alek! You know I wouldn't want to make no trouble for a friend of yourn."

"THE OLD MAN DREW HIMSELF TO A STATELY POSE"

"Yes, seh," cried the negro at once. "He's er frien' er mine. He is dat."

"Well, then, it seems as if about the only thing to do is for you to tell me his name so's I can send him his knife, and that's all there is to it."

Alek took off his hat, and in perplexity ran his hand over his wool. He studied the ground. But several times he raised his eyes to take a sly peep at the imperturbable visage of the white man. "Y—y—yes, Mist' Bryant. ...I raikon dat's erbout all what kin be done. I gwine tell you who b'longs ter dish yer knife."

"Of course," said the smooth Bryant, "it ain't a very nice thing to have to do, but—"

"No, seh," cried Alek, brightly; "I'm gwine tell you, Mist' Bryant. I gwine tell you erbout dat knife. Mist' Bryant," he asked, solemnly, "does you know who b'longs ter dat knife?"

"No, I—"

"Well, I gwine tell. I gwine tell who, Mr Bryant—" The old man drew himself to a stately pose and held forth his arm. "I gwine tell who, Mist' Bryant, *dish yer knife b'longs ter Sam Jackson!*"

Bryant *was* startled into indignation. "Who in hell is Sam Jackson?" he growled.

"He's a nigger," said Alek, impressively, "and he wuks in er lumber-yawd up yere in Hoswego."

IX. THE STOVE

I

THEY'LL bring her," said Mrs. Trescott, dubiously. Her cousin, the painter, the bewildered father of the angel child, had written to say that if they were asked, he and his wife would come to the Trescotts for the Christmas holidays. But he had not officially stated that the angel child would form part of the expedition. "But of course they'll bring her," said Mrs. Trescott to her husband.

The doctor assented. "Yes, they'll have to bring her. They wouldn't dare leave New York at her mercy."

"Well," sighed Mrs. Trescott, after a pause, "the neighbors will be pleased. When they see her they'll immediately lock up their children for safety."

"Anyhow," said Trescott, "the devastation of the Margate twins was complete. She can't do that particular thing again. I shall be interested to note what form her energy will take this time."

"Oh yes! that's it!" cried the wife. "You'll be interested. You've hit it exactly. You'll be interested to note what form her energy will take this time. And then, when the real crisis comes, you'll put on your hat and walk out of the house and leave me to straighten things out. This is not a scientific question; this is a practical matter."

"Well, as a practical man, I advocate chaining her out in the stable," answered the doctor.

When Jimmie Trescott was told that his old flame was again to appear, he remained calm. In fact, time had so mended his youthful heart that it was a regular apple of oblivion and peace. Her image in his thought was as the track of a bird on deep snow—it was an impression, but it did not concern the depths. However, he did what befitted his state. He went out and bragged in the street: "My cousin is comin' next week f'om New York." ..."My cousin is comin' to-morrow f'om New York."

"Girl or boy?" said the populace, bluntly; but, when enlightened, they speedily cried, "Oh, we remember *her!*" They were charmed, for they thought of her as an outlaw, and they surmised that she could lead them into a very ecstasy of sin. They thought of her as a brave bandit, because they had been whipped for various pranks into which she had led them. When Jimmie made his declaration, they fell into a state of pleased and shuddering expectancy.

Mrs. Trescott pronounced her point of view: "The child is a nice child, if only Caroline had some sense. But she hasn't. And Willis is like a wax figure. I don't see what can be done, unless—unless you simply go to Willis and put the whole thing right at him." Then, for purposes of indication, she improvised a speech: "Look here, Willis, you've got a little daughter, haven't you? But, confound it, man, she is not the only girl child ever brought into the sunlight. There are a lot of children. Children are an ordinary phenomenon. In China they drown girl babies. If you wish to submit to this frightful impostor and tyrant, that is all very well, but why in the name of humanity do you make us submit to it?"

Doctor Trescott laughed. "I wouldn't dare say it to him."

"Anyhow," said Mrs. Trescott, determinedly, "that is what you *should* say to him."

"It wouldn't do the slightest good. It would only make him very angry, and I would lay myself perfectly open to a suggestion that I had better attend to my own affairs with more rigor."

"Well, I suppose you are right," Mrs. Trescott again said.

"Why don't you speak to Caroline?" asked the doctor, humorously.

"Speak to Caroline! Why, I wouldn't for the *world!* She'd fly through the roof. She'd snap my head off! Speak to Caroline! You must be mad!"

One afternoon the doctor went to await his visitors on the platform of the railway station. He was thoughtfully smiling. For some quaint reason he was convinced that he was to be treated to a quick manifestation of little Cora's peculiar and interesting powers. And yet, when the train paused at the station, there appeared to him only a pretty little girl in a fur-lined hood, and with her nose reddening from the sudden cold, and—attended respectfully by her parents. He smiled again, reflecting that he had comically exaggerated the dangers of dear little Cora. It amused his philosophy to note that he had really been perturbed.

As the big sleigh sped homeward there was a sudden shrill outcry from the angel child: "Oh, mamma! mamma! They've forgotten my stove!"

"Hush, dear; hush!" said the mother. "It's all right."

"Oh, but, mamma, they've forgotten my stove!"

The doctor thrust his chin suddenly out of his top-coat collar. "Stove?" he said. "Stove? What stove?"

"Oh, just a toy of the child's," explained the mother. "She's grown so fond of it, she loves it so, that if we didn't take it everywhere with her she'd suffer dreadfully. So we always bring it."

"Oh!" said the doctor. He pictured a little tin trinket. But when the stove was really unmasked, it turned out to be an affair of cast iron, as big as a portmanteau, and, as the stage people say, practicable. There was some trouble that evening when came the hour of children's bedtime. Little Cora burst into a wild declaration that she could not retire for the night unless the stove was carried up-stairs and placed, at her bedside. While the mother was trying to dissuade the child, the Trescott's held their peace and gazed with awe. The incident closed when the lamb-eyed father gathered the stove in his arms and preceded the angel child to her chamber.

In the morning, Trescott was standing with his back to the dining room fire, awaiting breakfast, when he heard a noise of descending guests. Presently the door opened, and the party entered in regular order. First came the angel child, then the cooing mother, and last the great painter with his arm full of the stove. He deposited it gently in a corner, and sighed. Trescott wore a wide grin.

"THE LAMB-EYED FATHER PRECEDED THE ANGEL CHILD TO HER CHAMBER"

"What are you carting that thing all over the house for?" he said, brutally. "Why don't you put it some place where she can play with it, and leave it there?"

The mother rebuked him with a look. "Well, if it gives her pleasure, Ned?" she expostulated, softly. "If it makes the child happy to have the stove with her, why shouldn't she have it?"

"Just so," said the doctor, with calmness.

Jimmie's idea was the roaring fireplace in the cabin of the lone mountaineer. At first he was not able to admire a girl's stove built on well-known domestic lines. He eyed it and thought it was very pretty, but it did not move him immediately. But a certain respect grew to an interest, and he became the angel child's accomplice. And even if he had not

had an interest grow upon him, he was certain to have been implicated sooner or later, because of the imperious way of little Cora, who made a serf of him in a few swift sentences. Together they carried the stove out into the desolate garden and squatted it in the snow. Jimmie's snug little muscles had been pitted against the sheer nervous vigor of this little golden-haired girl, and he had not won great honors. When the mind blazed inside the small body, the angel child was pure force. She began to speak: "Now, Jim, get some paper. Get some wood-little sticks at first. Now we want a match. You got a match? Well, go get a match. Get some more wood. Hurry up, now! No. *No!* I'll light it my own self. You get some more wood. There! Isn't that splendid? You get a whole lot of wood an' pile it up here by the stove. An' now what'll we cook? We must have somethin' to cook, you know, else it ain't like the real."

"Potatoes," said Jimmie, at once.

The day was clear, cold, bright. An icy wind sped from over the waters of the lake. A grown person would hardly have been abroad save on compulsion of a kind, and yet, when they were called to luncheon, the two little simpletons protested with great cries.

II

The ladies of Whilomville were somewhat given to the pagan habit of tea parties. When a tea party was to befall a certain house one could read it in the manner of the prospective hostess, who for some previous days would go about twitching this and twisting that, and dusting here and polishing there; the ordinary habits of the household began then to disagree with her, and her unfortunate husband and children fled to the lengths of their tethers. Then there was a hush. Then there was a tea party. On the fatal afternoon a small picked company of latent enemies would meet. There would be a fanfare of affectionate greetings, during which everybody would measure to an inch the importance of what everybody else was wearing. Those who wore old dresses would wish then that they had not come; and those who saw that, in the company, they were well clad, would be pleased or exalted, or filled with the joys of cruelty. Then they had tea, which was a habit and a delight with none of them, their usual beverage being coffee with milk.

Usually the party jerked horribly in the beginning, while the hostess strove and pulled and pushed to make its progress smooth. Then suddenly it would be off like the wind, eight, fifteen, or twenty-five tongues clattering, with a noise like a cotton-mill combined with the noise of a few penny whistles. Then the hostess had nothing to do but to look glad, and see that everybody had enough tea and cake. When the door was closed behind the last guest, the hostess would usually drop into a chair and say: "Thank Heaven! They're gone!" There would be no malice in this expression. It simply would be that, womanlike, she had flung herself headlong at the accomplishment of a pleasure which she could not even define, and at the end she felt only weariness.

The value and beauty, or oddity, of the tea-cups was another element which entered largely into the spirit of these terrible enterprises. The quality of the tea was an element which did not enter at all. Uniformly it was rather bad. But the cups! Some of the more ambitious people aspired to have cups each of a different pattern, possessing, in fact, the sole similarity that with their odd curves and dips of form they each resembled anything but a teacup. Others of the more ambitious aspired to a quite severe and godly "set," which, when viewed, appalled one with its austere and rigid family resemblances, and made one desire to ask the hostess if the teapot was not the father of all the little cups, and at the same time protesting gallantly that such a young and charming cream-jug surely could not be their mother.

But of course the serious part is that these collections so differed in style and the obvious amount paid for them that nobody could be happy. The poorer ones envied; the richer ones feared; the poorer ones continually striving to overtake the leaders; the leaders always with their heads turned back to hear overtaking footsteps. And none of these things here written did they know. Instead of seeing that they were very stupid, they thought they were very fine. And they gave and took heart-bruises—fierce, deep heart-bruises—under the clear impression that of such kind of rubbish was the kingdom of nice people. The characteristics of outsiders of course emerged in shreds from these tea parties, and it is doubtful if the characteristics of insiders escaped entirely. In fact, these tea parties were in the large way the result of a conspiracy of certain unenlightened people to make life still more uncomfortable.

Mrs. Trescott was in the circle of tea-fighters largely through a sort of artificial necessity—a necessity, in short, which she had herself created in a spirit of femininity.

When the painter and his family came for the holidays, Mrs. Trescott had for some time been feeling that it was her turn to give a tea party, and she was resolved upon it now that she was reinforced by the beautiful wife of the painter, whose charms would make all the other women feel badly. And Mrs. Trescott further resolved that the affair should be notable in more than one way. The painter's wife suggested that, as an innovation, they give the people good tea; but Mrs. Trescott shook her head; she was quite sure they would not like it.

It was an impressive gathering. A few came to see if they could not find out the faults of the painter's wife, and these, added to those who would have attended even without that attractive prospect, swelled the company to a number quite large for Whilomville. There were the usual preliminary jolts, and then suddenly the tea party was in full swing, and looked like an unprecedented success.

Mrs. Trescott exchanged a glance with the painter's wife. They felt proud and superior. This tea party was almost perfection.

III

Jimmie and the angel child, after being oppressed by innumerable admonitions to behave correctly during the afternoon, succeeded in reaching the garden, where the stove awaited them. They were enjoying themselves grandly, when snow began to fall so heavily that it gradually dampened their ardor as well as extinguished the fire in the stove. They stood ruefully until the angel child devised the plan of carrying the stove into the stable, and there, safe from the storm, to continue the festivities. But they were met at the door of the stable by Peter Washington.

"What you 'bout, Jim?"

"Now—it's snowin' so hard, we thought we'd take the stove into the stable."

"An' have er fiah in it? No, seh! G'w'on 'way f'm heh!—g'w'on! Don' 'low no sech foolishin' round yer. No, seh!"

"Well, we ain't goin' to hurt your old stable, are we?" asked Jimmie, ironically.

"Dat you ain't, Jim! Not so long's I keep my two eyes right plumb squaah pinted at ol' Jim. No, seh!" Peter began to chuckle in derision.

The two vagabonds stood before him while he informed them of their iniquities as well as their absurdities, and further made clear his own masterly grasp of the spirit of their devices. Nothing affects children so much as rhetoric. It may not involve any definite presentation of common-sense, but if it is picturesque they surrender decently to its influence. Peter was by all means a rhetorician, and it was not long before the two children had dismally succumbed to him. They went away.

Depositing the stove in the snow, they straightened to look at each other. It did not enter either head to relinquish the idea of continuing the game. But the situation seemed invulnerable.

The angel child went on a scouting tour. Presently she returned, flying. "I know! Let's have it in the cellar! In the cellar! Oh, it'll be lovely!"

The outer door of the cellar was open, and they proceeded down some steps with their treasure. There was plenty of light; the cellar was high-walled, warm, and dry. They named it an ideal place. Two huge cylindrical furnaces were humming away, one at either end. Overhead the beams detonated with the different emotions which agitated the tea party.

Jimmie worked like a stoker, and soon there was a fine bright fire in the stove. The fuel was of small brittle sticks which did not make a great deal of smoke.

"Now what'll we cook?" cried little Cora. "What'll we cook, Jim? We must have something to cook, you know."

"Potatoes?" said Jimmie.

But the angel child made a scornful gesture. "No. I've cooked 'bout a million potatoes, I guess. Potatoes aren't nice any more."

Jimmie's mind was all said and done when the question of potatoes had been passed, and he looked weakly at his companion.

"Haven't you got any turnips in your house?" she inquired, contemptuously. "In my house we have *turnips.*"

"Oh, turnips!" exclaimed Jimmie, immensely relieved to find that the honor of his family was safe. "Turnips? Oh, bushels an' bushels an' bushels! Out in the shed."

"Well, go an' get a whole lot," commanded the angel child. "Go an' get a whole lot. Grea' big ones. *We* always have grea' big ones."

Jimmie went to the shed and kicked gently at a company of turnips which the frost had amalgamated. He made three journeys to and from the cellar, carrying always the very largest types from his father's store. Four of them filled the oven of little Cora's stove. This fact did not please her, so they placed three rows of turnips on the hot top. Then the angel child, profoundly moved by an inspiration, suddenly cried out,

"Oh, Jimmie, let's play we're keepin' a hotel, an' have got to cook for 'bout a thousand people, an' those two furnaces will be the ovens, an' I'll be the chief cook—"

"No; I want to be chief cook some of the time," interrupted Jimmie.

"No; I'll be chief cook my own self. You must be my 'sistant. Now I'll prepare 'em—see? An' then you put 'em in the ovens. Get the shovel. We'll play that's the pan. I'll fix 'em, an' then you put 'em in the oven. Hold it still now."

Jim held the coal-shovel while little Cora, with a frown of importance, arranged turnips in rows upon it. She patted each one daintily, and then backed away to view it, with her head critically sideways.

"There!" she shouted at last. "That'll do, I guess. Put 'em in the oven."

Jimmie marched with his shovelful of turnips to one of the furnaces. The door was already open, and he slid the shovel in upon the red coals.

"Come on," cried little Cora. "I've got another batch nearly ready."

"But what am I goin' to do with these?" asked Jimmie. "There ain't only one shovel."

"Leave 'm in there," retorted the girl, passionately. "Leave 'm in there, an' then play you're comin' with another pan. 'Tain't right to stand there an' *hold* the pan, you goose."

So Jimmie expelled all his turnips from his shovel out upon the furnace fire, and returned obediently for another batch.

"These are puddings," yelled the angel child, gleefully. "Dozens an' dozens of puddings for the thousand people at our grea' big hotel."

IV

At the first alarm the painter had fled to the doctor's office, where he hid his face behind a book and pretended that he did not hear the noise of feminine revelling. When the doctor came from a round of calls, he too retreated upon the office, and the men consoled each other as well as they were able. Once Mrs. Trescott dashed in to say delightedly that her tea party was not only the success of the season, but it was probably the very nicest tea party that had ever been held in Whilomville. After vainly beseeching them to return with her, she dashed away again, her face bright with happiness.

The doctor and the painter remained for a long time in silence, Trescott tapping reflectively upon the window-pane. Finally he turned to the painter, and sniffing, said: "What is that, Willis? Don't you smell something?"

The painter also sniffed. "Why, yes! It's like—it's like turnips."

"Turnips? No; it can't be.

"Well, it's very much like it."

The puzzled doctor opened the door into the hall, and at first it appeared that he was going to give back two paces. A result of frizzling turnips, which was almost as tangible as mist, had blown in upon his face and made him gasp. "Good God! Willis, what can this be?" he cried.

"Whee!" said the painter. "It's awful, isn't it?"

The doctor made his way hurriedly to his wife, but before he could speak with her he had to endure the business of greeting a score of women. Then he whispered, "Out in the hall there's an awful—"

"THE SOLEMN ODOR OF BURNING TURNIPS ROLLED IN LIKE A SEA-FOG"

But at that moment it came to them on the wings of a sudden draught. The solemn odor of burning turnips rolled in like a sea-fog, and fell upon that dainty, perfumed tea party. It was almost a personality; if some unbidden and extremely odious guest had entered the room, the effect would have been much the same. The sprightly talk stopped with a jolt, and people looked at each other. Then a few brave and considerate persons made the usual attempt to talk away as if nothing had happened. They all looked at their hostess, who wore an air of stupefaction.

The odor of burning turnips grew and grew. To Trescott it seemed to make a noise. He thought he could hear the dull roar of this outrage. Under some circumstances he might have been able to take the situation from a point of view of comedy, but the agony of his wife was too acute, and, for him, too visible. She was saying: "Yes, we saw the play the last time we were in New York. I liked it very much. That scene in the second act—the gloomy church, you know, and all that—and the organ playing—and then when the four singing little girls came in—" But Trescott comprehended that she did not know if she was talking of a play or a parachute.

He had not been in the room twenty seconds before his brow suddenly flushed with an angry inspiration. He left the room hastily, leaving behind him an incoherent phrase of apology, and charged upon his office, where he found the painter somnolent.

"Willis!" he cried, sternly, "come with me. It's that damn kid of yours!"

The painter was immediately agitated. He always seemed to feel more than any one else in the world the peculiar ability of his child to create resounding excitement, but he seemed always to exhibit his feelings very late. He arose hastily, and hurried after Trescott to the top of the inside cellar stairway. Trescott motioned him to pause, and for an instant they listened.

"Hurry up, Jim," cried the busy little Cora. "Here's another whole batch of lovely puddings. Hurry up now, an' put 'em in the oven."

Trescott looked at the painter; the painter groaned. Then they appeared violently in the middle of the great kitchen of the hotel with a thousand people in it. "Jimmie, go up-stairs!" said Trescott, and then he turned to watch the painter deal with the angel child.

With some imitation of wrath, the painter stalked to his daughter's side and grasped her by the arm.

"'HERE'S ANOTHER BATCH OF LOVELY PUDDINGS'"

"Oh, papa! papa!" she screamed. "You're pinching me! You're pinching me! You're pinching me, papa!"

At first the painter had seemed resolved to keep his grip, but suddenly he let go her arm in a panic. "I've hurt her," he said, turning to Trescott.

Trescott had swiftly done much towards the obliteration of the hotel kitchen, but he looked up now and spoke, after a short period of reflection. "You've hurt her, have you? Well, hurt her again. Spank her!" he cried, enthusiastically. "Spank her, confound you, man! She needs it. Here's your chance. Spank her, and spank her good. Spank her!"

113

The painter naturally wavered over this incendiary proposition, but at last, in one supreme burst of daring, he shut his eyes and again grabbed his precious offspring.

The spanking was lamentably the work of a perfect bungler. It couldn't have hurt at all; but the angel child raised to heaven a loud, clear soprano howl that expressed the last word in even mediæval anguish. Soon the painter was aghast. "Stop it, darling! I didn't mean—I didn't mean to—to hurt you so much, you know." He danced nervously. Trescott sat on a box, and devilishly smiled.

But the pasture call of suffering motherhood came down to them, and a moment later a splendid apparition appeared on the cellar stairs. She understood the scene at a glance. "Willis! What have you been doing?"

Trescott sat on his box, the painter guiltily moved from foot to foot, and the angel child advanced to her mother with arms outstretched, making a piteous wail of amazed and pained pride that would have moved Peter the Great. Regardless of her frock, the panting mother knelt on the stone floor and took her child to her bosom, and looked, then, bitterly, scornfully, at the cowering father and husband.

The painter, for his part, at once looked reproachfully at Trescott, as if to say: "There! You see?"

Trescott arose and extended his hands in a quiet but magnificent gesture of despair and weariness. He seemed about to say something classic, and, quite instinctively, they waited. The stillness was deep, and the wait was longer than a moment. "Well," he said, "we can't live in the cellar. Let's go up-stairs."

X. THE TRIAL, EXECUTION, AND BURIAL OF HOMER PHELPS

FROM time to time an enwearied pine bough let fall to the earth its load of melting snow, and the branch swung back glistening in the faint wintry sunlight. Down the gulch a brook clattered amid its ice with the sound of a perpetual breaking of glass. All the forest looked drenched and forlorn.

The sky-line was a ragged enclosure of gray cliffs and hemlocks and pines. If one had been miraculously set down in this gulch one could have imagined easily that the nearest human habitation was hundreds of miles away, if it were not for an old half-discernible wood-road that led towards the brook.

"Halt! Who's there?"

This low and gruff cry suddenly dispelled the stillness which lay upon the lonely gulch, but the hush which followed it seemed even more profound. The hush endured for some seconds, and then the voice of the challenger was again raised, this time with a distinctly querulous note in it.

"Halt! Who's there? Why don't you answer when I holler? Don't you know you're likely to get shot?"

A second voice answered, "Oh, you knew who I was easy enough."

"That don't make no diff'rence." One of the Margate twins stepped from a thicket and confronted Homer Phelps on the old wood-road. The majestic scowl of official wrath was upon the brow of Reeves Margate, a long stick was held in the hollow of his arm as one would hold a rifle, and he strode grimly to the other boy. "That don't make no diff'rence. You've got to answer when I holler, anyhow. Willie says so."

At the mention of the dread chieftain's name the Phelps boy daunted a trifle, but he still sulkily murmured, "Well, you knew it was me."

He started on his way through the snow, but the twin sturdily blocked the path. "You can't pass less'n you give the countersign."

"Huh?" said the Phelps boy. "Countersign?"

"Yes—countersign," sneered the twin, strong in his sense of virtue.

But the Phelps boy became very angry. "Can't I, hey? Can't I, hey? I'll show you whether I can or not! I'll show you, Reeves Margate!"

There was a short scuffle, and then arose the anguished clamor of the sentry: "Hey, fellers! Here's a man tryin' to run a-past the guard. Hey, fellers! Hey!"

There was a great noise in the adjacent underbrush. The voice of Willie could be heard exhorting his followers to charge swiftly and bravely. Then they appeared—Willie Dalzel, Jimmie Trescott, the other Margate twin, and Dan Earl. The chieftain's face was dark with wrath. "What's the matter? Can't you play it right? 'Ain't you got any sense?" he asked the Phelps boy.

The sentry was yelling out his grievance. "Now—he came along an' I hollered at 'im, an' he didn't pay no 'tention, an' when I ast 'im for the countersign, he wouldn't say nothin'. That ain't no way."

"Can't you play it right?" asked the chief again, with gloomy scorn.

"He knew it was me easy enough," said the Phelps boy.

"That 'ain't got nothin' to do with it," cried the chief, furiously. "That 'ain't got nothin' to do with it. If you're goin' to play, you've got to play it right. It ain't no fun if you go spoilin' the whole thing this way. Can't you play it right?"

"I forgot the countersign," lied the culprit, weakly.

Whereupon the remainder of the band yelled out, with one triumphant voice: "War to the knife! War to the knife! I remember it, Willie. Don't I, Willie?"

The leader was puzzled. Evidently he was trying to develop in his mind a plan for dealing correctly with this unusual incident. He felt, no doubt, that he must proceed according to the books, but unfortunately the books did not cover the point precisely. However, he finally said to Homer Phelps, "You are under arrest." Then with a stentorian voice he shouted, "Seize him!"

His loyal followers looked startled for a brief moment, but directly they began to move upon the Phelps boy. The latter clearly did not intend to be seized. He backed away, expostulating wildly. He even seemed somewhat frightened. "No, no; don't you touch me, I tell you; don't you dare touch me."

The others did not seem anxious to engage. They moved slowly, watching the desperate light in his eyes. The chieftain stood with folded arms, his face growing darker and darker with impatience. At length he burst out: "Oh, seize him, I tell you! Why don't you seize him? Grab him by the leg, Dannie! Hurry up, all of you! Seize him, I keep a-say-in'!"

Thus adjured, the Margate twins and Dan Earl made another pained effort, while Jimmie Trescott manœuvred to cut off a retreat. But, to tell the truth, there was a boyish law which held them back from laying hands of violence upon little Phelps under these conditions. Perhaps it was because they were only playing, whereas he was now undeniably serious. At any rate, they looked very sick of their occupation.

"Don't you dare!" snarled the Phelps boy, facing first one and then the other; he was almost in tears—"don't you dare touch me!"

The chieftain was now hopping with exasperation. "Oh, seize him, can't you? You're no good at all!" Then he loosed his wrath upon the Phelps boy: "Stand still, Homer, can't you? You've got to be seized, you know. That ain't the way. It ain't any fun if you keep a-dodgin' that way. Stand still, can't you! You've got to be seized."

"I don't want to be seized," retorted the Phelps boy, obstinate and bitter.

"But you've *got* to be seized!" yelled the maddened chief. "Don't you see? That's the way to play it."

The Phelps boy answered, promptly, "But I don't want to play that way."

"But that's the *right* way to play it. Don't you see? You've got to play it the right way. You've got to be seized, an' then we'll hold a trial on you, an'—an' all sorts of things."

But this prospect held no illusions for the Phelps boy. He continued doggedly to repeat, "I don't want to play that way!"

Of course in the end the chief stooped to beg and beseech this unreasonable lad. "Oh, come on, Homer! Don't be so mean. You're a-spoilin' everything. We won't hurt you any. Not the tintiest bit. It's all just playin'. What's the matter with you?"

The different tone of the leader made an immediate impression upon the other. He showed some signs of the beginning of weakness. "Well," he asked, "what you goin' to do?"

"Why, first we're goin' to put you in a dungeon, or tie you to a stake, or something like that—just pertend, you know," added the chief, hurriedly, "an' then we'll hold a trial, awful solemn, but there won't be anything what'll hurt you. Not a thing."

And so the game was readjusted. The Phelps boy was marched off between Dan Earl and a Margate twin. The party proceeded to their camp, which was hidden some hundred feet back in the thickets. There was a miserable little hut with a pine-bark roof, which so frankly and constantly leaked that existence in the open air was always preferable. At present it was noisily dripping melted snow into the black mouldy interior. In front of this hut a feeble fire was flickering through its unhappy career. Underfoot, the watery snow was of the color of lead.

The party having arrived at the camp, the chief leaned against a tree, and balancing on one foot, drew off a rubber boot. From this boot he emptied about a quart of snow. He squeezed his stocking, which had a hole from which protruded a lobster-red toe. He resumed his boot. "Bring up the prisoner," said he. They did it. "Guilty or not guilty?" he asked.

"FROM THIS BOOT HE EMPTIED ABOUT A QUART OF SNOW"

"Huh?" said the Phelps boy.

"Guilty or not guilty?" demanded the chief,

peremptorily. "Guilty or not guilty? Don't you understand?"

Homer Phelps looked profoundly puzzled. "Guilty or not guilty?" he asked, slowly and weakly.

The chief made a swift gesture, and turned in despair to the others. "Oh, he don't do it right! He does it all wrong!" He again faced the prisoner with an air of making a last attempt, "Now look-a-here, Homer, when I say, 'Guilty or not guilty?' you want to up an' say, 'Not Guilty.' Don't you see?"

"Not guilty," said Homer, at once.

"No, no, no. Wait till I ask you. Now wait." He called out, pompously, "Pards, if this prisoner before us is guilty, what shall be his fate?"

All those well-trained little infants with one voice sung out, "*Death!*"

"Prisoner," continued the chief, "are you guilty or not guilty?"

"But look-a-here," argued Homer, "you said it wouldn't be nothin' that would hurt. I—"

"Thunder an' lightnin'!" roared the wretched chief. "Keep your mouth shut, can't ye? What in the mischief—"

But there was an interruption from Jimmie Trescott, who shouldered a twin aside and stepped to the front. "Here," he said, very contemptuously, "let me be the prisoner. I'll show 'im how to do it."

"All right, Jim," cried the chief, delighted; "you be the prisoner, then. Now all you fellers with guns stand there in a row! Get out of the way, Homer!" He cleared his throat, and addressed Jimmie. "Prisoner, are you guilty or not guilty?"

"Not guilty," answered Jimmie, firmly. Standing there before his judge—unarmed, slim, quiet, modest—he was ideal.

The chief beamed upon him, and looked aside to cast a triumphant and withering glance upon Homer Phelps. He said: "There! That's the way to do it."

The twins and Dan Earl also much admired Jimmie.

"That's all right so far, anyhow," said the satisfied chief. "An' now we'll— now we'll—we'll perceed with the execution."

"That ain't right," said the new prisoner, suddenly. "That ain't the next thing. You've got to have a trial first. You've got to fetch up a lot of people first who'll say I done it."

"That's so," said the chief. "I didn't think. Here, Reeves, you be first witness. Did the prisoner do it?"

The twin gulped for a moment in his anxiety to make the proper reply. He was at the point where the roads forked. Finally he hazarded, "Yes."

"There," said the chief, "that's one of 'em. Now, Dan, you be a witness. Did he do it?"

Dan Earl, having before him the twin's example, did not hesitate. "Yes," he said.

"Well, then, pards, what shall be his fate?"

Again came the ringing answer, "*Death!*"

With Jimmie in the principal rôle, this drama, hidden deep in the hemlock thicket neared a kind of perfection. "You must blind-fold me," cried the condemned lad, briskly, "an' then I'll go off an' stand, an' you must all get in a row an' shoot me."

The chief gave this plan his urbane countenance, and the twins and Dan Earl were greatly pleased. They blindfolded Jimmie under his careful directions. He waded a few paces into snow, and then turned and stood with quiet dignity, awaiting his fate. The chief marshalled the twins and Dan Earl in line with their sticks. He gave the necessary commands: "Load! Ready! Aim! Fire!" At the last command the firing party all together yelled, "Bang!"

Jimmie threw his hands high, tottered in agony for a moment, and then crashed full length into the snow—into, one would think, a serious case of pneumonia. It was beautiful.

THE EXECUTION

He arose almost immediately and came back to them, wondrously pleased with himself. They acclaimed him joyously.

The chief was particularly grateful. He was always trying to bring off these little romantic affairs, and it seemed, after all, that the only boy who could ever really help him was Jimmie Trescott. "There," he said to the others, "that's the way it ought to be done."

They were touched to the heart by the whole thing, and they looked at Jimmie with big, smiling eyes. Jimmie, blown out like a balloon-fish with pride of his performance, swaggered to the fire and took seat on some wet hemlock boughs. "Fetch some more wood, one of you kids," he murmured, negligently. One of the twins came fortunately upon a small cedar-tree the lower branches of which were dead and dry. An armful of these branches flung upon the sick fire soon made a high, ruddy, warm blaze, which was like an illumination in honor of Jimmie's success.

The boys sprawled about the fire and talked the regular language of the game. "Waal, pards," remarked the chief, "it's many a night we've had together here in the Rockies among the b'ars an' the Indyuns, hey?"

"Yes, pard," replied Jimmie Trescott, "I reckon you're right. Our wild, free life is—there ain't nothin' to compare with our wild, free life."

Whereupon the two lads arose and magnificently shook hands, while the others watched them in an ecstasy. "I'll allus stick by ye, pard," said Jimmie, earnestly. "When yer in trouble, don't forget that Lightnin' Lou is at yer back."

"Thanky, pard," quoth Willie Dalzel, deeply affected. "I'll not forget it, pard. An' don't you forget, either, that Dead-shot Demon, the leader of the Red Raiders, never forgits a friend."

But Homer Phelps was having none of this great fun. Since his disgraceful refusal to be seized and executed he had been hovering unheeded on the outskirts of the band. He seemed very sorry; he cast a wistful eye at the romantic scene. He knew too well that if he went near at that particular time he would be certain to encounter a pitiless snubbing. So he vacillated modestly in the background.

At last the moment came when he dared venture near enough to the fire to gain some warmth, for he was now bitterly suffering with the cold. He sidled close to Willie Dalzel. No one heeded him. Eventually he looked at his chief, and with a bright face said,

"Now—if I was seized now to be executed, I could do it as well as Jimmie Trescott, I could."

The chief gave a crow of scorn, in which he was followed by the other boys. "Ho!" he cried, "why didn't you do it, then? Why didn't you do it?" Homer Phelps felt upon him many pairs of disdainful eyes. He wagged his shoulders in misery.

"You're dead," said the chief, frankly. "That's what you are. We executed you, we did."

"When?" demanded the Phelps boy, with some spirit.

"Just a little while ago. Didn't we, fellers? Hey, fellers, didn't we?"

The trained chorus cried: "Yes, of course we did. You're dead, Homer. You can't play any more. You're dead."

"That wasn't me. It was Jimmie Trescott," he said, in a low and bitter voice, his eyes on the ground. He would have given the world if he could have retracted his mad refusals of the early part of the drama.

"No," said the chief, "it was you. We're playin' it was you, an' it *was* you. You're dead, you are." And seeing the cruel effect of his words, he did not refrain from administering some advice: "The next time, don't be such a chuckle-head."

Presently the camp imagined that it was attacked by Indians, and the boys dodged behind trees with their stick-rifles, shouting out, "Bang!" and encouraging each other to resist until the last. In the mean time the dead lad hovered near the fire, looking moodily at the gay and exciting scene. After the fight the gallant defenders returned one by one to the fire, where they grandly clasped hands, calling each other "old pard," and boasting of their deeds.

Parenthetically, one of the twins had an unfortunate inspiration. "I killed the Indy-un chief, fellers. Did you see me kill the Indy-un chief?"

But Willie Dalzel, his own chief, turned upon him wrathfully: "*You* didn't kill no chief. *I* killed 'im with me own hand."

"Oh!" said the twin, apologetically, at once. "It must have been some other Indy-un."

"Who's wounded?" cried Willie Dalzel. "Ain't anybody wounded?" The party professed themselves well and sound. The roving and inventive eye of the chief chanced upon Homer Phelps. "Ho! Here's a dead man! Come on, fellers, here's a dead man! We've got to bury him, you know." And at his bidding they pounced upon the dead Phelps lad. The unhappy boy saw clearly his road to rehabilitation, but mind and body revolted at the idea of burial, even as they had revolted at the thought of execution. "No!" he said, stubbornly. "No! I don't want to be buried! I don't want to be buried!"

THE FUNERAL ORATION

"You've *got* to be buried!" yelled the chief, passionately. "'Tain't goin' to hurt ye, is it? Think you're made of glass? Come on, fellers, get the grave ready!"

They scattered hemlock boughs upon the snow in the form of a rectangle, and piled other boughs near at hand. The victim surveyed these preparations with a glassy eye. When all was ready, the chief turned determinedly to him: "Come on now, Homer. We've got to carry you to the grave. Get him by the legs, Jim!"

Little Phelps had now passed into that state which may be described as a curious and temporary childish fatalism. He still objected, but it was only feeble muttering, as if he did not know what he spoke. In some confusion

they carried him to the rectangle of hemlock boughs and dropped him. Then they piled other boughs upon him until he was not to be seen. The chief stepped forward to make a short address, but before proceeding with it he thought it expedient, from certain indications, to speak to the grave itself. "Lie still, can't ye? Lie still until I get through." There was a faint movement of the boughs, and then a perfect silence.

The chief took off his hat. Those who watched him could see that his face was harrowed with emotion. "Pards," he began, brokenly—"pards, we've got one more debt to pay them murderin' red-skins. Bowie-knife Joe was a brave man an' a good pard, but—he's gone now—gone." He paused for a moment, overcome, and the stillness was only broken by the deep manly grief of Jimmie Trescott.

XI. THE FIGHT

I

THE child life of the neighborhood was sometimes moved in its deeps at the sight of wagon-loads of furniture arriving in front of some house which, with closed blinds and barred doors, had been for a time a mystery, or even a fear. The boys often expressed this fear by stamping bravely and noisily on the porch of the house, and then suddenly darting away with screams of nervous laughter, as if they expected to be pursued by something uncanny. There was a group who held that the cellar of a vacant house was certainly the abode of robbers, smugglers, assassins, mysterious masked men in council about the dim rays of a candle, and possessing skulls, emblematic bloody daggers, and owls. Then, near the first of April, would come along a wagon-load of furniture, and children would assemble on the walk by the gate and make serious examination of everything that passed into the house, and taking no thought whatever of masked men.

One day it was announced in the neighborhood that a family was actually moving into the Hannigan house, next door to Dr. Trescott's. Jimmie was one of the first to be informed, and by the time some of his friends came dashing up he was versed in much.

"Any boys?" they demanded, eagerly.

"Yes," answered Jimmie, proudly. "One's a little feller, and one's most as big as me. I saw 'em, I did."

"Where are they?" asked Willie Dalzel, as if under the circumstances he could not take Jimmie's word, but must have the evidence of his senses.

"Oh, they're in there," said Jimmie, carelessly. It was evident he owned these new boys.

Willie Dalzel resented Jimmie's proprietary way.

"Ho!" he cried, scornfully. "Why don't they come out, then? Why don't they come out?"

"How d' I know?" said Jimmie.

"STAMPING BRAVELY AND NOISILY ON THE PORCH"

"Well," retorted Willie Dalzel, "you seemed to know so thundering much about 'em."

At the moment a boy came strolling down the gravel walk which led from the front door to the gate. He was about the height and age of Jimmie Trescott, but he was thick through the chest and had fat legs. His face was round and rosy and plump, but his hair was curly black, and his brows were naturally darkling, so that he resembled both a pudding and a young bull.

He approached slowly the group of older inhabitants, and they had grown profoundly silent. They looked him over; he looked them over. They might have been savages observing the first white man, or white men observing the first savage. The silence held steady.

128

As he neared the gate the strange boy wandered off to the left in a definite way, which proved his instinct to make a circular voyage when in doubt. The motionless group stared at him. In time this unsmiling scrutiny worked upon him somewhat, and he leaned against the fence and fastidiously examined one shoe.

In the end Willie Dalzel authoritatively broke the stillness. "What's your name?" said he, gruffly.

"Johnnie Hedge 'tis," answered the new boy. Then came another great silence while Whilomville pondered this intelligence.

Again came the voice of authority—"Where'd you live b'fore?"

"Jersey City."

These two sentences completed the first section of the formal code. The second section concerned itself with the establishment of the new-comer's exact position in the neighborhood.

"I kin lick you," announced Willie Dalzel, and awaited the answer.

The Hedge boy had stared at Willie Dalzel, but he stared at him again. After a pause he said, "I know you kin."

"Well," demanded Willie, "kin *he* lick you?" And he indicated Jimmie Trescott with a sweep which announced plainly that Jimmie was the next in prowess.

Whereupon the new boy looked at Jimmie respectfully but carefully, and at length said, "I dun'no'."

This was the signal for an outburst of shrill screaming, and everybody pushed Jimmie forward. He knew what he had to say, and, as befitted the occasion, he said it fiercely: "Kin you lick me?"

The new boy also understood what he had to say, and, despite his unhappy and lonely state, he said it bravely: "Yes."

"Well," retorted Jimmie, bluntly, "come out and do it, then! Jest come out and do it!" And these words were greeted with cheers. These little rascals yelled that there should be a fight at once. They were in bliss over the prospect. "Go on, Jim! Make 'im come out. He said he could lick you. Aw-aw-aw! He said he could lick you!" There probably never was a fight among this class in Whilomville which was not the result of the goading and guying of two proud lads by a populace of urchins who simply wished to see a show.

Willie Dalzel was very busy. He turned first to the one and then to the other. "You said you could lick him. Well, why don't you come out and do it, then? You said you could lick him, didn't you?"

"Yes," answered the new boy, dogged and dubious.

Willie tried to drag Jimmie by the arm. "Aw, go on, Jimmie! You ain't afraid, are you?"

"No," said Jimmie.

The two victims opened wide eyes at each other. The fence separated them, and so it was impossible for them to immediately engage; but they seemed to understand that they were ultimately to be sacrificed to the ferocious aspirations of the other boys, and each scanned the other to learn something of his spirit. They were not angry at all. They were merely two little gladiators who were being clamorously told to hurt each other. Each displayed hesitation and doubt without displaying fear. They did not exactly understand what were their feelings, and they moodily kicked the ground and made low and sullen answers to Willie Dalzel, who worked like a circus-manager.

"Aw, go on, Jim! What's the matter with you? You ain't afraid, are you? Well, then, say something." This sentiment received more cheering from the abandoned little wretches who wished to be entertained, and in this cheering there could be heard notes of derision of Jimmie Trescott. The latter had a position to sustain; he was well known; he often bragged of his willingness and ability to thrash other boys; well, then, here was a boy of his size who said that he could not thrash him. What was he going to do about it? The crowd made these arguments very clear, and repeated them again and again.

Finally Jimmie, driven to aggression, walked close to the fence and said to the new boy, "The first time I catch you out of your own yard I'll lam the head off'n you!" This was received with wild plaudits by the Whilomville urchins.

But the new boy stepped back from the fence. He was awed by Jimmie's formidable mien. But he managed to get out a semi-defiant sentence. "Maybe you will, and maybe you won't," said he.

However, his short retreat was taken as a practical victory for Jimmie, and the boys hooted him bitterly. He remained inside the fence, swinging one foot and scowling, while Jimmie was escorted off down the street amid acclamations. The new boy turned and walked back towards the house, his face gloomy, lined deep with discouragement, as if he felt that the new environment's antagonism and palpable cruelty were sure to prove too much for him.

II

The mother of Johnnie Hedge was a widow, and the chief theory of her life was that her boy should be in school on the greatest possible number of days. He himself had no sympathy with this ambition, but she detected the truth of his diseases with an unerring eye, and he was required to be really ill before he could win the right to disregard the first bell, morning and noon. The chicken-pox and the mumps had given him vacations—vacations of misery, wherein he nearly died between pain and nursing. But bad colds in the head did nothing for him, and he was not able to invent a satisfactory hacking cough. His mother was not consistently a tartar. In most things he swayed her to his will. He was allowed to have more jam, pickles, and pie than most boys; she respected his profound loathing of Sunday-school; on summer evenings he could remain out-of-doors until 8.30; but in this matter of school she was inexorable. This single point in her character was of steel.

The Hedges arrived in Whilomville on a Saturday, and on the following Monday Johnnie wended his way to school with a note to the principal and his Jersey City school-books. He knew perfectly well that he would be told to buy new and different books, but in those days mothers always had an idea that old books would "do," and they invariably sent boys off to a new school with books which would not meet the selected and unchangeable views of the new administration. The old books never would "do." Then the boys brought them home to annoyed mothers and asked for ninety cents or sixty cents or eighty-five cents or some number of cents for another outfit. In the garret of every house holding a large family there was a collection of effete school-books, with mother rebellious because James could not inherit his books from Paul, who should properly be Peter's heir, while Peter should be a beneficiary under Henry's will.

"'THE FIRST TIME I CATCH YOU I'LL LAM THE HEAD OFF'N YOU'"

But the matter of the books was not the measure of Johnnie Hedge's unhappiness. This whole business of changing schools was a complete torture. Alone he had to go among a new people, a new tribe, and he apprehended his serious time. There were only two fates for him. One meant victory. One meant a kind of serfdom in which he would subscribe to every word of some superior boy and support his every word. It was not anything like an English system of fagging, because boys invariably drifted into the figurative service of other boys whom they devotedly admired, and if they were obliged to subscribe to everything, it is true that they would have done so freely in any case. One means to suggest that Johnnie Hedge had to find his place. Willie Dalzel was a type of the little chieftain, and Willie was a master, but he was not a bully in a special physical sense. He did not drag little boys by the ears until they cried, nor make them tearfully fetch and carry for him. They fetched and carried, but it was because of their worship of his prowess and genius. And so all through the strata of boy life were chieftains and subchieftains and assistant subchieftains. There was no question of little Hedge being towed about by the nose; it was, as one has said, that he had to find his place in a new school. And this in itself was a problem which awed his boyish heart. He was a stranger cast away upon the moon. None knew him, understood him, felt for him. He would be surrounded for this initiative time by a horde of jackal creatures who might turn out in the end to be little boys like himself, but this last point his philosophy could not understand in its fulness.

He came to a white meeting-house sort of a place, in the squat tower of which a great bell was clanging impressively. He passed through an iron gate into a play-ground worn bare as the bed of a mountain brook by the endless runnings and scufflings of little children. There was still a half-hour before the final clangor in the squat tower, but the play-ground held a number of frolicsome imps. A loitering boy espied Johnnie Hedge, and he howled: "Oh! oh! Here's a new feller! Here's a new feller!" He advanced upon the strange arrival. "What's your name?" he demanded, belligerently, like a particularly offensive custom-house officer.

"Johnnie Hedge," responded the new-comer, shyly.

133

This name struck the other boy as being very comic. All new names strike boys as being comic. He laughed noisily.

"Oh, fellers, he says his name is Johnnie Hedge! Haw! haw! haw!"

The new boy felt that his name was the most disgraceful thing which had ever been attached to a human being.

"Johnnie Hedge! Haw! haw! What room you in?" said the other lad.

"I dun'no'," said Johnnie. In the mean time a small flock of interested vultures had gathered about him. The main thing was his absolute strangeness. He even would have welcomed the sight of his tormentors of Saturday; he had seen them before at least. These creatures were only so many incomprehensible problems. He diffidently began to make his way towards the main door of the school, and the other boys followed him. They demanded information.

"Are you through subtraction yet? We study jogerfre—did you, ever? You live here now? You goin' to school here now?"

To many questions he made answer as well as the clamor would permit, and at length he reached the main door and went quaking unto his new kings. As befitted them, the rabble stopped at the door. A teacher strolling along a corridor found a small boy holding in his hand a note. The boy palpably did not know what to do with the note, but the teacher knew, and took it. Thereafter this little boy was in harness.

A splendid lady in gorgeous robes gave him a seat at a double desk, at the end of which sat a hoodlum with grimy finger-nails, who eyed the inauguration with an extreme and personal curiosity. The other desks were gradually occupied by children, who first were told of the new boy, and then turned upon him a speculative and somewhat derisive eye. The school opened; little classes went forward to a position in front of the teacher's platform and tried to explain that they knew something. The new boy was not requisitioned a great deal; he was allowed to lie dormant until he became used to the scenes and until the teacher found, approximately, his mental position. In the mean time he suffered a shower of stares and whispers and giggles, as if he were a man-ape, whereas he was precisely like other children. From time to time he made funny and pathetic little overtures to other boys, but these overtures could not yet be received; he was not known; he was a foreigner. The village school was like a nation. It was tight. Its amiability or friendship must be won in certain ways.

At recess he hovered in the school-room around the weak lights of society and around the teacher, in the hope that somebody might be good to him, but none considered him save as some sort of a specimen. The teacher of course had a secondary interest in the fact that he was an additional one to a class of sixty-three.

At twelve o'clock, when the ordered files of boys and girls marched towards the door, he exhibited—to no eye—the tremblings of a coward in a charge. He exaggerated the lawlessness of the play-ground and the street.

But the reality was hard enough. A shout greeted him:

"Oh, here's the new feller! Here's the new feller!"

Small and utterly obscure boys teased him. He had a hard time of it to get to the gate. There never was any actual hurt, but everything was competent to smite the lad with shame. It was a curious, groundless shame, but nevertheless it was shame. He was a new-comer, and he definitely felt the disgrace of the fact. In the street he was seen and recognized by some lads who had formed part of the group of Saturday. They shouted:

"Oh, Jimmie! Jimmie! Here he is! Here's that new feller!"

Jimmie Trescott was going virtuously towards his luncheon when he heard these cries behind him. He pretended not to hear, and in this deception he was assisted by the fact that he was engaged at the time in a furious argument with a friend over the relative merits of two "Uncle Tom's Cabin" companies. It appeared that one company had only two bloodhounds, while the other had ten. On the other hand, the first company had two Topsys and two Uncle Toms, while the second had only one Topsy and one Uncle Tom.

But the shouting little boys were hard after him. Finally they were even pulling at his arms.

"Jimmie—"

"What?" he demanded, turning with a snarl. "What d'you want? Leggo my arm!"

"Here he is! Here's the new feller! Here's the new feller! Now!"

"I don't care if he is," said Jimmie, with grand impatience. He tilted his chin. "I don't care if he is."

Then they reviled him. "Thought you was goin' to lick him first time you caught him! Yah! You're a 'fraid-cat!" They began to sing "'Fraid-cat! 'Fraidcat! 'Fraid-cat!" He expostulated hotly, turning from one to the other, but they would not listen. In the mean time the Hedge boy slunk on his way, looking with deep anxiety upon this attempt to send Jimmie against him. But Jimmie would have none of the plan.

III

When the children met again on the play-ground, Jimmie was openly challenged with cowardice. He had made a big threat in the hearing of comrades, and when invited by them to take advantage of an opportunity, he had refused. They had been fairly sure of their amusement, and they were indignant. Jimmie was finally driven to declare that as soon as school was out for the day, he would thrash the Hedge boy.

When finally the children came rushing out of the iron gate, filled with the delights of freedom, a hundred boys surrounded Jimmie in high spirits, for he had said that he was determined. They waited for the lone lad from Jersey City. When he appeared, Jimmie wasted no time. He walked straight to him and said, "Did you say you kin lick me?"

Johnnie Hedge was cowed, shrinking, affrighted, and the roars of a hundred boys thundered in his ears, but again he knew what he had to say. "Yes," he gasped, in anguish.

136

"Then," said Jimmie, resolutely, "you've got to fight." There was a joyous clamor by the mob. The beleaguered lad looked this way and that way for succor, as Willie Dalzel and other officious youngsters policed an irregular circle in the crowd. He saw Jimmie facing him; there was no help for it; he dropped his books—the old books which would not "do."

Now it was the fashion among tiny Whilomville belligerents to fight much in the manner of little bear cubs. Two boys would rush upon each other, immediately grapple, and—the best boy having probably succeeded in getting the coveted "under hold"—there would presently be a crash to the earth of the inferior boy, and he would probably be mopped around in the dust, or the mud, or the snow, or whatever the material happened to be, until the engagement was over. Whatever havoc was dealt out to him was ordinarily the result of his wild endeavors to throw off his opponent and arise. Both infants wept during the fight, as a common thing, and if they wept very hard, the fight was a harder fight. The result was never very bloody, but the complete dishevelment of both victor and vanquished was extraordinary. As for the spectacle, it more resembled a collision of boys in a fog than it did the manly art of hammering another human being into speechless inability.

The fight began when Jimmie made a mad, bear-cub rush at the new boy, amid savage cries of encouragement. Willie Dalzel, for instance, almost howled his head off. Very timid boys on the outskirts of the throng felt their hearts leap to their throats. It was a time when certain natures were impressed that only man is vile.

But it appeared that bear-cub rushing was no part of the instruction received by boys in Jersey City. Boys in Jersey City were apparently schooled curiously. Upon the onslaught of Jimmie, the stranger had gone wild with rage—boylike. Some spark had touched his fighting-blood, and in a moment he was a cornered, desperate, fire-eyed little man. He began to swing his arms, to revolve them so swiftly that one might have considered him a small, working model of an extra-fine patented windmill which was caught in a gale. For a moment this defence surprised Jimmie more than it damaged him, but two moments later a small, knotty fist caught him squarely in the eye, and with a shriek he went down in defeat. He lay on the ground so stunned that he could not even cry; but if he had been able to cry, he would have cried over his prestige—or something—not over his eye.

There was a dreadful tumult. The boys cast glances of amazement and terror upon the victor, and thronged upon the beaten Jimmie Trescott. It was a moment of excitement so intense that one cannot say what happened. Never before had Whilomville seen such a thing—not the little tots. They were aghast, dumfounded, and they glanced often over their shoulders at the new boy, who stood alone, his clinched fists at his side, his face crimson, his lips still working with the fury of battle.

But there was another surprise for Whilomville. It might have been seen that the little victor was silently debating against an impulse.

"NO TIME FOR ACADEMICS—HE RAN"

But the impulse won, for the lone lad from Jersey City suddenly wheeled, sprang like a demon, and struck another boy.

A curtain should be drawn before this deed. A knowledge of it is really too much for the heart to bear. The other boy was Willie Dalzel. The lone lad from Jersey City had smitten him full sore.

There is little to say of it. It must have been that a feeling worked gradually to the top of the little stranger's wrath that Jimmie Trescott had been a mere tool, that the front and centre of his persecutors had been Willie Dalzel, and being rendered temporarily lawless by his fighting-blood, he raised his hand and smote for revenge.

Willie Dalzel had been in the middle of a vandal's cry, which screeched out over the voices of everybody. The new boy's fist cut it in half, so to say. And then arose the howl of an amazed and terrorized walrus.

One wishes to draw a second curtain. Without discussion or inquiry or brief retort, Willie Dalzel ran away. He ran like a hare straight for home, this redoubtable chieftain. Following him at a heavy and slow pace ran the impassioned new boy. The scene was long remembered.

Willie Dalzel was no coward; he had been panic-stricken into running away from a new thing. He ran as a man might run from the sudden appearance of a vampire or a ghoul or a gorilla. This was no time for academics—he ran.

Jimmie slowly gathered himself and came to his feet. "Where's Willie?" said he, first of all. The crowd sniggered. "Where's Willie?" said Jimmie again.

"Why, he licked him *too!*" answered a boy suddenly.

"He did?" said Jimmie. He sat weakly down on the roadway. "He did?" After allowing a moment for the fact to sink into him, he looked up at the crowd with his one good eye and his one bunged eye, and smiled cheerfully

XII. THE CITY URCHIN AND THE CHASTE VILLAGERS

AFTER the brief encounters between the Hedge boy and Jimmie Trescott and the Hedge boy and Willie Dalzel, the neighborhood which contained the homes of the boys was, as far as child life is concerned, in a state resembling anarchy. This was owing to the signal overthrow and shameful retreat of the boy who had for several years led a certain little clan by the nose. The adherence of the little community did not go necessarily to the boy who could whip all the others, but it certainly could not go to a boy who had run away in a manner that made his shame patent to the whole world. Willie Dalzel found himself in a painful position. This tiny tribe which had followed him with such unwavering faith was now largely engaged in whistling and catcalling and hooting. He chased a number of them into the sanctity of their own yards, but from these coigns they continued to ridicule him.

But it must not be supposed that the fickle tribe went over in a body to the new light. They did nothing of the sort. They occupied themselves with avenging all which they had endured—gladly enough, too—for many months. As for the Hedge boy, he maintained a curious timid reserve, minding his own business with extreme care, and going to school with that deadly punctuality of which his mother was the genius. Jimmie Trescott suffered no adverse criticism from his fellows. He was entitled to be beaten by a boy who had made Willie Dalzel bellow like a bull-calf and run away. Indeed, he received some honors. He had confronted a very superior boy and received a bang in the eye which for a time was the wonder of the children, and he had not bellowed like a bull-calf. As a matter of fact, he was often invited to tell how it had felt, and this he did with some pride, claiming arrogantly that he had been superior to any particular pain.

Early in the episode he and the Hedge boy had patched up a treaty. Living next door to each other, they could not fail to have each other often in sight. One afternoon they wandered together in the strange indefinite diplomacy of boyhood. As they drew close the new boy suddenly said, "Napple?"

"Yes," said Jimmie, and the new boy bestowed upon him an apple. It was one of those green-coated winter-apples which lie for many months in safe and dry places, and can at any time be brought forth for the persecution of the unwary and inexperienced. An older age would have fled from this apple, but to the unguided youth of Jimmie Trescott it was a thing to be possessed and cherished. Wherefore this apple was the emblem of something more than a truce, despite the fact that it tasted like wet Indian meal; and Jimmie looked at the Hedge boy out of one good eye and one bunged eye. The long-drawn animosities of men have no place in the life of a boy. The boy's mind is flexible; he readjusts his position with an ease which is derived from the fact—simply—that he is not yet a man.

But there were other and more important matters. Johnnie Hedge's exploits had brought him into such prominence among the school-boys that it was necessary to settle a number of points once and for all. There was the usual number of boys in the school who were popularly known to be champions in their various classes. Among these Johnnie Hedge now had to thread his way, every boy taking it upon himself to feel anxious that Johnnie's exact position should be soon established. His fame as a fighter had gone forth to the world, but there were other boys who had fame as fighters, and the world was extremely anxious to know where to place the new-comer. Various heroes were urged to attempt this classification. Usually it was not accounted a matter of supreme importance, but in this boy life it was essential.

In all cases the heroes were backward enough. It was their followings who agitated the question. And so Johnnie Hedge was more or less beset.

He maintained his bashfulness. He backed away from altercation. It was plain that to bring matters to a point he must be forced into a quarrel. It was also plain that the proper person for the business was some boy who could whip Willie Dalzel, and these formidable warriors were distinctly averse to undertaking the new contract. It is a kind of a law in boy life that a quiet, decent, peace-loving lad is able to thrash a wide-mouthed talker. And so it had transpired that by a peculiar system of elimination most of the real chiefs were quiet, decent, peace-loving boys, and they had no desire to engage in a fight with a boy on the sole grounds that it was not known who could whip. Johnnie Hedge attended his affairs, they attended their affairs, and around them waged this discussion of relative merit. Jimmie Trescott took a prominent part in these arguments. He contended that Johnnie Hedge could thrash any boy in the world. He was certain of it, and to any one who opposed him he said, "You just get one of those smashes in the eye, and then you'll see." In the mean time there was a grand and impressive silence in the direction of Willie Dalzel. He had gathered remnants of his clan, but the main parts of his sovereignty were scattered to the winds. He was an enemy.

Owing to the circumspect behavior of the new boy, the commotions on the school grounds came to nothing. He was often asked, "Kin you lick him?" And he invariably replied, "I dun'no'." This idea of waging battle with the entire world appalled him.

A war for complete supremacy of the tribe which had been headed by Willie Dalzel was fought out in the country of the tribe. It came to pass that a certain half-dime blood-and-thunder pamphlet had a great vogue in the tribe at this particular time. This story relates the experience of a lad who began his career as cabin-boy on a pirate ship. Throughout the first fifteen chapters he was rope's-ended from one end of the ship to the other end, and very often he was felled to the deck by a heavy fist. He lived through enough hardships to have killed a battalion of Turkish soldiers, but in the end he rose upon them. Yes, he rose upon them. Hordes of pirates fell before his intrepid arm, and in the last chapters of the book he is seen jauntily careering on his own hook as one of the most gallous pirate captains that ever sailed the seas.

Naturally, when this tale was thoroughly understood by the tribe, they had to dramatize it, although it was a dramatization that would gain no royalties for the author. Now it was plain that the urchin who was cast for the cabin-boy's part would lead a life throughout the first fifteen chapters which would attract few actors. Willie Dalzel developed a scheme by which some small lad would play cabin-boy during this period of misfortune and abuse, and then, when the cabin-boy came to the part where he slew all his enemies and reached his zenith, that he, Willie Dalzel, should take the part.

This fugitive and disconnected rendering of a great play opened in Jimmie Trescott's back garden. The path between the two lines of gooseberry-bushes was elected unanimously to be the ship. Then Willie Dalzel insisted that Homer Phelps should be the cabin-boy. Homer tried the position for a time, and then elected that he would resign in favor of some other victim. There was no other applicant to succeed him, whereupon it became necessary to press some boy. Jimmie Trescott was a great actor, as is well known, but he steadfastly refused to engage for the part. Ultimately they seized upon little Dan Earl, whose disposition was so milky and docile that he would do whatever anybody asked of him. But Dan Earl made the one firm revolt of his life after trying existence as cabin-boy for some ten minutes. Willie Dalzel was in despair. Then he suddenly sighted the little brother of Johnnie Hedge, who had come into the garden, and in a poor-little-stranger sort of fashion was looking wistfully at the play. When he was invited to become the cabin-boy he accepted joyfully, thinking that it was his initiation into the tribe. Then they proceeded to give him the rope's end and to punch him with a realism which was not altogether painless. Directly he began to cry out. They exhorted him not to cry out, not to mind it, but still they continued to hurt him.

There was a commotion among the gooseberry-bushes, two branches were swept aside, and Johnnie Hedge walked down upon them. Every boy stopped in his tracks. Johnnie was boiling with rage.

"Who hurt him?" he said, ferociously. "Did *you*?" He had looked at Willie Dalzel.

Willie Dalzel began to mumble: "We was on'y playin'. Wasn't nothin' fer him to cry fer."

The new boy had at his command some big phrases, and he used them. "I am goin' to whip you within an inch of your life. I am goin' to tan the hide off'n you." And immediately there was a mixture—an infusion of two boys which looked as if it had been done by a chemist. The other children stood back, stricken with horror. But out of this whirl they presently perceived the figure of Willie Dalzel seated upon the chest of the Hedge boy.

"Got enough?" asked Willie, hoarsely.

"No," choked out the Hedge boy. Then there was another flapping and floundering, and finally another calm.

"'WHO HURT HIM?' HE SAID FEROCIOUSLY"

"Got enough?" asked Willie.

"No," said the Hedge boy. A sort of war-cloud again puzzled the sight of the observers. Both combatants were breathless, bloodless in their faces, and very weak.

"Got enough?" said Willie.

"No," said the Hedge boy. The carnage was again renewed. All the spectators were silent but Johnnie Hedge's little brother, who shrilly exhorted him to continue the struggle. But it was not plain that the Hedge boy needed any encouragement, for he was crying bitterly, and it has been explained that when a boy cried it was a bad time to hope for peace. He had managed to wriggle over upon his hands and knees. But Willie Dalzel was tenaciously gripping him from the back, and it seemed that his strength would spend

144

itself in futility. The bear cub seemed to have the advantage of the working model of the windmill. They heaved, uttered strange words, wept, and the sun looked down upon them with steady, unwinking eye.

Peter Washington came out of the stable and observed this tragedy of the back garden. He stood transfixed for a moment, and then ran towards it, shouting: "Hi! What's all dish yere? Hi! Stopper dat, stopper dat, you two! For lan' sake, what's all dish yere?" He grabbed the struggling boys and pulled them apart. He was stormy and fine in his indignation. "For lan' sake! You two kids act like you gwine mad dogs. Stopper dat!" The whitened, tearful, soiled combatants, their clothing all awry, glared fiercely at each other as Peter stood between them, lecturing. They made several futile attempts to circumvent him and again come to battle. As he fended them off with his open hands he delivered his reproaches at Jimmie. "I's s'prised at you! I suhtainly is!"

"Why?" said Jimmie. "I 'ain't done nothin'. What have I done?"

"Y-y-you done 'courage dese yere kids ter scrap," said Peter, virtuously.

"Me?" cried Jimmie. "I 'ain't had nothin' to do with it."

"I raikon you 'ain't," retorted Peter, with heavy sarcasm. "I raikon you been er-prayin', 'ain't you?" Turning to Willie Dalzel, he said, "You jest take an' run erlong outer dish yere or I'll jest nachually take an' damnearkill you." Willie Dalzel went. To the new boy Peter said: "You look like you had some saince, but I raikon you don't know no more'n er rabbit. You jest take an' trot erlong off home, an' don' lemme caitch you round yere er-fightin' or I'll break yer back." The Hedge boy moved away with dignity, followed by his little brother. The latter, when he had placed a sufficient distance between himself and Peter, played his fingers at his nose and called out:

"Nig-ger-r-r! Nig-ger-r-r!"

Peter Washington's resentment poured out upon Jimmie.

"'Pears like you never would understan' you ain't reg'lar common trash. You take an' 'sociate with an'body what done come erlong."

"Aw, go on," retorted Jimmie, profanely. "Go soak your head, Pete."

"'NIG-GER-R-R! NIG-GER-R-R!'"

The remaining boys retired to the street, whereupon they perceived Willie Dalzel in the distance. He ran to them.

"I licked him!" he shouted, exultantly. "I licked him! Didn't I, now?"

From the Whilomville point of view he was entitled to a favorable answer. They made it. "Yes," they said, "you did."

"I run in," cried Willie, "an' I grabbed 'im, an' afore he knew what it was I throwed 'im. An' then it was easy." He puffed out his chest and smiled like an English recruiting-sergeant. "An' now," said he, suddenly facing Jimmie Trescott, "whose side were you on?"

The question was direct and startling. Jimmie gave back two paces. "He licked you once," he explained, haltingly.

"He never saw the day when he could lick one side of me. I could lick him with my left hand tied behind me. Why, I could lick him when I was asleep." Willie Dalzel was magnificent.

A gate clicked, and Johnnie Hedge was seen to be strolling towards them.

"You said," he remarked, coldly, "you licked me, didn't you?"

Willie Dalzel stood his ground. "Yes," he said, stoutly.

"Well, you're a liar," said the Hedge boy.

"You're another," retorted Willie.

"No, I ain't, either, but you're a liar."

"You're another," retorted Willie.

"Don't you dare tell me I'm a liar, or I'll smack your mouth for you," said the Hedge boy.

"Well, I did, didn't I?" barked Willie. "An' whatche goin' to do about it?"

"I'm goin' to lam you," said the Hedge boy.

He approached to attack warily, and the other boys held their breaths. Willie Dalzel winced back a pace. "Hol' on a minute," he cried, raising his palm. "I'm not—"

"ONE APPROACHING FROM BEHIND LAID HOLD OF HIS EAR"

But the comic windmill was again in motion, and between gasps from his exertions Johnnie Hedge remarked, "I'll show—you—whether—you kin—lick me—or not."

The first blows did not reach home on Willie, for he backed away with expedition, keeping up his futile cry, "Hol' on a minute." Soon enough a swinging fist landed on his cheek. It did not knock him down, but it hurt him a little and frightened him a great deal. He suddenly opened his mouth to an amazing and startling extent, tilted back his head, and howled, while his eyes, glittering with tears, were fixed upon this scowling butcher of a Johnnie

Hedge. The latter was making slow and vicious circles, evidently intending to renew the massacre.

But the spectators really had been desolated and shocked by the terrible thing which had happened to Willie Dalzel. They now cried out: "No, no; don't hit 'im any more! Don't hit 'im any more!"

Jimmie Trescott, in a panic of bravery, yelled, "We'll all jump on you if you do."

The Hedge boy paused, at bay. He breathed angrily, and flashed his glance from lad to lad.

They still protested: "No, no; don't hit 'im any more. Don't hit 'im no more."

"I'll hammer him until he can't stand up," said Johnnie, observing that they all feared him. "I'll fix him so he won't know hisself, an' if any of you kids bother with me—"

Suddenly he ceased, he trembled, he collapsed. The hand of one approaching from behind had laid hold upon his ear, and it was the hand of one whom he knew.

The other lads heard a loud, iron-filing voice say, "Caught ye at it again, ye brat, ye." They saw a dreadful woman with gray hair, with a sharp red nose, with bare arms, with spectacles of such magnifying quality that her eyes shone through them like two fierce white moons. She was Johnnie Hedge's mother. Still holding Johnnie by the ear, she swung out swiftly and dexterously, and succeeded in boxing the ears of two boys before the crowd regained its presence of mind and stampeded. Yes, the war for supremacy was over, and the question was never again disputed. The supreme power was Mrs. Hedge.

XIII. A LITTLE PILGRIMAGE

ONE November it became clear to childish minds in certain parts of Whilomville that the Sunday-school of the Presbyterian church would not have for the children the usual tree on Christmas eve. The funds free for that ancient festival would be used for the relief of suffering among the victims of the Charleston earthquake.

The plan had been born in the generous head of the superintendent of the Sunday-school, and during one session he had made a strong plea that the children should forego the vain pleasures of a tree and, in glorious application of the Golden Rule, refuse a local use of the fund, and will that it be sent where dire pain might be alleviated. At the end of a tearfully eloquent speech the question was put fairly to a vote, and the children in a burst of virtuous abandon carried the question for Charleston. Many of the teachers had been careful to preserve a finely neutral attitude, but even if they had cautioned the children against being too impetuous they could not have checked the wild impulses.

But this was a long time before Christmas.

Very early, boys held important speech together. "Huh! you ain't goin' to have no Christmas tree at the Presbyterian Sunday-school."

Sullenly the victim answered, "No, we ain't."

"Huh!" scoffed the other denomination, "we are goin' to have the all-firedest biggest tree that you ever saw in the world."

The little Presbyterians were greatly downcast.

It happened that Jimmie Trescott had regularly attended the Presbyterian Sunday-school. The Trescotts were consistently undenominational, but they had sent their lad on Sundays to one of the places where they thought he would receive benefits. However, on one day in December, Jimmie appeared before his father and made a strong spiritual appeal to be forthwith attached to the Sunday-school of the Big Progressive church. Doctor Trescott mused this question considerably. "Well, Jim," he said, "why do you conclude that the Big Progressive Sunday-school is better for you than the Presbyterian Sunday-school?"

"Now—it's nicer," answered Jimmie, looking at his father with an anxious eye.

"How do you mean?"

"Why—now—some of the boys what go to the Presbyterian place, they ain't very nice," explained the flagrant Jimmie.

Trescott mused the question considerably once more. In the end he said: "Well, you may change if you wish, this one time, but you must not be changing to and fro. You decide now, and then you must abide by your decision."

"Yessir," said Jimmie, brightly. "Big Progressive."

"All right," said the father. "But remember what I've told you."

On the following Sunday morning Jimmie presented himself at the door of the basement of the Big Progressive church. He was conspicuously washed, notably raimented, prominently polished. And, incidentally, he was very uncomfortable because of all these virtues.

A number of acquaintances greeted him contemptuously. "Hello, Jimmie! What you doin' here? Thought you was a Presbyterian?"

Jimmie cast down his eyes and made no reply. He was too cowed by the change. However, Homer Phelps, who was a regular patron of the Big Progressive Sunday-school, suddenly appeared and said, "Hello, Jim!" Jimmie seized upon him. Homer Phelps was amenable to Trescott laws, tribal if you like, but iron-bound, almost compulsory.

"Hello, Homer!" said Jimmie, and his manner was so good that Homer felt a great thrill in being able to show his superior a new condition of life.

151

"You 'ain't never come here afore, have you?" he demanded, with a new arrogance.

"No, I 'ain't," said Jimmie. Then they stared at each other and manœuvred.

"You don't know my teacher," said Homer.

"No, I don't know her" admitted Jimmie, but in a way which contended, modestly, that he knew countless other Sunday-school teachers.

"Better join our class," said Homer, sagely. "She wears spectacles; don't see very well. Sometimes we do almost what we like."

"All right," said Jimmie, glad to place himself in the hands of his friends. In due time they entered the Sunday-school room, where a man with benevolent whiskers stood on a platform and said, "We will now sing No. 33—'Pull for the Shore, Sailor, Pull for the Shore.'" And as the obedient throng burst into melody the man on the platform indicated the time with a fat, white, and graceful hand. He was an ideal Sunday-school superintendent—one who had never felt hunger or thirst or the wound of the challenge of dishonor; a man, indeed, with beautiful flat hands who waved them in greasy victorious beneficence over a crowd of children.

Jimmie, walking carefully on his toes, followed Homer Phelps. He felt that the kingly superintendent might cry out and blast him to ashes before he could reach a chair. It was a desperate journey. But at last he heard Homer muttering to a young lady, who looked at him through glasses which greatly magnified her eyes. "A new boy," she said, in an oily and deeply religious voice.

"Yes'm," said Jimmie, trembling. The five other boys of the class scanned him keenly and derided his condition.

"We will proceed to the lesson," said the young lady. Then she cried sternly, like a sergeant, "The seventh chapter of Jeremiah!"

There was a swift fluttering of leaflets. Then the name of Jeremiah, a wise man, towered over the feelings of these boys. Homer Phelps was doomed to read the fourth verse. He took a deep breath, he puffed out his lips, he gathered his strength for a great effort. His beginning was childishly explosive. He hurriedly said:

"*Trust ye not in lying words, saying The temple of the Lord, the temple of the Lord, the temple of the Lord, are these.*"

"Now," said the teacher, "Johnnie Scanlan, tell us what these words mean." The Scanlan boy shamefacedly muttered that he did not know. The teacher's countenance saddened. Her heart was in her work; she wanted to make a success of this Sunday-school class. "Perhaps Homer Phelps can tell us," she remarked.

Homer gulped; he looked at Jimmie. Through the great room hummed a steady hum. A little circle, very near, was being told about Daniel in the lion's den. They were deeply moved. At the moment they liked Sunday-school.

"Why—now—it means," said Homer, with a grand pomposity born of a sense of hopeless ignorance—"it means—why it means that they were in the wrong place."

"No," said the teacher, profoundly; "it means that we should be good, very good indeed. That is what it means. It means that we should love the Lord and be good. Love the Lord and be good. That is what it means."

The little boys suddenly had a sense of black wickedness as their teacher looked austerely upon them. They gazed at her with the wide-open eyes of simplicity. They were stirred again. This thing of being good—this great business of life—apparently it was always successful. They knew from the fairy tales. But it was difficult, wasn't it? It was said to be the most heartbreaking task to be generous, wasn't it? One had to pay the price of one's eyes in order to be pacific, didn't one? As for patience, it was tortured martyrdom to be patient, wasn't it? Sin was simple, wasn't it? But virtue was so difficult that it could only be practised by heavenly beings, wasn't it?

And the angels, the Sunday-school superintendent, and the teacher swam in the high visions of the little boys as beings so good that if a boy scratched his shin in the same room he was a profane and sentenced devil.

"THE PROFESSIONAL BRIGHT BOY OF THE CLASS SUDDENLY AWOKE"

"And," said the teacher, "'The temple of the Lord'—what does that mean? I'll ask the new boy. What does that mean?"

"I dun'no'," said Jimmie, blankly.

But here the professional bright boy of the class suddenly awoke to his obligations. "Teacher," he cried, "it means church, same as this."

"Exactly," said the teacher, deeply satisfied with this reply. "You know your lesson well, Clarence. I am much pleased."

The other boys, instead of being envious, looked with admiration upon Clarence, while he adopted an air of being habituated to perform such feats every day of his life. Still, he was not much of a boy. He had the virtue of being able to walk on very high stilts, but when the season of stilts had passed he possessed no rank save this Sunday-school rank, this clever-little-Clarence business of knowing the Bible and the lesson better than the other boys. The other boys, sometimes looking at him meditatively, did not actually decide to thrash him as soon as he cleared the portals of the church, but they certainly decided to molest him in such ways as would re-establish their self-respect. Back of the superintendent's chair hung a lithograph of the martyrdom of St. Stephen.

Jimmie, feeling stiff and encased in his best clothes, waited for the ordeal to end. A bell pealed: the fat hand of the superintendent had tapped a bell. Slowly the rustling and murmuring dwindled to silence. The benevolent man faced the school. "I have to announce," he began, waving his body from side to side in the conventional bows of his kind, "that—" Bang went the bell. "Give me your attention, please, children. I have to announce that the Board has decided that this year there will be no Christmas tree, but the—"

Instantly the room buzzed with the subdued clamor of the children. Jimmie was speechless. He stood morosely during the singing of the closing hymn. He passed out into the street with the others, pushing no more than was required.

Speedily the whole idea left him. If he remembered Sunday-school at all, it was to remember that he did not like it.

MAGGIE

Chapter 1

A very little boy stood upon a heap of gravel for the honor of Rum Alley. He was throwing stones at howling urchins from Devil's Row who were circling madly about the heap and pelting at him.

His infantile countenance was livid with fury. His small body was writhing in the delivery of great, crimson oaths.

"Run, Jimmie, run! Dey'll get yehs," screamed a retreating Rum Alley child.

"Naw," responded Jimmie with a valiant roar, "dese micks can't make me run."

Howls of renewed wrath went up from Devil's Row throats. Tattered gamins on the right made a furious assault on the gravel heap. On their small, convulsed faces there shone the grins of true assassins. As they charged, they threw stones and cursed in shrill chorus.

The little champion of Rum Alley stumbled precipitately down the other side. His coat had been torn to shreds in a scuffle, and his hat was gone. He had bruises on twenty parts of his body, and blood was dripping from a cut in his head. His wan features wore a look of a tiny, insane demon.

On the ground, children from Devil's Row closed in on their antagonist. He crooked his left arm defensively about his head and fought with cursing fury. The little boys ran to and fro, dodging, hurling stones and swearing in barbaric trebles.

From a window of an apartment house that upreared its form from amid squat, ignorant stables, there leaned a curious woman. Some laborers, unloading a scow at a dock at the river, paused for a moment and regarded the fight. The engineer of a passive tugboat hung lazily to a railing and watched. Over on the Island, a worm of yellow convicts came from the shadow of a building and crawled slowly along the river's bank.

A stone had smashed into Jimmie's mouth. Blood was bubbling over his chin and down upon his ragged shirt. Tears made furrows on his dirt-stained cheeks. His thin legs had begun to tremble and turn weak, causing his small body to reel. His roaring curses of the first part of the fight had changed to a blasphemous chatter.

In the yells of the whirling mob of Devil's Row children there were notes of joy like songs of triumphant savagery. The little boys seemed to leer gloatingly at the blood upon the other child's face.

Down the avenue came boastfully sauntering a lad of sixteen years, although the chronic sneer of an ideal manhood already sat upon his lips. His hat was tipped with an air of challenge over his eye. Between his teeth, a cigar stump was tilted at the angle of defiance. He walked with a certain swing of the shoulders which appalled the timid. He glanced over into the vacant lot in which the little raving boys from Devil's Row seethed about the shrieking and tearful child from Rum Alley.

"Gee!" he murmured with interest. "A scrap. Gee!"

He strode over to the cursing circle, swinging his shoulders in a manner which denoted that he held victory in his fists. He approached at the back of one of the most deeply engaged of the Devil's Row children.

"Ah, what deh hell," he said, and smote the deeply-engaged one on the back of the head. The little boy fell to the ground and gave a hoarse, tremendous howl. He scrambled to his feet, and perceiving, evidently, the size of his assailant, ran quickly off, shouting alarms. The entire Devil's Row party followed him. They came to a stand a short distance away and yelled taunting oaths at the boy with the chronic sneer. The latter, momentarily, paid no attention to them.

"What deh hell, Jimmie?" he asked of the small champion.

Jimmie wiped his blood-wet features with his sleeve.

"Well, it was dis way, Pete, see! I was goin' teh lick dat Riley kid and dey all pitched on me."

Some Rum Alley children now came forward. The party stood for a moment exchanging vainglorious remarks with Devil's Row. A few stones were thrown at long distances, and words of challenge passed between small warriors. Then the Rum Alley contingent turned slowly in the direction of their home street. They began to give, each to each, distorted versions of the fight. Causes of retreat in particular cases were magnified. Blows dealt in the fight were enlarged to catapultian power, and stones thrown were alleged to have hurtled with infinite accuracy. Valor grew strong again, and the little boys began to swear with great spirit.

"Ah, we blokies kin lick deh hull damn Row," said a child, swaggering.

Little Jimmie was striving to stanch the flow of blood from his cut lips. Scowling, he turned upon the speaker.

"Ah, where deh hell was yeh when I was doin' all deh fightin?" he demanded. "Youse kids makes me tired."

"Ah, go ahn," replied the other argumentatively.

Jimmie replied with heavy contempt. "Ah, youse can't fight, Blue Billie! I kin lick yeh wid one han'."

"Ah, go ahn," replied Billie again.

"Ah," said Jimmie threateningly.

"Ah," said the other in the same tone.

They struck at each other, clinched, and rolled over on the cobble stones.

"Smash 'im, Jimmie, kick deh damn guts out of 'im," yelled Pete, the lad with the chronic sneer, in tones of delight.

The small combatants pounded and kicked, scratched and tore. They began to weep and their curses struggled in their throats with sobs. The other little boys clasped their hands and wriggled their legs in excitement. They formed a bobbing circle about the pair.

A tiny spectator was suddenly agitated.

"Cheese it, Jimmie, cheese it! Here comes yer fader," he yelled.

The circle of little boys instantly parted. They drew away and waited in ecstatic awe for that which was about to happen. The two little boys fighting in the modes of four thousand years ago, did not hear the warning.

Up the avenue there plodded slowly a man with sullen eyes. He was carrying a dinner pail and smoking an apple-wood pipe.

As he neared the spot where the little boys strove, he regarded them listlessly. But suddenly he roared an oath and advanced upon the rolling fighters.

"Here, you Jim, git up, now, while I belt yer life out, you damned disorderly brat."

He began to kick into the chaotic mass on the ground. The boy Billie felt a heavy boot strike his head. He made a furious effort and disentangled himself from Jimmie. He tottered away, damning.

Jimmie arose painfully from the ground and confronting his father, began to curse him. His parent kicked him. "Come home, now," he cried, "an' stop yer jawin', er I'll lam the everlasting head off yehs."

They departed. The man paced placidly along with the apple-wood emblem of serenity between his teeth. The boy followed a dozen feet in the rear. He swore luridly, for he felt that it was degradation for one who aimed to be some vague soldier, or a man of blood with a sort of sublime license, to be taken home by a father.

Chapter II

Eventually they entered into a dark region where, from a careening building, a dozen gruesome doorways gave up loads of babies to the street and the gutter. A wind of early autumn raised yellow dust from cobbles and swirled it against an hundred windows. Long streamers of garments fluttered from fire-escapes. In all unhandy places there were buckets, brooms, rags and bottles. In the street infants played or fought with other infants or sat stupidly in the way of vehicles. Formidable women, with uncombed hair and disordered dress, gossiped while leaning on railings, or screamed in frantic quarrels. Withered persons, in curious postures of submission to something, sat smoking pipes in obscure corners. A thousand odors of cooking food came forth to the street. The building quivered and creaked from the weight of humanity stamping about in its bowels.

A small ragged girl dragged a red, bawling infant along the crowded ways. He was hanging back, baby-like, bracing his wrinkled, bare legs.

The little girl cried out: "Ah, Tommie, come ahn. Dere's Jimmie and fader. Don't be a-pullin' me back."

She jerked the baby's arm impatiently. He fell on his face, roaring. With a second jerk she pulled him to his feet, and they went on. With the obstinacy of his order, he protested against being dragged in a chosen direction. He made heroic endeavors to keep on his legs, denounce his sister and consume a bit of orange peeling which he chewed between the times of his infantile orations.

As the sullen-eyed man, followed by the blood-covered boy, drew near, the little girl burst into reproachful cries. "Ah, Jimmie, youse bin fightin' agin."

The urchin swelled disdainfully.

"Ah, what deh hell, Mag. See?"

The little girl upbraided him, "Youse allus fightin', Jimmie, an' yeh knows it puts mudder out when yehs come home half dead, an' it's like we'll all get a poundin'."

She began to weep. The babe threw back his head and roared at his prospects.

"Ah, what deh hell!" cried Jimmie. "Shut up er I'll smack yer mout'. See?"

As his sister continued her lamentations, he suddenly swore and struck her. The little girl reeled and, recovering herself, burst into tears and quaveringly cursed him. As she slowly retreated her brother advanced dealing her cuffs. The father heard and turned about.

"Stop that, Jim, d'yeh hear? Leave yer sister alone on the street. It's like I can never beat any sense into yer damned wooden head."

The urchin raised his voice in defiance to his parent and continued his attacks. The babe bawled tremendously, protesting with great violence. During his sister's hasty manoeuvres, he was dragged by the arm.

Finally the procession plunged into one of the gruesome doorways. They crawled up dark stairways and along cold, gloomy halls. At last the father pushed open a door and they entered a lighted room in which a large woman was rampant.

She stopped in a career from a seething stove to a pan-covered table. As the father and children filed in she peered at them.

"Eh, what? Been fightin' agin, by Gawd!" She threw herself upon Jimmie. The urchin tried to dart behind the others and in the scuffle the babe, Tommie, was knocked down. He protested with his usual vehemence, because they had bruised his tender shins against a table leg.

The mother's massive shoulders heaved with anger. Grasping the urchin by the neck and shoulder she shook him until he rattled. She dragged him to an unholy sink, and, soaking a rag in water, began to scrub his lacerated face with it. Jimmie screamed in pain and tried to twist his shoulders out of the clasp of the huge arms.

The babe sat on the floor watching the scene, his face in contortions like that of a woman at a tragedy. The father, with a newly-ladened pipe in his mouth, crouched on a backless chair near the stove. Jimmie's cries annoyed him. He turned about and bellowed at his wife:

"Let the damned kid alone for a minute, will yeh, Mary? Yer allus poundin' 'im. When I come nights I can't git no rest 'cause yer allus poundin' a kid. Let up, d'yeh hear? Don't be allus poundin' a kid."

The woman's operations on the urchin instantly increased in violence. At last she tossed him to a corner where he limply lay cursing and weeping.

The wife put her immense hands on her hips and with a chieftain-like stride approached her husband.

"Ho," she said, with a great grunt of contempt. "An' what in the devil are you stickin' your nose for?"

The babe crawled under the table and, turning, peered out cautiously. The ragged girl retreated and the urchin in the corner drew his legs carefully beneath him.

The man puffed his pipe calmly and put his great mudded boots on the back part of the stove.

"Go teh hell," he murmured, tranquilly.

The woman screamed and shook her fists before her husband's eyes. The rough yellow of her face and neck flared suddenly crimson. She began to howl.

He puffed imperturbably at his pipe for a time, but finally arose and began to look out at the window into the darkening chaos of back yards.

"You've been drinkin', Mary," he said. "You'd better let up on the bot', ol' woman, or you'll git done."

"You're a liar. I ain't had a drop," she roared in reply.

They had a lurid altercation, in which they damned each other's souls with frequence.

The babe was staring out from under the table, his small face working in his excitement.

The ragged girl went stealthily over to the corner where the urchin lay.

"Are yehs hurted much, Jimmie?" she whispered timidly.

"Not a damn bit! See?" growled the little boy.

"Will I wash deh blood?"

"Naw!"

"Will I—"

"When I catch dat Riley kid I'll break 'is face! Dat's right! See?"

He turned his face to the wall as if resolved to grimly bide his time.

In the quarrel between husband and wife, the woman was victor. The man grabbed his hat and rushed from the room, apparently determined upon a vengeful drunk. She followed to the door and thundered at him as he made his way down stairs.

She returned and stirred up the room until her children were bobbing about like bubbles.

"Git outa deh way," she persistently bawled, waving feet with their dishevelled shoes near the heads of her children. She shrouded herself, puffing and snorting, in a cloud of steam at the stove, and eventually extracted a frying-pan full of potatoes that hissed.

She flourished it. "Come teh yer suppers, now," she cried with sudden exasperation. "Hurry up, now, er I'll help yeh!"

The children scrambled hastily. With prodigious clatter they arranged themselves at table. The babe sat with his feet dangling high from a precarious infant chair and gorged his small stomach. Jimmie forced, with feverish rapidity, the grease-enveloped pieces between his wounded lips. Maggie, with side glances of fear of interruption, ate like a small pursued tigress.

The mother sat blinking at them. She delivered reproaches, swallowed potatoes and drank from a yellow-brown bottle. After a time her mood changed and she wept as she carried little Tommie into another room and laid him to sleep with his fists doubled in an old quilt of faded red and green grandeur. Then she came and moaned by the stove. She rocked to and fro upon a chair, shedding tears and crooning miserably to the two children about their "poor mother" and "yer fader, damn 'is soul."

The little girl plodded between the table and the chair with a dish-pan on it. She tottered on her small legs beneath burdens of dishes.

Jimmie sat nursing his various wounds. He cast furtive glances at his mother. His practised eye perceived her gradually emerge from a muddled mist of sentiment until her brain burned in drunken heat. He sat breathless.

Maggie broke a plate.

The mother started to her feet as if propelled.

"Good Gawd," she howled. Her eyes glittered on her child with sudden hatred. The fervent red of her face turned almost to purple. The little boy ran to the halls, shrieking like a monk in an earthquake.

He floundered about in darkness until he found the stairs. He stumbled, panic-stricken, to the next floor. An old woman opened a door. A light behind her threw a flare on the urchin's quivering face.

"Eh, Gawd, child, what is it dis time? Is yer fader beatin' yer mudder, or yer mudder beatin' yer fader?"

Chapter III

Jimmie and the old woman listened long in the hall. Above the muffled roar of conversation, the dismal wailings of babies at night, the thumping of feet in unseen corridors and rooms, mingled with the sound of varied hoarse shoutings in the street and the rattling of wheels over cobbles, they heard the screams of the child and the roars of the mother die away to a feeble moaning and a subdued bass muttering.

The old woman was a gnarled and leathery personage who could don, at will, an expression of great virtue. She possessed a small music-box capable of one tune, and a collection of "God bless yehs" pitched in assorted keys of fervency. Each day she took a position upon the stones of Fifth Avenue, where she crooked her legs under her and crouched immovable and hideous, like an idol. She received daily a small sum in pennies. It was contributed, for the most part, by persons who did not make their homes in that vicinity.

Once, when a lady had dropped her purse on the sidewalk, the gnarled woman had grabbed it and smuggled it with great dexterity beneath her cloak. When she was arrested she had cursed the lady into a partial swoon, and with her aged limbs, twisted from rheumatism, had almost kicked the stomach out of a huge policeman whose conduct upon that occasion she referred to when she said: "The police, damn 'em."

"Eh, Jimmie, it's cursed shame," she said. "Go, now, like a dear an' buy me a can, an' if yer mudder raises 'ell all night yehs can sleep here."

Jimmie took a tendered tin-pail and seven pennies and departed. He passed into the side door of a saloon and went to the bar. Straining up on his toes he raised the pail and pennies as high as his arms would let him. He saw two hands thrust down and take them. Directly the same hands let down the filled pail and he left.

In front of the gruesome doorway he met a lurching figure. It was his father, swaying about on uncertain legs.

"Give me deh can. See?" said the man, threateningly.

"Ah, come off! I got dis can fer dat ol' woman an' it 'ud be dirt teh swipe it. See?" cried Jimmie.

The father wrenched the pail from the urchin. He grasped it in both hands and lifted it to his mouth. He glued his lips to the under edge and tilted his head. His hairy throat swelled until it seemed to grow near his chin. There was a tremendous gulping movement and the beer was gone.

The man caught his breath and laughed. He hit his son on the head with the empty pail. As it rolled clanging into the street, Jimmie began to scream and kicked repeatedly at his father's shins.

"Look at deh dirt what yeh done me," he yelled. "Deh ol' woman 'ill be raisin' hell."

He retreated to the middle of the street, but the man did not pursue. He staggered toward the door.

"I'll club hell outa yeh when I ketch yeh," he shouted, and disappeared.

During the evening he had been standing against a bar drinking whiskies and declaring to all comers, confidentially: "My home reg'lar livin' hell! Damndes' place! Reg'lar hell! Why do I come an' drin' whisk' here thish way? 'Cause home reg'lar livin' hell!"

Jimmie waited a long time in the street and then crept warily up through the building. He passed with great caution the door of the gnarled woman, and finally stopped outside his home and listened.

He could hear his mother moving heavily about among the furniture of the room. She was chanting in a mournful voice, occasionally interjecting bursts of volcanic wrath at the father, who, Jimmie judged, had sunk down on the floor or in a corner.

"Why deh blazes don' chere try teh keep Jim from fightin'? I'll break her jaw," she suddenly bellowed.

The man mumbled with drunken indifference. "Ah, wha' deh hell. W'a's odds? Wha' makes kick?"

"Because he tears 'is clothes, yeh damn fool," cried the woman in supreme wrath.

The husband seemed to become aroused. "Go teh hell," he thundered fiercely in reply. There was a crash against the door and something broke into clattering fragments. Jimmie partially suppressed a howl and darted down the stairway. Below he paused and listened. He heard howls and curses, groans and shrieks, confusingly in chorus as if a battle were raging. With all was the crash of splintering furniture. The eyes of the urchin glared in fear that one of them would discover him.

Curious faces appeared in doorways, and whispered comments passed to and fro. "Ol' Johnson's raisin' hell agin."

Jimmie stood until the noises ceased and the other inhabitants of the tenement had all yawned and shut their doors. Then he crawled upstairs with the caution of an invader of a panther den. Sounds of labored breathing came through the broken door-panels. He pushed the door open and entered, quaking.

A glow from the fire threw red hues over the bare floor, the cracked and soiled plastering, and the overturned and broken furniture.

In the middle of the floor lay his mother asleep. In one corner of the room his father's limp body hung across the seat of a chair.

The urchin stole forward. He began to shiver in dread of awakening his parents. His mother's great chest was heaving painfully. Jimmie paused and looked down at her. Her face was inflamed and swollen from drinking. Her yellow brows shaded eyelids that had brown blue. Her tangled hair tossed in waves over her forehead. Her mouth was set in the same lines of vindictive hatred that it had, perhaps, borne during the fight. Her bare, red arms were thrown out above her head in positions of exhaustion, something, mayhap, like those of a sated villain.

The urchin bended over his mother. He was fearful lest she should open her eyes, and the dread within him was so strong, that he could not forbear to stare, but hung as if fascinated over the woman's grim face.

170

Suddenly her eyes opened. The urchin found himself looking straight into that expression, which, it would seem, had the power to change his blood to salt. He howled piercingly and fell backward.

The woman floundered for a moment, tossed her arms about her head as if in combat, and again began to snore.

Jimmie crawled back in the shadows and waited. A noise in the next room had followed his cry at the discovery that his mother was awake. He grovelled in the gloom, the eyes from out his drawn face riveted upon the intervening door.

He heard it creak, and then the sound of a small voice came to him. "Jimmie! Jimmie! Are yehs dere?" it whispered. The urchin started. The thin, white face of his sister looked at him from the door-way of the other room. She crept to him across the floor.

The father had not moved, but lay in the same death-like sleep. The mother writhed in uneasy slumber, her chest wheezing as if she were in the agonies of strangulation. Out at the window a florid moon was peering over dark roofs, and in the distance the waters of a river glimmered pallidly.

The small frame of the ragged girl was quivering. Her features were haggard from weeping, and her eyes gleamed from fear. She grasped the urchin's arm in her little trembling hands and they huddled in a corner. The eyes of both were drawn, by some force, to stare at the woman's face, for they thought she need only to awake and all fiends would come from below.

They crouched until the ghost-mists of dawn appeared at the window, drawing close to the panes, and looking in at the prostrate, heaving body of the mother.

Chapter IV

The babe, Tommie, died. He went away in a white, insignificant coffin, his small waxen hand clutching a flower that the girl, Maggie, had stolen from an Italian.

She and Jimmie lived.

The inexperienced fibres of the boy's eyes were hardened at an early age. He became a young man of leather. He lived some red years without laboring. During that time his sneer became chronic. He studied human nature in the gutter, and found it no worse than he thought he had reason to believe it. He never conceived a respect for the world, because he had begun with no idols that it had smashed.

He clad his soul in armor by means of happening hilariously in at a mission church where a man composed his sermons of "yous." While they got warm at the stove, he told his hearers just where he calculated they stood with the Lord. Many of the sinners were impatient over the pictured depths of their degradation. They were waiting for soup-tickets.

A reader of words of wind-demons might have been able to see the portions of a dialogue pass to and fro between the exhorter and his hearers.

"You are damned," said the preacher. And the reader of sounds might have seen the reply go forth from the ragged people: "Where's our soup?"

Jimmie and a companion sat in a rear seat and commented upon the things that didn't concern them, with all the freedom of English gentlemen. When they grew thirsty and went out their minds confused the speaker with Christ.

Momentarily, Jimmie was sullen with thoughts of a hopeless altitude where grew fruit. His companion said that if he should ever meet God he would ask for a million dollars and a bottle of beer.

Jimmie's occupation for a long time was to stand on streetcorners and watch the world go by, dreaming blood-red dreams at the passing of pretty women. He menaced mankind at the intersections of streets.

On the corners he was in life and of life. The world was going on and he was there to perceive it.

He maintained a belligerent attitude toward all well-dressed men. To him fine raiment was allied to weakness, and all good coats covered faint hearts. He and his order were kings, to a certain extent, over the men of untarnished clothes, because these latter dreaded, perhaps, to be either killed or laughed at.

Above all things he despised obvious Christians and ciphers with the chrysanthemums of aristocracy in their button-holes. He considered himself above both of these classes. He was afraid of neither the devil nor the leader of society.

When he had a dollar in his pocket his satisfaction with existence was the greatest thing in the world. So, eventually, he felt obliged to work. His father died and his mother's years were divided up into periods of thirty days.

He became a truck driver. He was given the charge of a painstaking pair of horses and a large rattling truck. He invaded the turmoil and tumble of the down-town streets and learned to breathe maledictory defiance at the police who occasionally used to climb up, drag him from his perch and beat him.

In the lower part of the city he daily involved himself in hideous tangles. If he and his team chanced to be in the rear he preserved a demeanor of serenity, crossing his legs and bursting forth into yells when foot passengers took dangerous dives beneath the noses of his champing horses. He smoked his pipe calmly for he knew that his pay was marching on.

If in the front and the key-truck of chaos, he entered terrifically into the quarrel that was raging to and fro among the drivers on their high seats, and sometimes roared oaths and violently got himself arrested.

After a time his sneer grew so that it turned its glare upon all things. He became so sharp that he believed in nothing. To him the police were always actuated by malignant impulses and the rest of the world was composed, for the most part, of despicable creatures who were all trying to take advantage of him and with whom, in defense, he was obliged to quarrel on all possible occasions. He himself occupied a down-trodden position that had a private but distinct element of grandeur in its isolation.

The most complete cases of aggravated idiocy were, to his mind, rampant upon the front platforms of all the street cars. At first his tongue strove with these beings, but he eventually was superior. He became immured like an African cow. In him grew a majestic contempt for those strings of street cars that followed him like intent bugs.

He fell into the habit, when starting on a long journey, of fixing his eye on a high and distant object, commanding his horses to begin, and then going into a sort of a trance of observation. Multitudes of drivers might howl in his rear, and passengers might load him with opprobrium, he would not awaken until some blue policeman turned red and began to frenziedly tear bridles and beat the soft noses of the responsible horses.

When he paused to contemplate the attitude of the police toward himself and his fellows, he believed that they were the only men in the city who had no rights. When driving about, he felt that he was held liable by the police for anything that might occur in the streets, and was the common prey of all energetic officials. In revenge, he resolved never to move out of the way of anything, until formidable circumstances, or a much larger man than himself forced him to it.

Foot-passengers were mere pestering flies with an insane disregard for their legs and his convenience. He could not conceive their maniacal desires to cross the streets. Their madness smote him with eternal amazement. He was continually storming at them from his throne. He sat aloft and denounced their frantic leaps, plunges, dives and straddles.

When they would thrust at, or parry, the noses of his champing horses, making them swing their heads and move their feet, disturbing a solid dreamy repose, he swore at the men as fools, for he himself could perceive that Providence had caused it clearly to be written, that he and his team had the unalienable right to stand in the proper path of the sun chariot, and if they so minded, obstruct its mission or take a wheel off.

And, perhaps, if the god-driver had an ungovernable desire to step down, put up his flame-colored fists and manfully dispute the right of way, he would have probably been immediately opposed by a scowling mortal with two sets of very hard knuckles.

It is possible, perhaps, that this young man would have derided, in an axle-wide alley, the approach of a flying ferry boat. Yet he achieved a respect for a fire engine. As one charged toward his truck, he would drive fearfully upon a sidewalk, threatening untold people with annihilation. When an engine would strike a mass of blocked trucks, splitting it into fragments, as a blow annihilates a cake of ice, Jimmie's team could usually be observed high and safe, with whole wheels, on the sidewalk. The fearful coming of the engine could break up the most intricate muddle of heavy vehicles at which the police had been swearing for the half of an hour.

A fire engine was enshrined in his heart as an appalling thing that he loved with a distant dog-like devotion. They had been known to overturn street-cars. Those leaping horses, striking sparks from the cobbles in their forward lunge, were creatures to be ineffably admired. The clang of the gong pierced his breast like a noise of remembered war.

When Jimmie was a little boy, he began to be arrested. Before he reached a great age, he had a fair record.

He developed too great a tendency to climb down from his truck and fight with other drivers. He had been in quite a number of miscellaneous fights, and in some general barroom rows that had become known to the police. Once he had been arrested for assaulting a Chinaman. Two women in different parts of the city, and entirely unknown to each other, caused him considerable annoyance by breaking forth, simultaneously, at fateful intervals, into wailings about marriage and support and infants.

Nevertheless, he had, on a certain star-lit evening, said wonderingly and quite reverently: "Deh moon looks like hell, don't it?"

Chapter V

The girl, Maggie, blossomed in a mud puddle. She grew to be a most rare and wonderful production of a tenement district, a pretty girl.

None of the dirt of Rum Alley seemed to be in her veins. The philosophers up-stairs, down-stairs and on the same floor, puzzled over it.

When a child, playing and fighting with gamins in the street, dirt disguised her. Attired in tatters and grime, she went unseen.

There came a time, however, when the young men of the vicinity said: "Dat Johnson goil is a puty good looker." About this period her brother remarked to her: "Mag, I'll tell yeh dis! See? Yeh've edder got teh go teh hell or go teh work!" Whereupon she went to work, having the feminine aversion of going to hell.

By a chance, she got a position in an establishment where they made collars and cuffs. She received a stool and a machine in a room where sat twenty girls of various shades of yellow discontent. She perched on the stool and treadled at her machine all day, turning out collars, the name of whose brand could be noted for its irrelevancy to anything in connection with collars. At night she returned home to her mother.

Jimmie grew large enough to take the vague position of head of the family. As incumbent of that office, he stumbled up-stairs late at night, as his father had done before him. He reeled about the room, swearing at his relations, or went to sleep on the floor.

The mother had gradually arisen to that degree of fame that she could bandy words with her acquaintances among the police-justices. Court-officials called her by her first name. When she appeared they pursued a course which had been theirs for months. They invariably grinned and cried out: "Hello, Mary, you here again?" Her grey head wagged in many a court. She always besieged the bench with voluble excuses, explanations, apologies and prayers. Her flaming face and rolling eyes were a sort of familiar sight on the island. She measured time by means of sprees, and was eternally swollen and dishevelled.

One day the young man, Pete, who as a lad had smitten the Devil's Row urchin in the back of the head and put to flight the antagonists of his friend, Jimmie, strutted upon the scene. He met Jimmie one day on the street, promised to take him to a boxing match in Williamsburg, and called for him in the evening.

Maggie observed Pete.

He sat on a table in the Johnson home and dangled his checked legs with an enticing nonchalance. His hair was curled down over his forehead in an oiled bang. His rather pugged nose seemed to revolt from contact with a bristling moustache of short, wire-like hairs. His blue double-breasted coat, edged with black braid, buttoned close to a red puff tie, and his patent-leather shoes looked like murder-fitted weapons.

His mannerisms stamped him as a man who had a correct sense of his personal superiority. There was valor and contempt for circumstances in the glance of his eye. He waved his hands like a man of the world, who dismisses religion and philosophy, and says "Fudge." He had certainly seen everything and with each curl of his lip, he declared that it amounted to nothing. Maggie thought he must be a very elegant and graceful bartender.

He was telling tales to Jimmie.

Maggie watched him furtively, with half-closed eyes, lit with a vague interest.

"Hully gee! Dey makes me tired," he said. "Mos' e'ry day some farmer comes in an' tries teh run deh shop. See? But dey gits t'rowed right out! I jolt dem right out in deh street before dey knows where dey is! See?"

"Sure," said Jimmie.

"Dere was a mug come in deh place deh odder day wid an idear he wus goin' teh own deh place! Hully gee, he wus goin' teh own deh place! I see he had a still on an' I didn' wanna giv 'im no stuff, so I says: 'Git deh hell outa here an' don' make no trouble,' I says like dat! See? 'Git deh hell outa here an' don' make no trouble'; like dat. 'Git deh hell outa here,' I says. See?"

Jimmie nodded understandingly. Over his features played an eager desire to state the amount of his valor in a similar crisis, but the narrator proceeded.

"Well, deh blokie he says: 'T'hell wid it! I ain' lookin' for no scrap,' he says (See?), 'but' he says, 'I'm 'spectable cit'zen an' I wanna drink an' purtydamnsoon, too.' See? 'Deh hell,' I says. Like dat! 'Deh hell,' I says. See? 'Don' make no trouble,' I says. Like dat. 'Don' make no trouble.' See? Den deh mug he squared off an' said he was fine as silk wid his dukes (See?) an' he wanned a drink damnquick. Dat's what he said. See?"

"Sure," repeated Jimmie.

Pete continued. "Say, I jes' jumped deh bar an' deh way I plunked dat blokie was great. See? Dat's right! In deh jaw! See? Hully gee, he t'rowed a spittoon true deh front windee. Say, I taut I'd drop dead. But deh boss, he comes in after an' he says, 'Pete, yehs done jes' right! Yeh've gota keep order an' it's all right.' See? 'It's all right,' he says. Dat's what he said."

The two held a technical discussion.

"Dat bloke was a dandy," said Pete, in conclusion, "but he hadn' oughta made no trouble. Dat's what I says teh dem: 'Don' come in here an' make no trouble,' I says, like dat. 'Don' make no trouble.' See?"

As Jimmie and his friend exchanged tales descriptive of their prowess, Maggie leaned back in the shadow. Her eyes dwelt wonderingly and rather wistfully upon Pete's face. The broken furniture, grimey walls, and general disorder and dirt of her home of a sudden appeared before her and began to take a potential aspect. Pete's aristocratic person looked as if it might soil. She looked keenly at him, occasionally, wondering if he was feeling contempt. But Pete seemed to be enveloped in reminiscence.

"Hully gee," said he, "dose mugs can't phase me. Dey knows I kin wipe up deh street wid any t'ree of dem."

When he said, "Ah, what deh hell," his voice was burdened with disdain

178

for the inevitable and contempt for anything that fate might compel him to endure.

Maggie perceived that here was the beau ideal of a man. Her dim thoughts were often searching for far away lands where, as God says, the little hills sing together in the morning. Under the trees of her dream-gardens there had always walked a lover.

Chapter VI

Pete took note of Maggie.

"Say, Mag, I'm stuck on yer shape. It's outa sight," he said, parenthetically, with an affable grin.

As he became aware that she was listening closely, he grew still more eloquent in his descriptions of various happenings in his career. It appeared that he was invincible in fights.

"Why," he said, referring to a man with whom he had had a misunderstanding, "dat mug scrapped like a damn dago. Dat's right. He was dead easy. See? He tau't he was a scrapper. But he foun' out diff'ent! Hully gee."

He walked to and fro in the small room, which seemed then to grow even smaller and unfit to hold his dignity, the attribute of a supreme warrior. That swing of the shoulders that had frozen the timid when he was but a lad had increased with his growth and education at the ratio of ten to one. It, combined with the sneer upon his mouth, told mankind that there was nothing in space which could appall him. Maggie marvelled at him and surrounded him with greatness. She vaguely tried to calculate the altitude of the pinnacle from which he must have looked down upon her.

"I met a chump deh odder day way up in deh city," he said. "I was goin' teh see a frien' of mine. When I was a-crossin' deh street deh chump runned plump inteh me, an' den he turns aroun' an' says, 'Yer insolen' ruffin,' he says, like dat. 'Oh, gee,' I says, 'oh, gee, go teh hell and git off deh eart',' I says, like dat. See? 'Go teh hell an' git off deh eart',' like dat. Den deh blokie he got wild. He says I was a contempt'ble scoun'el, er somet'ing like dat, an' he says I was doom' teh everlastin' pe'dition an' all like dat. 'Gee,' I says, 'gee! Deh hell I am,' I says. 'Deh hell I am,' like dat. An' den I slugged 'im. See?"

With Jimmie in his company, Pete departed in a sort of a blaze of glory from the Johnson home. Maggie, leaning from the window, watched him as he walked down the street.

Here was a formidable man who disdained the strength of a world full of fists. Here was one who had contempt for brass-clothed power; one whose knuckles could defiantly ring against the granite of law. He was a knight.

The two men went from under the glimmering street-lamp and passed into shadows.

Turning, Maggie contemplated the dark, dust-stained walls, and the scant and crude furniture of her home. A clock, in a splintered and battered oblong box of varnished wood, she suddenly regarded as an abomination. She noted that it ticked raspingly. The almost vanished flowers in the carpet-pattern, she conceived to be newly hideous. Some faint attempts she had made with blue ribbon, to freshen the appearance of a dingy curtain, she now saw to be piteous.

She wondered what Pete dined on.

She reflected upon the collar and cuff factory. It began to appear to her mind as a dreary place of endless grinding. Pete's elegant occupation brought him, no doubt, into contact with people who had money and manners. It was probable that he had a large acquaintance of pretty girls. He must have great sums of money to spend.

To her the earth was composed of hardships and insults. She felt instant admiration for a man who openly defied it. She thought that if the grim angel of death should clutch his heart, Pete would shrug his shoulders and say: "Oh, ev'ryt'ing goes."

She anticipated that he would come again shortly. She spent some of her week's pay in the purchase of flowered cretonne for a lambrequin. She made it with infinite care and hung it to the slightly-careening mantel, over the stove, in the kitchen. She studied it with painful anxiety from different points in the room. She wanted it to look well on Sunday night when, perhaps, Jimmie's friend would come. On Sunday night, however, Pete did not appear.

Afterward the girl looked at it with a sense of humiliation. She was now convinced that Pete was superior to admiration for lambrequins.

A few evenings later Pete entered with fascinating innovations in his apparel. As she had seen him twice and he had different suits on each time, Maggie had a dim impression that his wardrobe was prodigiously extensive.

"Say, Mag," he said, "put on yer bes' duds Friday night an' I'll take yehs teh deh show. See?"

He spent a few moments in flourishing his clothes and then vanished, without having glanced at the lambrequin.

Over the eternal collars and cuffs in the factory Maggie spent the most of three days in making imaginary sketches of Pete and his daily environment. She imagined some half dozen women in love with him and thought he must lean dangerously toward an indefinite one, whom she pictured with great charms of person, but with an altogether contemptible disposition.

She thought he must live in a blare of pleasure. He had friends, and people who were afraid of him.

She saw the golden glitter of the place where Pete was to take her. An entertainment of many hues and many melodies where she was afraid she might appear small and mouse-colored.

Her mother drank whiskey all Friday morning. With lurid face and tossing hair she cursed and destroyed furniture all Friday afternoon. When Maggie came home at half-past six her mother lay asleep amidst the wreck of chairs and a table. Fragments of various household utensils were scattered about the floor. She had vented some phase of drunken fury upon the lambrequin. It lay in a bedraggled heap in the corner.

"Hah," she snorted, sitting up suddenly, "where deh hell yeh been? Why deh hell don' yeh come home earlier? Been loafin' 'round deh streets. Yer gettin' teh be a reg'lar devil."

When Pete arrived Maggie, in a worn black dress, was waiting for him in the midst of a floor strewn with wreckage. The curtain at the window had been pulled by a heavy hand and hung by one tack, dangling to and fro in the draft through the cracks at the sash. The knots of blue ribbons appeared like violated flowers. The fire in the stove had gone out. The displaced lids and open doors showed heaps of sullen grey ashes. The remnants of a meal, ghastly, like dead flesh, lay in a corner. Maggie's red mother, stretched on the floor, blasphemed and gave her daughter a bad name.

Chapter VII

An orchestra of yellow silk women and bald-headed men on an elevated stage near the centre of a great green-hued hall, played a popular waltz. The place was crowded with people grouped about little tables. A battalion of waiters slid among the throng, carrying trays of beer glasses and making change from the inexhaustible vaults of their trousers pockets. Little boys, in the costumes of French chefs, paraded up and down the irregular aisles vending fancy cakes. There was a low rumble of conversation and a subdued clinking of glasses. Clouds of tobacco smoke rolled and wavered high in air about the dull gilt of the chandeliers.

The vast crowd had an air throughout of having just quitted labor. Men with calloused hands and attired in garments that showed the wear of an endless trudge for a living, smoked their pipes contentedly and spent five, ten, or perhaps fifteen cents for beer. There was a mere sprinkling of kid-gloved men who smoked cigars purchased elsewhere. The great body of the crowd was composed of people who showed that all day they strove with their hands. Quiet Germans, with maybe their wives and two or three children, sat listening to the music, with the expressions of happy cows. An occasional party of sailors from a war-ship, their faces pictures of sturdy health, spent the earlier hours of the evening at the small round tables. Very infrequent tipsy men, swollen with the value of their opinions, engaged their companions in earnest and confidential conversation. In the balcony, and here and there below, shone the impassive faces of women. The nationalities of the Bowery beamed upon the stage from all directions.

Pete aggressively walked up a side aisle and took seats with Maggie at a table beneath the balcony.

"Two beehs!"

Leaning back he regarded with eyes of superiority the scene before them. This attitude affected Maggie strongly. A man who could regard such a sight with indifference must be accustomed to very great things.

It was obvious that Pete had been to this place many times before, and was very familiar with it. A knowledge of this fact made Maggie feel little and new.

He was extremely gracious and attentive. He displayed the consideration of a cultured gentleman who knew what was due.

"Say, what deh hell? Bring deh lady a big glass! What deh hell use is dat pony?"

"Don't be fresh, now," said the waiter, with some warmth, as he departed.

"Ah, git off deh eart'," said Pete, after the other's retreating form.

Maggie perceived that Pete brought forth all his elegance and all his knowledge of high-class customs for her benefit. Her heart warmed as she reflected upon his condescension.

The orchestra of yellow silk women and bald-headed men gave vent to a few bars of anticipatory music and a girl, in a pink dress with short skirts, galloped upon the stage. She smiled upon the throng as if in acknowledgment of a warm welcome, and began to walk to and fro, making profuse gesticulations and singing, in brazen soprano tones, a song, the words of which were inaudible. When she broke into the swift rattling measures of a chorus some half-tipsy men near the stage joined in the rollicking refrain and glasses were pounded rhythmically upon the tables. People leaned forward to watch her and to try to catch the words of the song. When she vanished there were long rollings of applause.

...ent to more anticipatory bars, she reappeared amidst the half- ... the tipsy men. The orchestra plunged into dance ...uttered and flew in the glare of gas jets. She ...ed in some half dozen skirts. It was patent ...proved adequate for the purpose for which ...al man bent forward, intent upon the pink ...the splendor of the costume and lost herself ...e silks and laces.

a vision
bonds. A
se, where the
ner." Instantly a

185

The dancer's smile of stereotyped enthusiasm was turned for ten minutes upon the faces of her audience. In the finale she fell into some of those grotesque attitudes which were at the time popular among the dancers in the theatres up-town, giving to the Bowery public the phantasies of the aristocratic theatre-going public, at reduced rates.

"Say, Pete," said Maggie, leaning forward, "dis is great."

"Sure," said Pete, with proper complacence.

A ventriloquist followed the dancer. He held two fantastic dolls on his knees. He made them sing mournful ditties and say funny things about geography and Ireland.

"Do dose little men talk?" asked Maggie.

"Naw," said Pete, "it's some damn fake. See?"

Two girls, on the bills as sisters, came forth and sang a duet that is heard occasionally at concerts given under church auspices. They supplemented it with a dance which of course can never be seen at concerts given under church auspices.

After the duettists had retired, a woman of debatable age sang a negro melody. The chorus necessitated some grotesque waddlings supposed to be an imitation of a plantation darkey, under the influence, probably, of music and the moon. The audience was just enthusiastic enough over it to have her return and sing a sorrowful lay, whose lines told of a mother's love and a sweetheart who waited and a young man who was lost at sea under the most harrowing circumstances. From the faces of a score or so in the crowd, the self-contained look faded. Many heads were bent forward with eagerness ar sympathy. As the last distressing sentiment of the piece was brought for was greeted by that kind of applause which rings as sincere.

As a final effort, the singer rendered some verses which describ of Britain being annihilated by America, and Ireland bursting ' carefully prepared crisis was reached in the last line of the last ' singer threw out her arms and cried, "The star-spangled ba

186

great cheer swelled from the throats of the assemblage of the masses. There was a heavy rumble of booted feet thumping the floor. Eyes gleamed with sudden fire, and calloused hands waved frantically in the air.

After a few moments' rest, the orchestra played crashingly, and a small fat man burst out upon the stage. He began to roar a song and stamp back and forth before the foot-lights, wildly waving a glossy silk hat and throwing leers, or smiles, broadcast. He made his face into fantastic grimaces until he looked like a pictured devil on a Japanese kite. The crowd laughed gleefully. His short, fat legs were never still a moment. He shouted and roared and bobbed his shock of red wig until the audience broke out in excited applause.

Pete did not pay much attention to the progress of events upon the stage. He was drinking beer and watching Maggie.

Her cheeks were blushing with excitement and her eyes were glistening. She drew deep breaths of pleasure. No thoughts of the atmosphere of the collar and cuff factory came to her.

When the orchestra crashed finally, they jostled their way to the sidewalk with the crowd. Pete took Maggie's arm and pushed a way for her, offering to fight with a man or two.

They reached Maggie's home at a late hour and stood for a moment in front of the gruesome doorway.

"Say, Mag," said Pete, "give us a kiss for takin' yeh teh deh show, will yer?"

Maggie laughed, as if startled, and drew away from him.

"Naw, Pete," she said, "dat wasn't in it."

"Ah, what deh hell?" urged Pete.

The girl retreated nervously.

"Ah, what deh hell?" repeated he.

Maggie darted into the hall, and up the stairs. She turned and smiled at him, then disappeared.

Pete walked slowly down the street. He had something of an astonished expression upon his features. He paused under a lamp-post and breathed a low breath of surprise.

"Gawd," he said, "I wonner if I've been played fer a duffer."

Chapter VIII

As thoughts of Pete came to Maggie's mind, she began to have an intense dislike for all of her dresses.

"What deh hell ails yeh? What makes yeh be allus fixin' and fussin'? Good Gawd," her mother would frequently roar at her.

She began to note, with more interest, the well-dressed women she met on the avenues. She envied elegance and soft palms. She craved those adornments of person which she saw every day on the street, conceiving them to be allies of vast importance to women.

Studying faces, she thought many of the women and girls she chanced to meet, smiled with serenity as though forever cherished and watched over by those they loved.

The air in the collar and cuff establishment strangled her. She knew she was gradually and surely shrivelling in the hot, stuffy room. The begrimed windows rattled incessantly from the passing of elevated trains. The place was filled with a whirl of noises and odors.

She wondered as she regarded some of the grizzled women in the room, mere mechanical contrivances sewing seams and grinding out, with heads bended over their work, tales of imagined or real girlhood happiness, past drunks, the baby at home, and unpaid wages. She speculated how long her youth would endure. She began to see the bloom upon her cheeks as valuable.

She imagined herself, in an exasperating future, as a scrawny woman with an eternal grievance. Too, she thought Pete to be a very fastidious person concerning the appearance of women.

She felt she would love to see somebody entangle their fingers in the oily beard of the fat foreigner who owned the establishment. He was a detestable creature. He wore white socks with low shoes.

He sat all day delivering orations, in the depths of a cushioned chair. His pocketbook deprived them of the power to retort.

"What een hell do you sink I pie fife dolla a week for? Play? No, py damn!" Maggie was anxious for a friend to whom she could talk about Pete. She would have liked to discuss his admirable mannerisms with a reliable mutual friend. At home, she found her mother often drunk and always raving. It seems that the world had treated this woman very badly, and she took a deep revenge upon such portions of it as came within her reach. She broke furniture as if she were at last getting her rights. She swelled with virtuous indignation as she carried the lighter articles of household use, one by one under the shadows of the three gilt balls, where Hebrews chained them with chains of interest.

Jimmie came when he was obliged to by circumstances over which he had no control. His well-trained legs brought him staggering home and put him to bed some nights when he would rather have gone elsewhere.

Swaggering Pete loomed like a golden sun to Maggie. He took her to a dime museum where rows of meek freaks astonished her. She contemplated their deformities with awe and thought them a sort of chosen tribe.

"What een hell do you sink I pie fife dolla a week for? Play? No, py damn!" Maggie was anxious for a friend to whom she could talk about Pete. She would have liked to discuss his admirable mannerisms with a reliable mutual friend. At home, she found her mother often drunk and always raving. It seems that the world had treated this woman very badly, and she took a deep revenge upon such portions of it as came within her reach. She broke furniture as if she were at last getting her rights. She swelled with virtuous indignation as she carried the lighter articles of household use, one by one under the shadows of the three gilt balls, where Hebrews chained them with chains of interest.

Jimmie came when he was obliged to by circumstances over which he had no control. His well-trained legs brought him staggering home and put him to bed some nights when he would rather have gone elsewhere.

Swaggering Pete loomed like a golden sun to Maggie. He took her to a dime museum where rows of meek freaks astonished her. She contemplated their deformities with awe and thought them a sort of chosen tribe.

Pete, raking his brains for amusement, discovered the Central Park Menagerie and the Museum of Arts. Sunday afternoons would sometimes find them at these places. Pete did not appear to be particularly interested in what he saw. He stood around looking heavy, while Maggie giggled in glee.

Once at the Menagerie he went into a trance of admiration before the spectacle of a very small monkey threatening to thrash a cageful because one of them had pulled his tail and he had not wheeled about quickly enough to discover who did it. Ever after Pete knew that monkey by sight and winked at him, trying to induce hime to fight with other and larger monkeys. At the Museum, Maggie said, "Dis is outa sight."

"Oh hell," said Pete, "wait 'till next summer an' I'll take yehs to a picnic."

While the girl wandered in the vaulted rooms, Pete occupied himself in returning stony stare for stony stare, the appalling scrutiny of the watch-dogs of the treasures. Occasionally he would remark in loud tones: "Dat jay has got glass eyes," and sentences of the sort.

When he tired of this amusement he would go to the mummies and moralize over them.

Usually he submitted with silent dignity to all which he had to go through, but, at times, he was goaded into comment.

"What deh hell," he demanded once. "Look at all dese little jugs! Hundred jugs in a row! Ten rows in a case an' 'bout a t'ousand cases! What deh blazes use is dem?"

Evenings during the week he took her to see plays in which the brain-clutching heroine was rescued from the palatial home of her guardian, who is cruelly after her bonds, by the hero with the beautiful sentiments. The latter spent most of his time out at soak in pale-green snow storms, busy with a nickel-plated revolver, rescuing aged strangers from villains.

Maggie lost herself in sympathy with the wanderers swooning in snow storms beneath happy-hued church windows. And a choir within singing "Joy to the World." To Maggie and the rest of the audience this was transcendental realism. Joy always within, and they, like the actor, inevitably without. Viewing it, they hugged themselves in ecstatic pity of their imagined or real condition.

The girl thought the arrogance and granite-heartedness of the magnate of the play was very accurately drawn. She echoed the maledictions that the occupants of the gallery showered on this individual when his lines compelled him to expose his extreme selfishness.

Shady persons in the audience revolted from the pictured villainy of the drama. With untiring zeal they hissed vice and applauded virtue. Unmistakably bad men evinced an apparently sincere admiration for virtue.

The loud gallery was overwhelmingly with the unfortunate and the oppressed. They encouraged the struggling hero with cries, and jeered the villain, hooting and calling attention to his whiskers. When anybody died in the pale-green snow storms, the gallery mourned. They sought out the painted misery and hugged it as akin.

In the hero's erratic march from poverty in the first act, to wealth and triumph in the final one, in which he forgives all the enemies that he has left, he was assisted by the gallery, which applauded his generous and noble sentiments and confounded the speeches of his opponents by making irrelevant but very sharp remarks. Those actors who were cursed with villainy parts were confronted at every turn by the gallery. If one of them rendered lines containing the most subtle distinctions between right and wrong, the gallery was immediately aware if the actor meant wickedness, and denounced him accordingly.

The last act was a triumph for the hero, poor and of the masses, the representative of the audience, over the villain and the rich man, his pockets stuffed with bonds, his heart packed with tyrannical purposes, imperturbable amid suffering.

Maggie always departed with raised spirits from the showing places of the melodrama. She rejoiced at the way in which the poor and virtuous eventually surmounted the wealthy and wicked. The theatre made her think.

She wondered if the culture and refinement she had seen imitated, perhaps grotesquely, by the heroine on the stage, could be acquired by a girl who lived in a tenement house and worked in a shirt factory.

Chapter IX

A group of urchins were intent upon the side door of a saloon. Expectancy gleamed from their eyes. They were twisting their fingers in excitement.

"Here she comes," yelled one of them suddenly.

The group of urchins burst instantly asunder and its individual fragments were spread in a wide, respectable half circle about the point of interest. The saloon door opened with a crash, and the figure of a woman appeared upon the threshold. Her grey hair fell in knotted masses about her shoulders. Her face was crimsoned and wet with perspiration. Her eyes had a rolling glare.

"Not a damn cent more of me money will yehs ever get, not a damn cent. I spent me money here fer t'ree years an' now yehs tells me yeh'll sell me no more stuff! T'hell wid yeh, Johnnie Murckre! 'Disturbance'? Disturbance be damned! T'hell wid yeh, Johnnie—"

The door received a kick of exasperation from within and the woman lurched heavily out on the sidewalk.

The gamins in the half-circle became violently agitated. They began to dance about and hoot and yell and jeer. Wide dirty grins spread over each face.

The woman made a furious dash at a particularly outrageous cluster of little boys. They laughed delightedly and scampered off a short distance, calling out over their shoulders to her. She stood tottering on the curb-stone and thundered at them.

"Yeh devil's kids," she howled, shaking red fists. The little boys whooped in glee. As she started up the street they fell in behind and marched uproariously. Occasionally she wheeled about and made charges on them. They ran nimbly out of reach and taunted her.

In the frame of a gruesome doorway she stood for a moment cursing them. Her hair straggled, giving her crimson features a look of insanity. Her great fists quivered as she shook them madly in the air.

The urchins made terrific noises until she turned and disappeared. Then they filed quietly in the way they had come.

The woman floundered about in the lower hall of the tenement house and finally stumbled up the stairs. On an upper hall a door was opened and a collection of heads peered curiously out, watching her. With a wrathful snort the woman confronted the door, but it was slammed hastily in her face and the key was turned.

She stood for a few minutes, delivering a frenzied challenge at the panels.

"Come out in deh hall, Mary Murphy, damn yeh, if yehs want a row. Come ahn, yeh overgrown terrier, come ahn."

She began to kick the door with her great feet. She shrilly defied the universe to appear and do battle. Her cursing trebles brought heads from all doors save the one she threatened. Her eyes glared in every direction. The air was full of her tossing fists.

"Come ahn, deh hull damn gang of yehs, come ahn," she roared at the spectators. An oath or two, cat-calls, jeers and bits of facetious advice were given in reply. Missiles clattered about her feet.

"What deh hell's deh matter wid yeh?" said a voice in the gathered gloom, and Jimmie came forward. He carried a tin dinner-pail in his hand and under his arm a brown truckman's apron done in a bundle. "What deh hell's wrong?" he demanded.

"Come out, all of yehs, come out," his mother was howling. "Come ahn an' I'll stamp her damn brains under me feet."

"Shet yer face, an' come home, yeh damned old fool," roared Jimmie at her. She strided up to him and twirled her fingers in his face. Her eyes were darting flames of unreasoning rage and her frame trembled with eagerness for a fight.

"T'hell wid yehs! An' who deh hell are yehs? I ain't givin' a snap of me fingers fer yehs," she bawled at him. She turned her huge back in tremendous disdain and climbed the stairs to the next floor.

Jimmie followed, cursing blackly. At the top of the flight he seized his mother's arm and started to drag her toward the door of their room.

"Come home, damn yeh," he gritted between his teeth.

"Take yer hands off me! Take yer hands off me," shrieked his mother.

She raised her arm and whirled her great fist at her son's face. Jimmie dodged his head and the blow struck him in the back of the neck. "Damn yeh," gritted he again. He threw out his left hand and writhed his fingers about her middle arm. The mother and the son began to sway and struggle like gladiators.

"Whoop!" said the Rum Alley tenement house. The hall filled with interested spectators.

"Hi, ol' lady, dat was a dandy!"

"T'ree to one on deh red!"

"Ah, stop yer damn scrappin'!"

The door of the Johnson home opened and Maggie looked out. Jimmie made a supreme cursing effort and hurled his mother into the room. He quickly followed and closed the door. The Rum Alley tenement swore disappointedly and retired.

The mother slowly gathered herself up from the floor. Her eyes glittered menacingly upon her children.

"Here, now," said Jimmie, "we've had enough of dis. Sit down, an' don' make no trouble."

He grasped her arm, and twisting it, forced her into a creaking chair.

"Keep yer hands off me," roared his mother again.

"Damn yer ol' hide," yelled Jimmie, madly. Maggie shrieked and ran into the other room. To her there came the sound of a storm of crashes and curses. There was a great final thump and Jimmie's voice cried: "Dere, damn yeh, stay still." Maggie opened the door now, and went warily out. "Oh, Jimmie."

196

He was leaning against the wall and swearing. Blood stood upon bruises on his knotty fore-arms where they had scraped against the floor or the walls in the scuffle. The mother lay screeching on the floor, the tears running down her furrowed face.

Maggie, standing in the middle of the room, gazed about her. The usual upheaval of the tables and chairs had taken place. Crockery was strewn broadcast in fragments. The stove had been disturbed on its legs, and now leaned idiotically to one side. A pail had been upset and water spread in all directions.

The door opened and Pete appeared. He shrugged his shoulders. "Oh, Gawd," he observed.

He walked over to Maggie and whispered in her ear. "Ah, what deh hell, Mag? Come ahn and we'll have a hell of a time."

The mother in the corner upreared her head and shook her tangled locks.

"Teh hell wid him and you," she said, glowering at her daughter in the gloom. Her eyes seemed to burn balefully. "Yeh've gone teh deh devil, Mag Johnson, yehs knows yehs have gone teh deh devil. Yer a disgrace teh yer people, damn yeh. An' now, git out an' go ahn wid dat doe-faced jude of yours. Go teh hell wid him, damn yeh, an' a good riddance. Go teh hell an' see how yeh likes it."

Maggie gazed long at her mother.

"Go teh hell now, an' see how yeh likes it. Git out. I won't have sech as yehs in me house! Get out, d'yeh hear! Damn yeh, git out!"

The girl began to tremble.

At this instant Pete came forward. "Oh, what deh hell, Mag, see," whispered he softly in her ear. "Dis all blows over. See? Deh ol' woman 'ill be all right in deh mornin'. Come ahn out wid me! We'll have a hell of a time."

The woman on the floor cursed. Jimmie was intent upon his bruised fore-arms. The girl cast a glance about the room filled with a chaotic mass of debris, and at the red, writhing body of her mother.

"Go teh hell an' good riddance."

She went.

Chapter X

Jimmie had an idea it wasn't common courtesy for a friend to come to one's home and ruin one's sister. But he was not sure how much Pete knew about the rules of politeness.

The following night he returned home from work at rather a late hour in the evening. In passing through the halls he came upon the gnarled and leathery old woman who possessed the music box. She was grinning in the dim light that drifted through dust-stained panes. She beckoned to him with a smudged forefinger.

"Ah, Jimmie, what do yehs t'ink I got onto las' night. It was deh funnies' t'ing I ever saw," she cried, coming close to him and leering. She was trembling with eagerness to tell her tale. "I was by me door las' night when yer sister and her jude feller came in late, oh, very late. An' she, the dear, she was a-cryin' as if her heart would break, she was. It was deh funnies' t'ing I ever saw. An' right out here by me door she asked him did he love her, did he. An' she was a-cryin' as if her heart would break, poor t'ing. An' him, I could see by deh way what he said it dat she had been askin' orften, he says: 'Oh, hell, yes,' he says, says he, 'Oh, hell, yes.'"

Storm-clouds swept over Jimmie's face, but he turned from the leathery old woman and plodded on up-stairs.

"Oh, hell, yes," called she after him. She laughed a laugh that was like a prophetic croak. "'Oh, hell, yes,' he says, says he, 'Oh, hell, yes.'"

There was no one in at home. The rooms showed that attempts had been made at tidying them. Parts of the wreckage of the day before had been repaired by an unskilful hand. A chair or two and the table, stood uncertainly upon legs. The floor had been newly swept. Too, the blue ribbons had been restored to the curtains, and the lambrequin, with its immense sheaves of yellow wheat and red roses of equal size, had been returned, in a worn and sorry state, to its position at the mantel. Maggie's jacket and hat were gone from the nail behind the door.

Jimmie walked to the window and began to look through the blurred glass. It occurred to him to vaguely wonder, for an instant, if some of the women of his acquaintance had brothers.

Suddenly, however, he began to swear.

"But he was me frien'! I brought 'im here! Dat's deh hell of it!"

He fumed about the room, his anger gradually rising to the furious pitch.

"I'll kill deh jay! Dat's what I'll do! I'll kill deh jay!"

He clutched his hat and sprang toward the door. But it opened and his mother's great form blocked the passage.

"What deh hell's deh matter wid yeh?" exclaimed she, coming into the rooms.

Jimmie gave vent to a sardonic curse and then laughed heavily.

"Well, Maggie's gone teh deh devil! Dat's what! See?"

"Eh?" said his mother.

"Maggie's gone teh deh devil! Are yehs deaf?" roared Jimmie, impatiently.

"Deh hell she has," murmured the mother, astounded.

Jimmie grunted, and then began to stare out at the window. His mother sat down in a chair, but a moment later sprang erect and delivered a maddened whirl of oaths. Her son turned to look at her as she reeled and swayed in the middle of the room, her fierce face convulsed with passion, her blotched arms raised high in imprecation.

"May Gawd curse her forever," she shrieked. "May she eat nothin' but stones and deh dirt in deh street. May she sleep in deh gutter an' never see deh sun shine agin. Deh damn—"

"Here, now," said her son. "Take a drop on yourself."

The mother raised lamenting eyes to the ceiling.

"She's deh devil's own chil', Jimmie," she whispered. "Ah, who would t'ink such a bad girl could grow up in our fambly, Jimmie, me son. Many deh hour I've spent in talk wid dat girl an' tol' her if she ever went on deh streets I'd see her damned. An' after all her bringin' up an' what I tol' her and talked wid her, she goes teh deh bad, like a duck teh water."

The tears rolled down her furrowed face. Her hands trembled.

"An' den when dat Sadie MacMallister next door to us was sent teh deh devil by dat feller what worked in deh soap-factory, didn't I tell our Mag dat if she—"

"Ah, dat's annuder story," interrupted the brother. "Of course, dat Sadie was nice an' all dat—but—see—it ain't dessame as if—well, Maggie was diff'ent—see—she was diff'ent."

He was trying to formulate a theory that he had always unconsciously held, that all sisters, excepting his own, could advisedly be ruined.

He suddenly broke out again. "I'll go t'ump hell outa deh mug what did her deh harm. I'll kill 'im! He t'inks he kin scrap, but when he gits me a-chasin' 'im he'll fin' out where he's wrong, deh damned duffer. I'll wipe up deh street wid 'im."

In a fury he plunged out of the doorway. As he vanished the mother raised her head and lifted both hands, entreating.

"May Gawd curse her forever," she cried.

In the darkness of the hallway Jimmie discerned a knot of women talking volubly. When he strode by they paid no attention to him.

"She allus was a bold thing," he heard one of them cry in an eager voice. "Dere wasn't a feller come teh deh house but she'd try teh mash 'im. My Annie says deh shameless t'ing tried teh ketch her feller, her own feller, what we useter know his fader."

"I could a' tol' yehs dis two years ago," said a woman, in a key of triumph. "Yessir, it was over two years ago dat I says teh my ol' man, I says,

'Dat Johnson girl ain't straight,' I says. 'Oh, hell,' he says. 'Oh, hell.' 'Dat's all right,' I says, 'but I know what I knows,' I says, 'an' it 'ill come out later. You wait an' see,' I says, 'you see.'"

"Anybody what had eyes could see dat dere was somethin' wrong wid dat girl. I didn't like her actions."

On the street Jimmie met a friend. "What deh hell?" asked the latter.

Jimmie explained. "An' I'll t'ump 'im till he can't stand."

"Oh, what deh hell," said the friend. "What's deh use! Yeh'll git pulled in! Everybody 'ill be onto it! An' ten plunks! Gee!"

Jimmie was determined. "He t'inks he kin scrap, but he'll fin' out diff'ent."

"Gee," remonstrated the friend. "What deh hell?"

ays as he assiduously polished away with a napkin at the gleaming
. He had a look of watchfulness upon his features.

Jimmie and his companion kept their eyes upon the bartender and
ersed loudly in tones of contempt.

"He's a dindy masher, ain't he, by Gawd?" laughed Jimmie.

"Oh, hell, yes," said the companion, sneering widely. "He's great, he is.
onto deh mug on deh blokie. Dat's enough to make a feller turn hand-
ngs in 'is sleep."

The quiet stranger moved himself and his glass a trifle further away and
ntained an attitude of oblivion.

"Gee! ain't he hot stuff!"

"Git onto his shape! Great Gawd!"

"Hey," cried Jimmie, in tones of command. Pete came along slowly, with
ullen dropping of the under lip.

"Well," he growled, "what's eatin' yehs?"

"Gin," said Jimmie.

"Gin," said the companion.

As Pete confronted them with the bottle and the glasses, they laughed in
s face. Jimmie's companion, evidently overcome with merriment, pointed a
imy forefinger in Pete's direction.

"Say, Jimmie," demanded he, "what deh hell is dat behind deh bar?"

"Damned if I knows," replied Jimmie. They laughed loudly. Pete put
own a bottle with a bang and turned a formidable face toward them. He
isclosed his teeth and his shoulders heaved restlessly.

"You fellers can't guy me," he said. "Drink yer stuff an' git out an' don'
make no trouble."

Instantly the laughter faded from the faces of the two men and
expressions of offended dignity immediately came.

Chapter XI

On a corner a glass-fronted building shed a yellow
pavements. The open mouth of a saloon called seductively
enter and annihilate sorrow or create rage.

The interior of the place was papered in olive and b
imitation leather. A shining bar of counterfeit massiveness e
the side of the room. Behind it a great mahogany-appear
reached the ceiling. Upon its shelves rested pyramids of shim
that were never disturbed. Mirrors set in the face of the sideboa
them. Lemons, oranges and paper napkins, arranged with
precision, sat among the glasses. Many-hued decanters of liqu
regular intervals on the lower shelves. A nickel-plated cash regis
a position in the exact centre of the general effect. The elementar
all seemed to be opulence and geometrical accuracy.

Across from the bar a smaller counter held a collection of
which swarmed frayed fragments of crackers, slices of boiled ham,
bits of cheese, and pickles swimming in vinegar. An odor o
begrimed hands and munching mouths pervaded.

Pete, in a white jacket, was behind the bar bending expectantl
quiet stranger. "A beeh," said the man. Pete drew a foam-topped gl
set it dripping upon the bar.

At this moment the light bamboo doors at the entrance swung
crashed against the siding. Jimmie and a companion entered. They sv
unsteadily but belligerently toward the bar and looked at Pete with
and blinking eyes.

"Gin," said Jimmie.

"Gin," said the companion.

Pete slid a bottle and two glasses along the bar. He bended hi

"Who deh hell has said anyt'ing teh you," cried they in the same breath.

The quiet stranger looked at the door calculatingly.

"Ah, come off," said Pete to the two men. "Don't pick me up for no jay. Drink yer rum an' git out an' don' make no trouble."

"Oh, deh hell," airily cried Jimmie.

"Oh, deh hell," airily repeated his companion.

"We goes when we git ready! See!" continued Jimmie.

"Well," said Pete in a threatening voice, "don' make no trouble."

Jimmie suddenly leaned forward with his head on one side. He snarled like a wild animal.

"Well, what if we does? See?" said he.

Dark blood flushed into Pete's face, and he shot a lurid glance at Jimmie.

"Well, den we'll see whose deh bes' man, you or me," he said.

The quiet stranger moved modestly toward the door.

Jimmie began to swell with valor.

"Don' pick me up fer no tenderfoot. When yeh tackles me yeh tackles one of deh bes' men in deh city. See? I'm a scrapper, I am. Ain't dat right, Billie?"

"Sure, Mike," responded his companion in tones of conviction.

"Oh, hell," said Pete, easily. "Go fall on yerself."

The two men again began to laugh.

"What deh hell is dat talkin'?" cried the companion.

"Damned if I knows," replied Jimmie with exaggerated contempt.

Pete made a furious gesture. "Git outa here now, an' don' make no trouble. See? Youse fellers er lookin' fer a scrap an' it's damn likely yeh'll fin'

205

one if yeh keeps on shootin' off yer mout's. I know yehs! See? I kin lick better men dan yehs ever saw in yer lifes. Dat's right! See? Don' pick me up fer no stuff er yeh might be jolted out in deh street before yeh knows where yeh is. When I comes from behind dis bar, I t'rows yehs bote inteh deh street. See?"

"Oh, hell," cried the two men in chorus.

The glare of a panther came into Pete's eyes. "Dat's what I said! Unnerstan'?"

He came through a passage at the end of the bar and swelled down upon the two men. They stepped promptly forward and crowded close to him.

They bristled like three roosters. They moved their heads pugnaciously and kept their shoulders braced. The nervous muscles about each mouth twitched with a forced smile of mockery.

"Well, what deh hell yer goin' teh do?" gritted Jimmie.

Pete stepped warily back, waving his hands before him to keep the men from coming too near.

"Well, what deh hell yer goin' teh do?" repeated Jimmie's ally. They kept close to him, taunting and leering. They strove to make him attempt the initial blow.

"Keep back, now! Don' crowd me," ominously said Pete.

Again they chorused in contempt. "Oh, hell!"

In a small, tossing group, the three men edged for positions like frigates contemplating battle.

"Well, why deh hell don' yeh try teh t'row us out?" cried Jimmie and his ally with copious sneers.

The bravery of bull-dogs sat upon the faces of the men. Their clenched fists moved like eager weapons.

The allied two jostled the bartender's elbows, glaring at him with feverish eyes and forcing him toward the wall.

Suddenly Pete swore redly. The flash of action gleamed from his eyes. He threw back his arm and aimed a tremendous, lightning-like blow at Jimmie's face. His foot swung a step forward and the weight of his body was behind his fist. Jimmie ducked his head, Bowery-like, with the quickness of a cat. The fierce, answering blows of him and his ally crushed on Pete's bowed head.

The quiet stranger vanished.

The arms of the combatants whirled in the air like flails. The faces of the men, at first flushed to flame-colored anger, now began to fade to the pallor of warriors in the blood and heat of a battle. Their lips curled back and stretched tightly over the gums in ghoul-like grins. Through their white, gripped teeth struggled hoarse whisperings of oaths. Their eyes glittered with murderous fire.

Each head was huddled between its owner's shoulders, and arms were swinging with marvelous rapidity. Feet scraped to and fro with a loud scratching sound upon the sanded floor. Blows left crimson blotches upon pale skin. The curses of the first quarter minute of the fight died away. The breaths of the fighters came wheezingly from their lips and the three chests were straining and heaving. Pete at intervals gave vent to low, labored hisses, that sounded like a desire to kill. Jimmie's ally gibbered at times like a wounded maniac. Jimmie was silent, fighting with the face of a sacrificial priest. The rage of fear shone in all their eyes and their blood-colored fists swirled.

At a tottering moment a blow from Pete's hand struck the ally and he crashed to the floor. He wriggled instantly to his feet and grasping the quiet stranger's beer glass from the bar, hurled it at Pete's head.

High on the wall it burst like a bomb, shivering fragments flying in all directions. Then missiles came to every man's hand. The place had heretofore appeared free of things to throw, but suddenly glass and bottles went singing through the air. They were thrown point blank at bobbing heads. The pyramid of shimmering glasses, that had never been disturbed, changed to cascades as heavy bottles were flung into them. Mirrors splintered to nothing.

The three frothing creatures on the floor buried themselves in a frenzy for blood. There followed in the wake of missiles and fists some unknown prayers, perhaps for death.

The quiet stranger had sprawled very pyrotechnically out on the sidewalk. A laugh ran up and down the avenue for the half of a block.

"Dey've trowed a bloke inteh deh street."

People heard the sound of breaking glass and shuffling feet within the saloon and came running. A small group, bending down to look under the bamboo doors, watching the fall of glass, and three pairs of violent legs, changed in a moment to a crowd.

A policeman came charging down the sidewalk and bounced through the doors into the saloon. The crowd bended and surged in absorbing anxiety to see.

Jimmie caught first sight of the on-coming interruption. On his feet he had the same regard for a policeman that, when on his truck, he had for a fire engine. He howled and ran for the side door.

The officer made a terrific advance, club in hand. One comprehensive sweep of the long night stick threw the ally to the floor and forced Pete to a corner. With his disengaged hand he made a furious effort at Jimmie's coat-tails. Then he regained his balance and paused.

"Well, well, you are a pair of pictures. What in hell yeh been up to?"

Jimmie, with his face drenched in blood, escaped up a side street, pursued a short distance by some of the more law-loving, or excited individuals of the crowd.

Later, from a corner safely dark, he saw the policeman, the ally and the bartender emerge from the saloon. Pete locked the doors and then followed up the avenue in the rear of the crowd-encompassed policeman and his charge.

On first thoughts Jimmie, with his heart throbbing at battle heat, started to go desperately to the rescue of his friend, but he halted.

"Ah, what deh hell?" he demanded of himself.

Chapter XII

In a hall of irregular shape sat Pete and Maggie drinking beer. A submissive orchestra dictated to by a spectacled man with frowsy hair and a dress suit, industriously followed the bobs of his head and the waves of his baton. A ballad singer, in a dress of flaming scarlet, sang in the inevitable voice of brass. When she vanished, men seated at the tables near the front applauded loudly, pounding the polished wood with their beer glasses. She returned attired in less gown, and sang again. She received another enthusiastic encore. She reappeared in still less gown and danced. The deafening rumble of glasses and clapping of hands that followed her exit indicated an overwhelming desire to have her come on for the fourth time, but the curiosity of the audience was not gratified.

Maggie was pale. From her eyes had been plucked all look of self-reliance. She leaned with a dependent air toward her companion. She was timid, as if fearing his anger or displeasure. She seemed to beseech tenderness of him.

Pete's air of distinguished valor had grown upon him until it threatened stupendous dimensions. He was infinitely gracious to the girl. It was apparent to her that his condescension was a marvel.

He could appear to strut even while sitting still and he showed that he was a lion of lordly characteristics by the air with which he spat.

With Maggie gazing at him wonderingly, he took pride in commanding the waiters who were, however, indifferent or deaf.

"Hi, you, git a russle on yehs! What deh hell yehs lookin' at? Two more beehs, d'yeh hear?"

He leaned back and critically regarded the person of a girl with a straw-colored wig who upon the stage was flinging her heels in somewhat awkward imitation of a well-known danseuse.

At times Maggie told Pete long confidential tales of her former home life, dwelling upon the escapades of the other members of the family and the difficulties she had to combat in order to obtain a degree of comfort. He responded in tones of philanthropy. He pressed her arm with an air of reassuring proprietorship.

"Dey was damn jays," he said, denouncing the mother and brother.

The sound of the music which, by the efforts of the frowsy-headed leader, drifted to her ears through the smoke-filled atmosphere, made the girl dream. She thought of her former Rum Alley environment and turned to regard Pete's strong protecting fists. She thought of the collar and cuff manufactory and the eternal moan of the proprietor: "What een hell do you sink I pie fife dolla a week for? Play? No, py damn." She contemplated Pete's man-subduing eyes and noted that wealth and prosperity was indicated by his clothes. She imagined a future, rose-tinted, because of its distance from all that she previously had experienced.

As to the present she perceived only vague reasons to be miserable. Her life was Pete's and she considered him worthy of the charge. She would be disturbed by no particular apprehensions, so long as Pete adored her as he now said he did. She did not feel like a bad woman. To her knowledge she had never seen any better.

At times men at other tables regarded the girl furtively. Pete, aware of it, nodded at her and grinned. He felt proud.

"Mag, yer a bloomin' good-looker," he remarked, studying her face through the haze. The men made Maggie fear, but she blushed at Pete's words as it became apparent to her that she was the apple of his eye.

Grey-headed men, wonderfully pathetic in their dissipation, stared at her through clouds. Smooth-cheeked boys, some of them with faces of stone and mouths of sin, not nearly so pathetic as the grey heads, tried to find the girl's eyes in the smoke wreaths. Maggie considered she was not what they thought her. She confined her glances to Pete and the stage.

The orchestra played negro melodies and a versatile drummer pounded, whacked, clattered and scratched on a dozen machines to make noise.

Those glances of the men, shot at Maggie from under half-closed lids, made her tremble. She thought them all to be worse men than Pete.

"Come, let's go," she said.

As they went out Maggie perceived two women seated at a table with some men. They were painted and their cheeks had lost their roundness. As she passed them the girl, with a shrinking movement, drew back her skirts.

Chapter XIII

Jimmie did not return home for a number of days after the fight with Pete in the saloon. When he did, he approached with extreme caution.

He found his mother raving. Maggie had not returned home. The parent continually wondered how her daughter could come to such a pass. She had never considered Maggie as a pearl dropped unstained into Rum Alley from Heaven, but she could not conceive how it was possible for her daughter to fall so low as to bring disgrace upon her family. She was terrific in denunciation of the girl's wickedness.

The fact that the neighbors talked of it, maddened her. When women came in, and in the course of their conversation casually asked, "Where's Maggie dese days?" the mother shook her fuzzy head at them and appalled them with curses. Cunning hints inviting confidence she rebuffed with violence.

"An' wid all deh bringin' up she had, how could she?" moaningly she asked of her son. "Wid all deh talkin' wid her I did an' deh t'ings I tol' her to remember? When a girl is bringed up deh way I bringed up Maggie, how kin she go teh deh devil?"

Jimmie was transfixed by these questions. He could not conceive how under the circumstances his mother's daughter and his sister could have been so wicked.

His mother took a drink from a squdgy bottle that sat on the table. She continued her lament.

"She had a bad heart, dat girl did, Jimmie. She was wicked teh deh heart an' we never knowed it."

Jimmie nodded, admitting the fact.

"We lived in deh same house wid her an' I brought her up an' we never knowed how bad she was."

Jimmie nodded again.

"Wid a home like dis an' a mudder like me, she went teh deh bad," cried the mother, raising her eyes.

One day, Jimmie came home, sat down in a chair and began to wriggle about with a new and strange nervousness. At last he spoke shamefacedly.

"Well, look-a-here, dis t'ing queers us! See? We're queered! An' maybe it 'ud be better if I—well, I t'ink I kin look 'er up an'—maybe it 'ud be better if I fetched her home an'—"

The mother started from her chair and broke forth into a storm of passionate anger.

"What! Let 'er come an' sleep under deh same roof wid her mudder agin! Oh, yes, I will, won't I? Sure? Shame on yehs, Jimmie Johnson, for sayin' such a t'ing teh yer own mudder—teh yer own mudder! Little did I t'ink when yehs was a babby playin' about me feet dat ye'd grow up teh say sech a t'ing teh yer mudder—yer own mudder. I never taut—"

Sobs choked her and interrupted her reproaches.

"Dere ain't nottin' teh raise sech hell about," said Jimmie. "I on'y says it 'ud be better if we keep dis t'ing dark, see? It queers us! See?"

His mother laughed a laugh that seemed to ring through the city and be echoed and re-echoed by countless other laughs. "Oh, yes, I will, won't I! Sure!"

"Well, yeh must take me fer a damn fool," said Jimmie, indignant at his mother for mocking him. "I didn't say we'd make 'er inteh a little tin angel, ner nottin', but deh way it is now she can queer us! Don' che see?"

"Aye, she'll git tired of deh life atter a while an' den she'll wanna be a-comin' home, won' she, deh beast! I'll let 'er in den, won' I?"

"Well, I didn' mean none of dis prod'gal bus'ness anyway," explained Jimmie.

"It wasn't no prod'gal dauter, yeh damn fool," said the mother. "It was prod'gal son, anyhow."

"I know dat," said Jimmie.

For a time they sat in silence. The mother's eyes gloated on a scene her imagination could call before her. Her lips were set in a vindictive smile.

"Aye, she'll cry, won' she, an' carry on, an' tell how Pete, or some odder feller, beats 'er an' she'll say she's sorry an' all dat an' she ain't happy, she ain't, an' she wants to come home agin, she does."

With grim humor, the mother imitated the possible wailing notes of the daughter's voice.

"Den I'll take 'er in, won't I, deh beast. She kin cry 'er two eyes out on deh stones of deh street before I'll dirty deh place wid her. She abused an' ill-treated her own mudder—her own mudder what loved her an' she'll never git anodder chance dis side of hell."

Jimmie thought he had a great idea of women's frailty, but he could not understand why any of his kin should be victims.

"Damn her," he fervidly said.

Again he wondered vaguely if some of the women of his acquaintance had brothers. Nevertheless, his mind did not for an instant confuse himself with those brothers nor his sister with theirs. After the mother had, with great difficulty, suppressed the neighbors, she went among them and proclaimed her grief. "May Gawd forgive dat girl," was her continual cry. To attentive ears she recited the whole length and breadth of her woes.

"I bringed 'er up deh way a dauter oughta be bringed up an' dis is how she served me! She went teh deh devil deh first chance she got! May Gawd forgive her."

When arrested for drunkenness she used the story of her daughter's downfall with telling effect upon the police justices. Finally one of them said to her, peering down over his spectacles: "Mary, the records of this and other

214

courts show that you are the mother of forty-two daughters who have been ruined. The case is unparalleled in the annals of this court, and this court thinks—"

The mother went through life shedding large tears of sorrow. Her red face was a picture of agony.

Of course Jimmie publicly damned his sister that he might appear on a higher social plane. But, arguing with himself, stumbling about in ways that he knew not, he, once, almost came to a conclusion that his sister would have been more firmly good had she better known why. However, he felt that he could not hold such a view. He threw it hastily aside.

Chapter XIV

In a hilarious hall there were twenty-eight tables and twenty-eight women and a crowd of smoking men. Valiant noise was made on a stage at the end of the hall by an orchestra composed of men who looked as if they had just happened in. Soiled waiters ran to and fro, swooping down like hawks on the unwary in the throng; clattering along the aisles with trays covered with glasses; stumbling over women's skirts and charging two prices for everything but beer, all with a swiftness that blurred the view of the cocoanut palms and dusty monstrosities painted upon the walls of the room. A bouncer, with an immense load of business upon his hands, plunged about in the crowd, dragging bashful strangers to prominent chairs, ordering waiters here and there and quarreling furiously with men who wanted to sing with the orchestra.

The usual smoke cloud was present, but so dense that heads and arms seemed entangled in it. The rumble of conversation was replaced by a roar. Plenteous oaths heaved through the air. The room rang with the shrill voices of women bubbling o'er with drink-laughter. The chief element in the music of the orchestra was speed. The musicians played in intent fury. A woman was singing and smiling upon the stage, but no one took notice of her. The rate at which the piano, cornet and violins were going, seemed to impart wildness to the half-drunken crowd. Beer glasses were emptied at a gulp and conversation became a rapid chatter. The smoke eddied and swirled like a shadowy river hurrying toward some unseen falls. Pete and Maggie entered the hall and took chairs at a table near the door. The woman who was seated there made an attempt to occupy Pete's attention and, failing, went away.

Three weeks had passed since the girl had left home. The air of spaniel-like dependence had been magnified and showed its direct effect in the peculiar off-handedness and ease of Pete's ways toward her.

She followed Pete's eyes with hers, anticipating with smiles gracious looks from him.

A woman of brilliance and audacity, accompanied by a mere boy, came into the place and took seats near them.

At once Pete sprang to his feet, his face beaming with glad surprise.

"By Gawd, there's Nellie," he cried.

He went over to the table and held out an eager hand to the woman.

"Why, hello, Pete, me boy, how are you," said she, giving him her fingers.

Maggie took instant note of the woman. She perceived that her black dress fitted her to perfection. Her linen collar and cuffs were spotless. Tan gloves were stretched over her well-shaped hands. A hat of a prevailing fashion perched jauntily upon her dark hair. She wore no jewelry and was painted with no apparent paint. She looked clear-eyed through the stares of the men.

"Sit down, and call your lady-friend over," she said cordially to Pete. At his beckoning Maggie came and sat between Pete and the mere boy.

"I thought yeh were gone away fer good," began Pete, at once. "When did yeh git back? How did dat Buff'lo bus'ness turn out?"

The woman shrugged her shoulders. "Well, he didn't have as many stamps as he tried to make out, so I shook him, that's all."

"Well, I'm glad teh see yehs back in deh city," said Pete, with awkward gallantry.

He and the woman entered into a long conversation, exchanging reminiscences of days together. Maggie sat still, unable to formulate an intelligent sentence upon the conversation and painfully aware of it.

She saw Pete's eyes sparkle as he gazed upon the handsome stranger. He listened smilingly to all she said. The woman was familiar with all his affairs, asked him about mutual friends, and knew the amount of his salary.

She paid no attention to Maggie, looking toward her once or twice and apparently seeing the wall beyond.

The mere boy was sulky. In the beginning he had welcomed with acclamations the additions.

"Let's all have a drink! What'll you take, Nell? And you, Miss what's-your-name. Have a drink, Mr. ——, you, I mean."

He had shown a sprightly desire to do the talking for the company and tell all about his family. In a loud voice he declaimed on various topics. He assumed a patronizing air toward Pete. As Maggie was silent, he paid no attention to her. He made a great show of lavishing wealth upon the woman of brilliance and audacity.

"Do keep still, Freddie! You gibber like an ape, dear," said the woman to him. She turned away and devoted her attention to Pete.

"We'll have many a good time together again, eh?"

"Sure, Mike," said Pete, enthusiastic at once.

"Say," whispered she, leaning forward, "let's go over to Billie's and have a heluva time."

"Well, it's dis way! See?" said Pete. "I got dis lady frien' here."

"Oh, t'hell with her," argued the woman.

Pete appeared disturbed.

"All right," said she, nodding her head at him. "All right for you! We'll see the next time you ask me to go anywheres with you."

Pete squirmed.

"Say," he said, beseechingly, "come wid me a minit an' I'll tell yer why."

The woman waved her hand.

"Oh, that's all right, you needn't explain, you know. You wouldn't come merely because you wouldn't come, that's all there is of it."

To Pete's visible distress she turned to the mere boy, bringing him speedily from a terrific rage. He had been debating whether it would be the part of a man to pick a quarrel with Pete, or would he be justified in striking him savagely with his beer glass without warning. But he recovered himself when the woman turned to renew her smilings. He beamed upon her with an expression that was somewhat tipsy and inexpressibly tender.

"Say, shake that Bowery jay," requested he, in a loud whisper.

"Freddie, you are so droll," she replied.

Pete reached forward and touched the woman on the arm.

"Come out a minit while I tells yeh why I can't go wid yer. Yer doin' me dirt, Nell! I never taut ye'd do me dirt, Nell. Come on, will yer?" He spoke in tones of injury.

"Why, I don't see why I should be interested in your explanations," said the woman, with a coldness that seemed to reduce Pete to a pulp.

His eyes pleaded with her. "Come out a minit while I tells yeh."

The woman nodded slightly at Maggie and the mere boy, "'Scuse me."

The mere boy interrupted his loving smile and turned a shrivelling glare upon Pete. His boyish countenance flushed and he spoke, in a whine, to the woman:

"Oh, I say, Nellie, this ain't a square deal, you know. You aren't goin' to leave me and go off with that duffer, are you? I should think—"

"Why, you dear boy, of course I'm not," cried the woman, affectionately. She bended over and whispered in his ear. He smiled again and settled in his chair as if resolved to wait patiently.

As the woman walked down between the rows of tables, Pete was at her shoulder talking earnestly, apparently in explanation. The woman waved her hands with studied airs of indifference. The doors swung behind them, leaving Maggie and the mere boy seated at the table.

Maggie was dazed. She could dimly perceive that something stupendous had happened. She wondered why Pete saw fit to remonstrate with the woman, pleading for forgiveness with his eyes. She thought she noted an air of submission about her leonine Pete. She was astounded.

The mere boy occupied himself with cock-tails and a cigar. He was tranquilly silent for half an hour. Then he bestirred himself and spoke.

"Well," he said, sighing, "I knew this was the way it would be." There was another stillness. The mere boy seemed to be musing.

"She was pulling m'leg. That's the whole amount of it," he said, suddenly. "It's a bloomin' shame the way that girl does. Why, I've spent over two dollars in drinks to-night. And she goes off with that plug-ugly who looks as if he had been hit in the face with a coin-die. I call it rocky treatment for a fellah like me. Here, waiter, bring me a cock-tail and make it damned strong."

Maggie made no reply. She was watching the doors. "It's a mean piece of business," complained the mere boy. He explained to her how amazing it was that anybody should treat him in such a manner. "But I'll get square with her, you bet. She won't get far ahead of yours truly, you know," he added, winking. "I'll tell her plainly that it was bloomin' mean business. And she won't come it over me with any of her 'now-Freddie-dears.' She thinks my name is Freddie, you know, but of course it ain't. I always tell these people some name like that, because if they got onto your right name they might use it sometime. Understand? Oh, they don't fool me much."

Maggie was paying no attention, being intent upon the doors. The mere boy relapsed into a period of gloom, during which he exterminated a number of cock-tails with a determined air, as if replying defiantly to fate. He occasionally broke forth into sentences composed of invectives joined together in a long string.

The girl was still staring at the doors. After a time the mere boy began to see cobwebs just in front of his nose. He spurred himself into being agreeable and insisted upon her having a charlotte-russe and a glass of beer.

"They's gone," he remarked, "they's gone." He looked at her through the smoke wreaths. "Shay, lil' girl, we mightish well make bes' of it. You ain't such bad-lookin' girl, y'know. Not half bad. Can't come up to Nell, though. No, can't do it! Well, I should shay not! Nell fine-lookin' girl! F—i—n—ine. You look damn bad longsider her, but by y'self ain't so bad. Have to do anyhow. Nell gone. On'y you left. Not half bad, though."

Maggie stood up.

"I'm going home," she said.

The mere boy started.

"Eh? What? Home," he cried, struck with amazement. "I beg pardon, did hear say home?"

"I'm going home," she repeated.

"Great Gawd, what hava struck," demanded the mere boy of himself, stupefied.

In a semi-comatose state he conducted her on board an up-town car, ostentatiously paid her fare, leered kindly at her through the rear window and fell off the steps.

Chapter XV

A forlorn woman went along a lighted avenue. The street was filled with people desperately bound on missions. An endless crowd darted at the elevated station stairs and the horse cars were thronged with owners of bundles.

The pace of the forlorn woman was slow. She was apparently searching for some one. She loitered near the doors of saloons and watched men emerge from them. She scanned furtively the faces in the rushing stream of pedestrians. Hurrying men, bent on catching some boat or train, jostled her elbows, failing to notice her, their thoughts fixed on distant dinners.

The forlorn woman had a peculiar face. Her smile was no smile. But when in repose her features had a shadowy look that was like a sardonic grin, as if some one had sketched with cruel forefinger indelible lines about her mouth.

Jimmie came strolling up the avenue. The woman encountered him with an aggrieved air.

"Oh, Jimmie, I've been lookin' all over fer yehs—," she began.

Jimmie made an impatient gesture and quickened his pace.

"Ah, don't bodder me! Good Gawd!" he said, with the savageness of a man whose life is pestered.

The woman followed him along the sidewalk in somewhat the manner of a suppliant.

"But, Jimmie," she said, "yehs told me ye'd—"

Jimmie turned upon her fiercely as if resolved to make a last stand for comfort and peace.

"Say, fer Gawd's sake, Hattie, don' foller me from one end of deh city teh deh odder. Let up, will yehs! Give me a minute's res', can't yehs? Yehs makes me tired, allus taggin' me. See? Ain' yehs got no sense. Do yehs want people teh get onto me? Go chase yerself, fer Gawd's sake."

The woman stepped closer and laid her fingers on his arm. "But, look-a-here—"

Jimmie snarled. "Oh, go teh hell."

He darted into the front door of a convenient saloon and a moment later came out into the shadows that surrounded the side door. On the brilliantly lighted avenue he perceived the forlorn woman dodging about like a scout. Jimmie laughed with an air of relief and went away.

When he arrived home he found his mother clamoring. Maggie had returned. She stood shivering beneath the torrent of her mother's wrath.

"Well, I'm damned," said Jimmie in greeting.

His mother, tottering about the room, pointed a quivering forefinger.

"Lookut her, Jimmie, lookut her. Dere's yer sister, boy. Dere's yer sister. Lookut her! Lookut her!"

She screamed in scoffing laughter.

The girl stood in the middle of the room. She edged about as if unable to find a place on the floor to put her feet.

"Ha, ha, ha," bellowed the mother. "Dere she stands! Ain' she purty? Lookut her! Ain' she sweet, deh beast? Lookut her! Ha, ha, lookut her!"

She lurched forward and put her red and seamed hands upon her daughter's face. She bent down and peered keenly up into the eyes of the girl.

"Oh, she's jes' dessame as she ever was, ain' she? She's her mudder's purty darlin' yit, ain' she? Lookut her, Jimmie! Come here, fer Gawd's sake, and lookut her."

The loud, tremendous sneering of the mother brought the denizens of the Rum Alley tenement to their doors. Women came in the hallways. Children scurried to and fro.

"What's up? Dat Johnson party on anudder tear?"

"Naw! Young Mag's come home!"

"Deh hell yeh say?"

Through the open door curious eyes stared in at Maggie. Children ventured into the room and ogled her, as if they formed the front row at a theatre. Women, without, bended toward each other and whispered, nodding their heads with airs of profound philosophy. A baby, overcome with curiosity concerning this object at which all were looking, sidled forward and touched her dress, cautiously, as if investigating a red-hot stove. Its mother's voice rang out like a warning trumpet. She rushed forward and grabbed her child, casting a terrible look of indignation at the girl.

Maggie's mother paced to and fro, addressing the doorful of eyes, expounding like a glib showman at a museum. Her voice rang through the building.

"Dere she stands," she cried, wheeling suddenly and pointing with dramatic finger. "Dere she stands! Lookut her! Ain' she a dindy? An' she was so good as to come home teh her mudder, she was! Ain' she a beaut'? Ain' she a dindy? Fer Gawd's sake!"

The jeering cries ended in another burst of shrill laughter.

The girl seemed to awaken. "Jimmie—"

He drew hastily back from her.

"Well, now, yer a hell of a t'ing, ain' yeh?" he said, his lips curling in scorn. Radiant virtue sat upon his brow and his repelling hands expressed horror of contamination.

Maggie turned and went.

The crowd at the door fell back precipitately. A baby falling down in front of the door, wrenched a scream like a wounded animal from its mother. Another woman sprang forward and picked it up, with a chivalrous air, as if rescuing a human being from an oncoming express train.

As the girl passed down through the hall, she went before open doors framing more eyes strangely microscopic, and sending broad beams of inquisitive light into the darkness of her path. On the second floor she met the gnarled old woman who possessed the music box.

"So," she cried, "'ere yehs are back again, are yehs? An' dey've kicked yehs out? Well, come in an' stay wid me teh-night. I ain' got no moral standin'."

From above came an unceasing babble of tongues, over all of which rang the mother's derisive laughter.

Chapter XVI

Pete did not consider that he had ruined Maggie. If he had thought that her soul could never smile again, he would have believed the mother and brother, who were pyrotechnic over the affair, to be responsible for it.

Besides, in his world, souls did not insist upon being able to smile. "What deh hell?"

He felt a trifle entangled. It distressed him. Revelations and scenes might bring upon him the wrath of the owner of the saloon, who insisted upon respectability of an advanced type.

"What deh hell do dey wanna raise such a smoke about it fer?" demanded he of himself, disgusted with the attitude of the family. He saw no necessity for anyone's losing their equilibrium merely because their sister or their daughter had stayed away from home.

Searching about in his mind for possible reasons for their conduct, he came upon the conclusion that Maggie's motives were correct, but that the two others wished to snare him. He felt pursued.

The woman of brilliance and audacity whom he had met in the hilarious hall showed a disposition to ridicule him.

"A little pale thing with no spirit," she said. "Did you note the expression of her eyes? There was something in them about pumpkin pie and virtue. That is a peculiar way the left corner of her mouth has of twitching, isn't it? Dear, dear, my cloud-compelling Pete, what are you coming to?"

Pete asserted at once that he never was very much interested in the girl. The woman interrupted him, laughing.

"Oh, it's not of the slightest consequence to me, my dear young man. You needn't draw maps for my benefit. Why should I be concerned about it?"

But Pete continued with his explanations. If he was laughed at for his tastes in women, he felt obliged to say that they were only temporary or indifferent ones.

The morning after Maggie had departed from home, Pete stood behind the bar. He was immaculate in white jacket and apron and his hair was plastered over his brow with infinite correctness. No customers were in the place. Pete was twisting his napkined fist slowly in a beer glass, softly whistling to himself and occasionally holding the object of his attention between his eyes and a few weak beams of sunlight that had found their way over the thick screens and into the shaded room.

With lingering thoughts of the woman of brilliance and audacity, the bartender raised his head and stared through the varying cracks between the swaying bamboo doors. Suddenly the whistling pucker faded from his lips. He saw Maggie walking slowly past. He gave a great start, fearing for the previously-mentioned eminent respectability of the place.

He threw a swift, nervous glance about him, all at once feeling guilty. No one was in the room.

He went hastily over to the side door. Opening it and looking out, he perceived Maggie standing, as if undecided, on the corner. She was searching the place with her eyes.

As she turned her face toward him Pete beckoned to her hurriedly, intent upon returning with speed to a position behind the bar and to the atmosphere of respectability upon which the proprietor insisted.

Maggie came to him, the anxious look disappearing from her face and a smile wreathing her lips.

"Oh, Pete—," she began brightly.

The bartender made a violent gesture of impatience.

"Oh, my Gawd," cried he, vehemently. "What deh hell do yeh wanna hang aroun' here fer? Do yeh wanna git me inteh trouble?" he demanded with an air of injury.

227

Astonishment swept over the girl's features. "Why, Pete! yehs tol' me—"

Pete glanced profound irritation. His countenance reddened with the anger of a man whose respectability is being threatened.

"Say, yehs makes me tired. See? What deh hell deh yeh wanna tag aroun' atter me fer? Yeh'll git me inteh trouble wid deh ol' man an' dey'll be hell teh pay! If he sees a woman roun' here he'll go crazy an' I'll lose me job! See? Yer brudder come in here an' raised hell an' deh ol' man hada put up fer it! An' now I'm done! See? I'm done."

The girl's eyes stared into his face. "Pete, don't yeh remem—"

"Oh, hell," interrupted Pete, anticipating.

The girl seemed to have a struggle with herself. She was apparently bewildered and could not find speech. Finally she asked in a low voice: "But where kin I go?"

The question exasperated Pete beyond the powers of endurance. It was a direct attempt to give him some responsibility in a matter that did not concern him. In his indignation he volunteered information.

"Oh, go teh hell," cried he. He slammed the door furiously and returned, with an air of relief, to his respectability.

Maggie went away.

She wandered aimlessly for several blocks. She stopped once and asked aloud a question of herself: "Who?"

A man who was passing near her shoulder, humorously took the questioning word as intended for him.

"Eh? What? Who? Nobody! I didn't say anything," he laughingly said, and continued his way.

Soon the girl discovered that if she walked with such apparent aimlessness, some men looked at her with calculating eyes. She quickened her step, frightened. As a protection, she adopted a demeanor of intentness as if going somewhere.

After a time she left rattling avenues and passed between rows of houses with sternness and stolidity stamped upon their features. She hung her head for she felt their eyes grimly upon her.

Suddenly she came upon a stout gentleman in a silk hat and a chaste black coat, whose decorous row of buttons reached from his chin to his knees. The girl had heard of the Grace of God and she decided to approach this man.

His beaming, chubby face was a picture of benevolence and kind-heartedness. His eyes shone good-will.

But as the girl timidly accosted him, he gave a convulsive movement and saved his respectability by a vigorous side-step. He did not risk it to save a soul. For how was he to know that there was a soul before him that needed saving?

Chapter XVII

Upon a wet evening, several months after the last chapter, two interminable rows of cars, pulled by slipping horses, jangled along a prominent side-street. A dozen cabs, with coat-enshrouded drivers, clattered to and fro. Electric lights, whirring softly, shed a blurred radiance. A flower dealer, his feet tapping impatiently, his nose and his wares glistening with rain-drops, stood behind an array of roses and chrysanthemums. Two or three theatres emptied a crowd upon the storm-swept pavements. Men pulled their hats over their eyebrows and raised their collars to their ears. Women shrugged impatient shoulders in their warm cloaks and stopped to arrange their skirts for a walk through the storm. People having been comparatively silent for two hours burst into a roar of conversation, their hearts still kindling from the glowings of the stage.

The pavements became tossing seas of umbrellas. Men stepped forth to hail cabs or cars, raising their fingers in varied forms of polite request or imperative demand. An endless procession wended toward elevated stations. An atmosphere of pleasure and prosperity seemed to hang over the throng, born, perhaps, of good clothes and of having just emerged from a place of forgetfulness.

In the mingled light and gloom of an adjacent park, a handful of wet wanderers, in attitudes of chronic dejection, was scattered among the benches.

A girl of the painted cohorts of the city went along the street. She threw changing glances at men who passed her, giving smiling invitations to men of rural or untaught pattern and usually seeming sedately unconscious of the men with a metropolitan seal upon their faces.

Crossing glittering avenues, she went into the throng emerging from the places of forgetfulness. She hurried forward through the crowd as if intent upon reaching a distant home, bending forward in her handsome cloak, daintily lifting her skirts and picking for her well-shod feet the dryer spots upon the pavements.

The restless doors of saloons, clashing to and fro, disclosed animated rows of men before bars and hurrying barkeepers.

A concert hall gave to the street faint sounds of swift, machine-like music, as if a group of phantom musicians were hastening.

A tall young man, smoking a cigarette with a sublime air, strolled near the girl. He had on evening dress, a moustache, a chrysanthemum, and a look of ennui, all of which he kept carefully under his eye. Seeing the girl walk on as if such a young man as he was not in existence, he looked back transfixed with interest. He stared glassily for a moment, but gave a slight convulsive start when he discerned that she was neither new, Parisian, nor theatrical. He wheeled about hastily and turned his stare into the air, like a sailor with a search-light.

A stout gentleman, with pompous and philanthropic whiskers, went stolidly by, the broad of his back sneering at the girl.

A belated man in business clothes, and in haste to catch a car, bounced against her shoulder. "Hi, there, Mary, I beg your pardon! Brace up, old girl." He grasped her arm to steady her, and then was away running down the middle of the street.

The girl walked on out of the realm of restaurants and saloons. She passed more glittering avenues and went into darker blocks than those where the crowd travelled.

A young man in light overcoat and derby hat received a glance shot keenly from the eyes of the girl. He stopped and looked at her, thrusting his hands in his pockets and making a mocking smile curl his lips. "Come, now, old lady," he said, "you don't mean to tel me that you sized me up for a farmer?"

A labouring man marched along; with bundles under his arms. To her remarks, he replied, "It's a fine evenin', ain't it?"

She smiled squarely into the face of a boy who was hurrying by with his hands buried in his overcoat pockets, his blonde locks bobbing on his youthful temples, and a cheery smile of unconcern upon his lips. He turned his head and smiled back at her, waving his hands.

"Not this eve—some other eve!"

A drunken man, reeling in her pathway, began to roar at her. "I ain' ga no money!" he shouted, in a dismal voice. He lurched on up the street, wailing to himself: "I ain' ga no money. Ba' luck. Ain' ga no more money."

The girl went into gloomy districts near the river, where the tall black factories shut in the street and only occasional broad beams of light fell across the pavements from saloons. In front of one of these places, whence came the sound of a violin vigorously scraped, the patter of feet on boards and the ring of loud laughter, there stood a man with blotched features.

Further on in the darkness she met a ragged being with shifting, bloodshot eyes and grimy hands.

She went into the blackness of the final block. The shutters of the tall buildings were closed like grim lips. The structures seemed to have eyes that looked over them, beyond them, at other things. Afar off the lights of the avenues glittered as if from an impossible distance. Street-car bells jingled with a sound of merriment.

At the feet of the tall buildings appeared the deathly black hue of the river. Some hidden factory sent up a yellow glare, that lit for a moment the waters lapping oilily against timbers. The varied sounds of life, made joyous by distance and seeming unapproachableness, came faintly and died away to a silence.

Chapter XVIII

In a partitioned-off section of a saloon sat a man with a half dozen women, gleefully laughing, hovering about him. The man had arrived at that stage of drunkenness where affection is felt for the universe.

"I'm good f'ler, girls," he said, convincingly. "I'm damn good f'ler. An'body treats me right, I allus trea's zem right! See?"

The women nodded their heads approvingly. "To be sure," they cried out in hearty chorus. "You're the kind of a man we like, Pete. You're outa sight! What yeh goin' to buy this time, dear?"

"An't'ing yehs wants, damn it," said the man in an abandonment of good will. His countenance shone with the true spirit of benevolence. He was in the proper mode of missionaries. He would have fraternized with obscure Hottentots. And above all, he was overwhelmed in tenderness for his friends, who were all illustrious.

"An't'ing yehs wants, damn it," repeated he, waving his hands with beneficent recklessness. "I'm good f'ler, girls, an' if an'body treats me right I—here," called he through an open door to a waiter, "bring girls drinks, damn it. What 'ill yehs have, girls? An't'ing yehs wants, damn it!"

The waiter glanced in with the disgusted look of the man who serves intoxicants for the man who takes too much of them. He nodded his head shortly at the order from each individual, and went.

"Damn it," said the man, "we're havin' heluva time. I like you girls! Damn'd if I don't! Yer right sort! See?"

He spoke at length and with feeling, concerning the excellencies of his assembled friends.

"Don' try pull man's leg, but have a heluva time! Das right! Das way teh do! Now, if I sawght yehs tryin' work me fer drinks, wouldn' buy damn t'ing! But yer right sort, damn it! Yehs know how ter treat a f'ler, an' I stays by yehs 'til spen' las' cent! Das right! I'm good f'ler an' I knows when an'body treats me right!"

Between the times of the arrival and departure of the waiter, the man discoursed to the women on the tender regard he felt for all living things. He laid stress upon the purity of his motives in all dealings with men in the world and spoke of the fervor of his friendship for those who were amiable. Tears welled slowly from his eyes. His voice quavered when he spoke to them.

Once when the waiter was about to depart with an empty tray, the man drew a coin from his pocket and held it forth.

"Here," said he, quite magnificently, "here's quar'."

The waiter kept his hands on his tray.

"I don' want yer money," he said.

The other put forth the coin with tearful insistence.

"Here, damn it," cried he, "tak't! Yer damn goo' f'ler an' I wan' yehs tak't!"

"Come, come, now," said the waiter, with the sullen air of a man who is forced into giving advice. "Put yer mon in yer pocket! Yer loaded an' yehs on'y makes a damn fool of yerself."

As the latter passed out of the door the man turned pathetically to the women.

"He don' know I'm damn goo' f'ler," cried he, dismally.

"Never you mind, Pete, dear," said a woman of brilliance and audacity, laying her hand with great affection upon his arm. "Never you mind, old boy! We'll stay by you, dear!"

"Das ri'," cried the man, his face lighting up at the soothing tones of the woman's voice. "Das ri', I'm damn goo' f'ler an' w'en anyone trea's me ri', I treats zem ri'! Shee!"

"Sure!" cried the women. "And we're not goin' back on you, old man."

234

The man turned appealing eyes to the woman of brilliance and audacity. He felt that if he could be convicted of a contemptible action he would die.

"Shay, Nell, damn it, I allus trea's yehs shquare, didn' I? I allus been goo' f'ler wi' yehs, ain't I, Nell?"

"Sure you have, Pete," assented the woman. She delivered an oration to her companions. "Yessir, that's a fact. Pete's a square fellah, he is. He never goes back on a friend. He's the right kind an' we stay by him, don't we, girls?"

"Sure," they exclaimed. Looking lovingly at him they raised their glasses and drank his health.

"Girlsh," said the man, beseechingly, "I allus trea's yehs ri', didn' I? I'm goo' f'ler, ain' I, girlsh?"

"Sure," again they chorused.

"Well," said he finally, "le's have nozzer drink, zen."

"That's right," hailed a woman, "that's right. Yer no bloomin' jay! Yer spends yer money like a man. Dat's right."

The man pounded the table with his quivering fists.

"Yessir," he cried, with deep earnestness, as if someone disputed him. "I'm damn goo' f'ler, an' w'en anyone trea's me ri', I allus trea's—le's have nozzer drink."

He began to beat the wood with his glass.

"Shay," howled he, growing suddenly impatient. As the waiter did not then come, the man swelled with wrath.

"Shay," howled he again.

The waiter appeared at the door.

"Bringsh drinksh," said the man.

The waiter disappeared with the orders.

"Zat f'ler damn fool," cried the man. "He insul' me! I'm ge'man! Can' stan' be insul'! I'm goin' lickim when comes!"

"No, no," cried the women, crowding about and trying to subdue him. "He's all right! He didn't mean anything! Let it go! He's a good fellah!"

"Din' he insul' me?" asked the man earnestly.

"No," said they. "Of course he didn't! He's all right!"

"Sure he didn' insul' me?" demanded the man, with deep anxiety in his voice.

"No, no! We know him! He's a good fellah. He didn't mean anything."

"Well, zen," said the man, resolutely, "I'm go' 'pol'gize!"

When the waiter came, the man struggled to the middle of the floor.

"Girlsh shed you insul' me! I shay damn lie! I 'pol'gize!"

"All right," said the waiter.

The man sat down. He felt a sleepy but strong desire to straighten things out and have a perfect understanding with everybody.

"Nell, I allus trea's yeh shquare, din' I? Yeh likes me, don' yehs, Nell? I'm goo' f'ler?"

"Sure," said the woman of brilliance and audacity.

"Yeh knows I'm stuck on yehs, don' yehs, Nell?"

"Sure," she repeated, carelessly.

Overwhelmed by a spasm of drunken adoration, he drew two or three bills from his pocket, and, with the trembling fingers of an offering priest, laid them on the table before the woman.

"Yehs knows, damn it, yehs kin have all got, 'cause I'm stuck on yehs, Nell, damn't, I—I'm stuck on yehs, Nell—buy drinksh—damn't—we're havin' heluva time—w'en anyone trea's me ri'—I—damn't, Nell—we're havin' heluva—time."

236

Shortly he went to sleep with his swollen face fallen forward on his chest.

The women drank and laughed, not heeding the slumbering man in the corner. Finally he lurched forward and fell groaning to the floor.

The women screamed in disgust and drew back their skirts.

"Come ahn," cried one, starting up angrily, "let's get out of here."

The woman of brilliance and audacity stayed behind, taking up the bills and stuffing them into a deep, irregularly-shaped pocket. A guttural snore from the recumbent man caused her to turn and look down at him.

She laughed. "What a damn fool," she said, and went.

The smoke from the lamps settled heavily down in the little compartment, obscuring the way out. The smell of oil, stifling in its intensity, pervaded the air. The wine from an overturned glass dripped softly down upon the blotches on the man's neck.

Chapter XIX

In a room a woman sat at a table eating like a fat monk in a picture.

A soiled, unshaven man pushed open the door and entered.

"Well," said he, "Mag's dead."

"What?" said the woman, her mouth filled with bread.

"Mag's dead," repeated the man.

"Deh hell she is," said the woman. She continued her meal. When she finished her coffee she began to weep.

"I kin remember when her two feet was no bigger dan yer t'umb, and she weared worsted boots," moaned she.

"Well, whata dat?" said the man.

"I kin remember when she weared worsted boots," she cried.

The neighbors began to gather in the hall, staring in at the weeping woman as if watching the contortions of a dying dog. A dozen women entered and lamented with her. Under their busy hands the rooms took on that appalling appearance of neatness and order with which death is greeted.

Suddenly the door opened and a woman in a black gown rushed in with outstretched arms. "Ah, poor Mary," she cried, and tenderly embraced the moaning one.

"Ah, what ter'ble affliction is dis," continued she. Her vocabulary was derived from mission churches. "Me poor Mary, how I feel fer yehs! Ah, what a ter'ble affliction is a disobed'ent chil'."

Her good, motherly face was wet with tears. She trembled in eagerness to express her sympathy. The mourner sat with bowed head, rocking her body heavily to and fro, and crying out in a high, strained voice that sounded like a dirge on some forlorn pipe.

"I kin remember when she weared worsted boots an' her two feets was no bigger dan yer t'umb an' she weared worsted boots, Miss Smith," she cried, raising her streaming eyes.

"Ah, me poor Mary," sobbed the woman in black. With low, coddling cries, she sank on her knees by the mourner's chair, and put her arms about her. The other women began to groan in different keys.

"Yer poor misguided chil' is gone now, Mary, an' let us hope it's fer deh bes'. Yeh'll fergive her now, Mary, won't yehs, dear, all her disobed'ence? All her t'ankless behavior to her mudder an' all her badness? She's gone where her ter'ble sins will be judged."

The woman in black raised her face and paused. The inevitable sunlight came streaming in at the windows and shed a ghastly cheerfulness upon the faded hues of the room. Two or three of the spectators were sniffling, and one was loudly weeping. The mourner arose and staggered into the other room. In a moment she emerged with a pair of faded baby shoes held in the hollow of her hand.

"I kin remember when she used to wear dem," cried she. The women burst anew into cries as if they had all been stabbed. The mourner turned to the soiled and unshaven man.

"Jimmie, boy, go git yer sister! Go git yer sister an' we'll put deh boots on her feets!"

"Dey won't fit her now, yeh damn fool," said the man.

"Go git yer sister, Jimmie," shrieked the woman, confronting him fiercely.

The man swore sullenly. He went over to a corner and slowly began to put on his coat. He took his hat and went out, with a dragging, reluctant step.

The woman in black came forward and again besought the mourner.

"Yeh'll fergive her, Mary! Yeh'll fergive yer bad, bad, chil'! Her life was a curse an' her days were black an' yeh'll fergive yer bad girl? She's gone where her sins will be judged."

"She's gone where her sins will be judged," cried the other women, like a choir at a funeral.

"Deh Lord gives and deh Lord takes away," said the woman in black, raising her eyes to the sunbeams.

"Deh Lord gives and deh Lord takes away," responded the others.

"Yeh'll fergive her, Mary!" pleaded the woman in black. The mourner essayed to speak but her voice gave way. She shook her great shoulders frantically, in an agony of grief. Hot tears seemed to scald her quivering face. Finally her voice came and arose like a scream of pain.

"Oh, yes, I'll fergive her! I'll fergive her!"

About Author

Stephen Crane (November 1, 1871 – June 5, 1900) was an American poet, novelist, and short story writer. Prolific throughout his short life, he wrote notable works in the Realist tradition as well as early examples of American Naturalism and Impressionism. He is recognized by modern critics as one of the most innovative writers of his generation.

The ninth surviving child of Methodist parents, Crane began writing at the age of four and had published several articles by the age of 16. Having little interest in university studies though he was active in a fraternity, he left Syracuse University in 1891 to work as a reporter and writer. Crane's first novel was the 1893 Bowery tale Maggie: A Girl of the Streets, generally considered by critics to be the first work of American literary Naturalism. He won international acclaim in 1895 for his Civil War novel The Red Badge of Courage, which he wrote without having any battle experience.

In 1896, Crane endured a highly publicized scandal after appearing as a witness in the trial of a suspected prostitute, an acquaintance named Dora Clark. Late that year he accepted an offer to travel to Cuba as a war correspondent. As he waited in Jacksonville, Florida for passage, he met Cora Taylor, with whom he began a lasting relationship. En route to Cuba, Crane's vessel the SS Commodore sank off the coast of Florida, leaving him and others adrift for 30 hours in a dinghy. Crane described the ordeal in "The Open Boat". During the final years of his life, he covered conflicts in Greece (accompanied by Cora, recognized as the first woman war correspondent) and later lived in England with her. He was befriended by writers such as Joseph Conrad and H. G. Wells. Plagued by financial difficulties and ill health, Crane died of tuberculosis in a Black Forest sanatorium in Germany at the age of 28.

At the time of his death, Crane was considered an important figure in American literature. After he was nearly forgotten for two decades, critics revived interest in his life and work. Crane's writing is characterized by vivid intensity, distinctive dialects, and irony. Common themes involve fear, spiritual crises and social isolation. Although recognized primarily for The Red Badge of Courage, which has become an American classic, Crane is also known for his poetry, journalism, and short stories such as "The Open Boat", "The Blue Hotel", "The Bride Comes to Yellow Sky", and The Monster. His writing made a deep impression on 20th-century writers, most prominent among them Ernest Hemingway, and is thought to have inspired the Modernists and the Imagists.

Biography

Early years

Stephen Crane was born on November 1, 1871, in Newark, New Jersey, to Jonathan Townley Crane, a minister in the Methodist Episcopal church, and Mary Helen Peck Crane, daughter of a clergyman, George Peck. He was the fourteenth and last child born to the couple. At 45, Helen Crane had suffered the early deaths of her previous four children, each of whom died within one year of birth. Nicknamed "Stevie" by the family, he joined eight surviving brothers and sisters—Mary Helen, George Peck, Jonathan Townley, William Howe, Agnes Elizabeth, Edmund Byran, Wilbur Fiske, and Luther.

The Cranes were descended from Jaspar Crane, a founder of New Haven Colony, who had migrated there from England in 1639. Stephen was named for a putative founder of Elizabethtown, New Jersey, who had, according to family tradition, come from England or Wales in 1665, as well as his great-great-grandfather Stephen Crane (1709–1780), a Revolutionary War patriot who served as New Jersey delegate to the First Continental Congress in Philadelphia. Crane later wrote that his father, Dr. Crane, "was a great, fine, simple mind," who had written numerous tracts on theology. Although his mother was a popular spokeswoman for the Woman's Christian Temperance Union and a highly religious woman, Crane wrote that he did not believe "she was as narrow as most of her friends or family." The young Stephen was raised primarily by his sister Agnes, who was 15 years his senior. The family moved to Port Jervis, New York, in 1876, where Dr. Crane became the pastor of Drew Methodist Church, a position that he retained until his death.

As a child, Stephen was often sickly and afflicted by constant colds.

When the boy was almost two, his father wrote in his diary that his youngest son became "so sick that we are anxious about him." Despite his fragile nature, Crane was an intelligent child who taught himself to read before the age of four. His first known inquiry, recorded by his father, dealt with writing; at the age of three, while imitating his brother Townley's writing, he asked his mother, "how do you spell O?" In December 1879, Crane wrote a poem about wanting a dog for Christmas. Entitled "I'd Rather Have –", it is his first surviving poem. Stephen was not regularly enrolled in school until January 1880, but he had no difficulty in completing two grades in six weeks. Recalling this feat, he wrote that it "sounds like the lie of a fond mother at a teaparty, but I do remember that I got ahead very fast and that father was very pleased with me."

Dr. Crane died on February 16, 1880, at the age of 60; Stephen was eight years old. Some 1,400 people mourned Dr. Crane at his funeral, more than double the size of his congregation. After her husband's death, Mrs. Crane moved to Roseville, near Newark, leaving Stephen in the care of his older brother Edmund, with whom the young boy lived with cousins in Sussex County. He next lived with his brother William, a lawyer, in Port Jervis for several years.

His older sister Helen took him to Asbury Park to be with their brother Townley and his wife, Fannie. Townley was a professional journalist; he headed the Long Branch department of both the New-York Tribune and the Associated Press, and also served as editor of the Asbury Park Shore Press. Agnes, another Crane sister, joined the siblings in New Jersey. She took a position at Asbury Park's intermediate school and moved in with Helen to care for the young Stephen.

Within a couple of years, the Crane family suffered more losses. First, Townley and his wife lost their two young children. His wife Fannie died of Bright's disease in November 1883. Agnes Crane became ill and died on June 10, 1884, of meningitis at the age of 28.

Schooling

Crane wrote his first known story, "Uncle Jake and the Bell Handle", when he was 14. In late 1885, he enrolled at Pennington Seminary, a ministry-focused coeducational boarding school 7 miles (11 km) north of Trenton. His father had been principal there from 1849 to 1858. Soon after her youngest son left for school, Mrs. Crane began suffering what the Asbury Park Shore Press reported as "a temporary aberration of the mind." She had apparently recovered by early 1886, but later that year, her son, 23-year-old Luther Crane, died after falling in front of an oncoming train while working as a flagman for the Erie Railroad. It was the fourth death in six years among Stephen's immediate family.

After two years, Crane left Pennington for Claverack College, a quasi-military school. He later looked back on his time at Claverack as "the happiest period of my life although I was not aware of it." A classmate remembered him as a highly literate but erratic student, lucky to pass examinations in math and science, and yet "far in advance of his fellow students in his knowledge of History and Literature", his favorite subjects. While he held an impressive record on the drill field and baseball diamond, Crane generally did not excel in the classroom. Not having a middle name, as was customary among other students, he took to signing his name "Stephen T. Crane" in order "to win recognition as a regular fellow". Crane was seen as friendly, but also moody and rebellious. He sometimes skipped class in order to play baseball, a game in which he starred as catcher. He was also greatly interested in the school's military training program. He rose rapidly in the ranks of the student battalion. One classmate described him as "indeed physically attractive without being handsome", but he was aloof, reserved and not generally popular at Claverack. Although academically weak, Crane gained experience at Claverack that provided background (and likely some anecdotes from the Civil War veterans on the staff) that proved useful when he came to write The Red Badge of Courage.

In mid-1888, Crane became his brother Townley's assistant at a New Jersey shore news bureau, working there every summer until 1892. Crane's first publication under his byline was an article on the explorer Henry M. Stanley's famous quest to find the Scottish missionary David Livingstone in Africa. It appeared in the February 1890 Claverack College Vidette. Within a few months, Crane was persuaded by his family to forgo a military career and transfer to Lafayette College in Easton, Pennsylvania, in order to pursue a mining engineering degree. He registered at Lafayette on September 12, and promptly became involved in extracurricular activities; he took up baseball again and joined the largest fraternity, Delta Upsilon. He also joined both rival literary societies, named for (George) Washington and (Benjamin) Franklin. Crane infrequently attended classes and ended the semester with grades for four of the seven courses he had taken.

After one semester, Crane transferred to Syracuse University, where he enrolled as a non-degree candidate in the College of Liberal Arts. He roomed in the Delta Upsilon fraternity house and joined the baseball team. Attending just one class (English Literature) during the middle trimester, he remained in residence while taking no courses in the third semester.

Concentrating on his writing, Crane began to experiment with tone and style while trying out different subjects. He published his fictional story, "Great Bugs of Onondaga," simultaneously in the Syracuse Daily Standard and the New York Tribune. Declaring college "a waste of time", Crane decided to become a full-time writer and reporter. He attended a Delta Upsilon chapter meeting on June 12, 1891, but shortly afterward left college for good.

Full-time writer

In the summer of 1891, Crane often camped with friends in the nearby area of Sullivan County, New York, where his brother Edmund occupied a house obtained as part of their brother William's Hartwood Club (Association) land dealings. He used this area as the geographic setting for several short stories, which were posthumously published in a collection under the title Stephen Crane: Sullivan County Tales and Sketches. Crane showed two of these works to Tribune editor Willis Fletcher Johnson, a friend of the family, who accepted them for the publication. "Hunting Wild Dogs" and "The Last of the Mohicans" were the first of fourteen unsigned Sullivan County sketches and tales that were published in the Tribune between February and July 1892. Crane also showed Johnson an early draft of his first novel, Maggie: A Girl of the Streets.

Later that summer, Crane met and befriended author Hamlin Garland, who had been lecturing locally on American literature and the expressive arts; on August 17 he gave a talk on novelist William Dean Howells, which Crane wrote up for the Tribune. Garland became a mentor for and champion of the young writer, whose intellectual honesty impressed him. Their relationship suffered in later years, however, because Garland disapproved of Crane's alleged immorality, related to his living with a woman married to another man.

Stephen moved into his brother Edmund's house in Lakeview, a suburb of Paterson, New Jersey, in the fall of 1891. From here he made frequent trips into New York City, writing and reporting particularly on its impoverished tenement districts. Crane focused particularly on The Bowery, a small and once prosperous neighborhood in the southern part of Manhattan. After the Civil War, Bowery shops and mansions had given way to saloons, dance halls, brothels and flophouses, all of which Crane frequented. He later said he did so for research. He was attracted to the human nature found in the slums, considering it "open and plain, with nothing hidden". Believing nothing honest and unsentimental had been written about the Bowery, Crane became determined to do so himself; this was the setting of his first novel. On December 7, 1891, Crane's mother died at the age of 64, and the 20-year-old appointed Edmund as his guardian.

Despite being frail, undernourished and suffering from a hacking cough, which did not prevent him from smoking cigarettes, in the spring of 1892 Crane began a romance with Lily Brandon Munroe, a married woman who was estranged from her husband. Although Munroe later said Crane "was not a handsome man", she admired his "remarkable almond-shaped gray eyes." He begged her to elope with him, but her family opposed the match because Crane lacked money and prospects, and she declined. Their last meeting likely occurred in April 1898, when he again asked her to run away with him and she again refused.

Between July 2 and September 11, 1892, Crane published at least ten news reports on Asbury Park affairs. Although a Tribune colleague stated that Crane "was not highly distinguished above any other boy of twenty who had gained a reputation for saying and writing bright things," that summer his reporting took on a more skeptical, hypocrisy-deflating tone. A storm of controversy erupted over a report he wrote on the Junior Order of United American Mechanics' American Day Parade, entitled "Parades and Entertainments". Published on August 21, the report juxtaposes the "bronzed, slope-shouldered, uncouth" marching men "begrimed with dust" and the spectators dressed in "summer gowns, lace parasols, tennis trousers, straw hats and indifferent smiles". Believing they were being ridiculed, some JOUAM marchers were outraged and wrote to the editor. The owner of the Tribune, Whitelaw Reid, was that year's Republican vice-presidential candidate, and this likely increased the sensitivity of the paper's management to the issue. Although Townley wrote a piece for the Asbury Park Daily Press in his brother's defense, the Tribune quickly apologized to its readers, calling Stephen Crane's piece "a bit of random correspondence, passed inadvertently by the copy editor". Hamlin Garland and biographer John Barry attested that Crane told them he had been dismissed by the Tribune, although Willis Fletcher Johnson later denied this. The paper did not publish any of Crane's work after 1892.

Such an assemblage of the spraddle-legged men of the middle class, whose hands were bent and shoulders stooped from delving and constructing, had never appeared to an Asbury Park summer crowd, and the latter was vaguely amused.

— Stephen Crane, account of the JOUAM parade as it appeared in the Tribune.

Life in New York

Crane struggled to make a living as a free-lance writer, contributing sketches and feature articles to various New York newspapers. In October 1892, he moved into a rooming house in Manhattan whose boarders were a group of medical students. During this time, he expanded or entirely reworked Maggie: A Girl of the Streets, which is about a girl who "blossoms in a mud-puddle" and becomes a pitiful victim of circumstance. In the winter of 1893, Crane took the manuscript of Maggie to Richard Watson Gilder, who rejected it for publication in The Century Magazine.

Crane decided to publish it privately, with money he had inherited from his mother. The novel was published in late February or early March 1893 by a small printing shop that usually printed medical books and religious tracts. The typewritten title page for the Library of Congress copyright application read simply: "A Girl of the Streets, / A Story of New York. / —By—/Stephen Crane." The name "Maggie" was added to the title later. Crane used the pseudonym "Johnston Smith" for the novel's initial publication, later telling friend and artist Corwin Knapp Linson that the nom de plume was the "commonest name I could think of. I had an editor friend named Johnson, and put in the "t", and no one could find me in the mob of Smiths." Hamlin Garland reviewed the work in the June 1893 issue of The Arena, calling it "the most truthful and unhackneyed study of the slums I have yet read, fragment though it is." Despite this early praise, Crane became depressed and destitute from having spent $869 for 1,100 copies of a novel that did not sell; he ended up giving a hundred copies away. He would later remember "how I looked forward to publication and pictured the sensation I thought it would make. It fell flat. Nobody seemed to notice it or care for it... Poor Maggie! She was one of my first loves."

In March 1893, Crane spent hours lounging in Linson's studio while having his portrait painted. He became fascinated with issues of the Century that were largely devoted to famous battles and military leaders from the Civil War. Frustrated with the dryly written stories, Crane stated, "I wonder that some of those fellows don't tell how they felt in those scraps. They spout enough of what they did, but they're as emotionless as rocks." Crane returned to these magazines during subsequent visits to Linson's studio, and eventually the idea of writing a war novel overtook him. He would later state that he "had been unconsciously working the detail of the story out through most of his boyhood" and had imagined "war stories ever since he was out of knickerbockers." This novel would ultimately become The Red Badge of Courage.

A river, amber-tinted in the shadow of its banks, purled at the army's feet; and at night, when the stream had become of a sorrowful blackness, one could see across it the red, eyelike gleam of hostile camp-fires set in the low brows of distant hills.

— Stephen Crane, The Red Badge of Courage

From the beginning, Crane wished to show how it felt to be in a war by writing "a psychological portrayal of fear." Conceiving his story from the point of view of a young private who is at first filled with boyish dreams of the glory of war and then quickly becomes disillusioned by war's reality, Crane borrowed the private's surname, "Fleming", from his sister-in-law's maiden name. He later said that the first paragraphs came to him with "every word in place, every comma, every period fixed." Working mostly nights, he wrote from around midnight until four or five in the morning. Because he could not afford a typewriter, he wrote carefully in ink on legal-sized paper, seldom crossing through or interlining a word. If he did change something, he would rewrite the whole page.

While working on his second novel, Crane remained prolific, concentrating on publishing stories to stave off poverty; "An Experiment in Misery", based on Crane's experiences in the Bowery, was printed by the New York Press. He also wrote five or six poems a day. In early 1894, he showed some of his poems or "lines" as he called them, to Hamlin Garland, who said he read "some thirty in all" with "growing wonder." Although Garland and William Dean Howells encouraged him to submit his poetry for publication, Crane's free verse was too unconventional for most. After brief wrangling between poet and publisher, Copeland & Day accepted Crane's first book of poems, The Black Riders and Other Lines, although it would not be published until after The Red Badge of Courage. He received a 10 percent royalty and the publisher assured him that the book would be in a form "more severely classic than any book ever yet issued in America."

In the spring of 1894, Crane offered the finished manuscript of The Red Badge of Courage to McClure's Magazine, which had become the foremost magazine for Civil War literature. While McClure's delayed giving him an answer on his novel, they offered him an assignment writing about the Pennsylvania coal mines. "In the Depths of a Coal Mine", a story with pictures by Linson, was syndicated by McClure's in a number of newspapers, heavily edited. Crane was reportedly disgusted by the cuts, asking Linson: "Why the hell did they send me up there then? Do they want the public to think the coal mines gilded ball-rooms with the miners eating ice-cream in boiled shirt-fronts?"

Sources report that following an encounter with a male prostitute that spring, Crane began a novel on the subject entitled Flowers of Asphalt, which he later abandoned. The manuscript has never been recovered.

After discovering that McClure's could not afford to pay him, Crane took his war novel to Irving Bacheller of the Bacheller-Johnson Newspaper Syndicate, which agreed to publish The Red Badge of Courage in serial form. Between the third and the ninth of December 1894, The Red Badge of Courage was published in some half-dozen newspapers in the United States. Although it was greatly cut for syndication, Bacheller attested to its causing a stir, saying "its quality [was] immediately felt and recognized." The lead editorial in the Philadelphia Press of December 7 said that Crane "is a new name now and unknown, but everybody will be talking about him if he goes on as he has begun".

Travels and fame

At the end of January 1895, Crane left on what he called "a very long and circuitous newspaper trip" to the west. While writing feature articles for the Bacheller syndicate, he traveled to Saint Louis, Missouri, Nebraska, New Orleans, Galveston, Texas and then Mexico City. Irving Bacheller would later state that he "sent Crane to Mexico for new color", which the author found in the form of Mexican slum life. Whereas he found the lower class in New York pitiful, he was impressed by the "superiority" of the Mexican peasants' contentment and "even refuse[d] to pity them."

Returning to New York five months later, Crane joined the Lantern (alternately spelled "Lanthom" or "Lanthorne") Club organized by a group of young writers and journalists. The Club, located on the roof of an old house on William Street near the Brooklyn Bridge, served as a drinking establishment of sorts and was decorated to look like a ship's cabin. There Crane ate one good meal a day, although friends were troubled by his "constant smoking, too much coffee, lack of food and poor teeth", as Nelson Greene put it. Living in near-poverty and greatly anticipating the publication of his books, Crane began work on two more novels: The Third Violet and George's Mother.

The Black Riders was published by Copeland & Day shortly before his return to New York in May, but it received mostly criticism, if not abuse, for the poems' unconventional style and use of free verse. A piece in the Bookman called Crane "the Aubrey Beardsley of poetry," and a commentator from the Chicago Daily Inter-Ocean stated that "there is not a line of poetry from the opening to the closing page. Whitman's Leaves of Grass were luminous in comparison. Poetic lunacy would be a better name for the book." In June, the New York Tribune dismissed the book as "so much trash." Crane was pleased that the book was "making some stir".

In contrast to the reception for Crane's poetry, The Red Badge of Courage was welcomed with acclaim after its publication by Appleton in September 1895. For the next four months, the book was in the top six on various bestseller lists around the country. It arrived on the literary scene "like a flash of lightning out of a clear winter sky", according to H. L. Mencken, who was about 15 at the time. The novel also became popular in Britain; Joseph Conrad, a future friend of Crane, wrote that the novel "detonated... with the impact and force of a twelve-inch shell charged with a very high explosive." Appleton published two, possibly three, printings in 1895 and as many as eleven more in 1896. Although some critics considered the work overly graphic and profane, it was widely heralded for its realistic portrayal of war and unique writing style. The Detroit Free Press declared that The Red Badge would give readers "so vivid a picture of the emotions and the horrors of the battlefield that you will pray your eyes may never look upon the reality."

Wanting to capitalize on the success of The Red Badge, McClure Syndicate offered Crane a contract to write a series on Civil War battlefields. Because it was a wish of his to "visit the battlefield—which I was to describe— at the time of year when it was fought", Crane agreed to take the assignment. Visiting battlefields in Northern Virginia, including Fredericksburg, he would later produce five more Civil War tales: "Three Miraculous Soldiers",

"The Veteran", "An Indiana Campaign", "An Episode of War" and The Little Regiment.

Scandal

At the age of 24, Crane, who was reveling in his success, became involved in a highly publicized case involving a suspected prostitute named Dora Clark. At 2 a.m. on September 16, 1896, he escorted two chorus girls and Clark from New York City's Broadway Garden, a popular "resort" where he had interviewed the women for a series he was writing. As Crane saw one woman safely to a streetcar, a plainclothes policeman named Charles Becker arrested the other two for solicitation; Crane was threatened with arrest when he tried to interfere. One of the women was released after Crane confirmed her erroneous claim that she was his wife, but Clark was charged and taken to the precinct. Against the advice of the arresting sergeant, Crane made a statement confirming Dora Clark's innocence, stating that "I only know that while with me she acted respectably, and that the policeman's charge was false." On the basis of Crane's testimony, Clark was discharged. The media seized upon the story; news spread to Philadelphia, Boston and beyond, with papers focusing on Crane's courage. The Stephen Crane story, as it became known, soon became a source for ridicule; the Chicago Dispatch in particular quipped that "Stephen Crane is respectfully informed that association with women in scarlet is not necessarily a 'Red Badge of Courage' ".

A couple of weeks after her trial, Clark pressed charges of false arrest against the officer who had arrested her. The next day, the officer physically attacked Clark in the presence of witnesses for having brought charges against him. Crane, who initially went briefly to Philadelphia to escape the pressure of publicity, returned to New York to give testimony at Becker's trial despite advice given to him from Theodore Roosevelt, who was Police Commissioner at the time and a new acquaintance of Crane. The defense targeted Crane: police raided his apartment and interviewed people who knew him, trying to find incriminating evidence in order to lessen the effect of his testimony. A vigorous cross-examination took place that sought to portray Crane as a man of dubious morals; while the prosecution proved that he frequented brothels, Crane claimed this was merely for research purposes. After the trial ended on

October 16, the arresting officer was exonerated, and Crane's reputation was ruined.

Cora Taylor and the Commodore shipwreck

None of them knew the color of the sky. Their eyes glanced level and were fastened upon the waves that swept toward them. These waves were of the hue of slate, save for the tops, which were of foaming white, and all of the men knew the colors of the sea.

— Stephen Crane, "The Open Boat"

Given $700 in Spanish gold by the Bacheller-Johnson syndicate to work as a war correspondent in Cuba as the Spanish–American War was pending, the 25-year-old Crane left New York on November 27, 1896, on a train bound for Jacksonville, Florida. Upon arrival in Jacksonville, he registered at the St. James Hotel under the alias of Samuel Carleton to maintain anonymity while seeking passage to Cuba. While waiting for a boat, he toured the city and visited the local brothels. Within days he met 31-year-old Cora Taylor, proprietor of the downtown bawdy house Hotel de Dream. Born into a respectable Boston family, Taylor (whose legal name was Cora Ethel Stewart) had already had two brief marriages; her first husband, Vinton Murphy, divorced her on grounds of adultery. In 1889, she had married British Captain Donald William Stewart. She left him in 1892 for another man, but was still legally married. By the time Crane arrived, Taylor had been in Jacksonville for two years. She lived a bohemian lifestyle, owned a hotel of assignation, and was a well-known and respected local figure. The two spent much time together while Crane awaited his departure. He was finally cleared to leave for the Cuban port of Cienfuegos on New Year's Eve aboard the SS Commodore.

The ship sailed from Jacksonville with 27 or 28 men and a cargo of supplies and ammunition for the Cuban rebels. On the St. Johns River and less than 2 miles (3.2 km) from Jacksonville, Commodore struck a sandbar in a dense fog and damaged its hull. Although towed off the sandbar the following day, it was beached again in Mayport and again damaged. A leak began in the boiler room that evening and, as a result of malfunctioning water pumps, the ship came to a standstill about 16 miles (26 km) from Mosquito Inlet. As the ship took on more water, Crane described the engine room as resembling "a scene at this time taken from the middle kitchen of hades." Commodore's lifeboats were lowered in the early hours of the morning on January 2, 1897 and the ship ultimately sank at 7 a.m. Crane was one of the last to leave the ship in a 10-foot (3.0 m) dinghy. In an ordeal that he recounted in the short story "The Open Boat", Crane and three other men (including the ship's Captain) foundered off the coast of Florida for a day and a half before trying to land the dinghy at Daytona Beach. The small boat overturned in the surf, forcing the exhausted men to swim to shore; one of them died. Having lost the gold given to him for his journey, Crane wired Cora Taylor for help. She traveled to Daytona and returned to Jacksonville with Crane the next day, only four days after he had left on the Commodore.

The disaster was reported on the front pages of newspapers across the country. Rumors that the ship had been sabotaged were widely circulated but never substantiated. Portrayed favorably and heroically by the press, Crane emerged from the ordeal with his reputation enhanced, if not restored, after the battering he had received in the Dora Clark affair. Meanwhile, Crane's affair with Taylor blossomed.

Three seasons of archaeological investigation were conducted in 2002-04 to examine and document the exposed remains of a wreck near Ponce Inlet, FL conjectured to be that of the SS Commodore. The collected data, and other accumulated evidence, finally substantiated the identification of the Commodore beyond a reasonable doubt.

Greco-Turkish War

Despite contentment in Jacksonville and the need for rest after his ordeal, Crane became restless. He left Jacksonville on January 11 for New York City, where he applied for a passport to Cuba, Mexico and the West Indies. Spending three weeks in New York, he completed "The Open Boat" and periodically visited Port Jervis to see family. By this time, however, blockades had formed along the Florida coast as tensions rose with Spain, and Crane concluded that he would never be able to travel to Cuba. He sold "The Open

Boat" to Scribner's for $300 in early March. Determined to work as a war correspondent, Crane signed on with William Randolph Hearst's New York Journal to cover the impending Greco-Turkish conflict. He brought along Taylor, who had sold the Hotel de Dream in order to follow him.

On March 20, they sailed first to England, where Crane was warmly received. They arrived in Athens in early April; between April 17 (when Turkey declared war on Greece) and April 22, Crane wrote his first published report of the war, "An Impression of the 'Concert' ". When he left for Epirus in the northwest, Taylor remained in Athens, where she became the Greek war's first woman war correspondent. She wrote under the pseudonym "Imogene Carter" for the New York Journal, a job that Crane had secured for her. They wrote frequently, traveling throughout the country separately and together. The first large battle that Crane witnessed was the Turks' assault on General Constantine Smolenski's Greek forces at Velestino. Crane wrote, "It is a great thing to survey the army of the enemy. Just where and how it takes hold upon the heart is difficult of description." During this battle, Crane encountered "a fat waddling puppy" that he immediately claimed, dubbing it "Velestino, the Journal dog". Greece and Turkey signed an armistice on May 20, ending the 30-day war; Crane and Taylor left Greece for England, taking two Greek brothers as servants and Velestino the dog with them.

Spanish–American War

After staying in Limpsfield, Surrey, for a few days, Crane and Taylor settled in Ravensbrook, a plain brick villa in Oxted. Referring to themselves as Mr. and Mrs. Crane, the couple lived openly in England, but Crane concealed the relationship from his friends and family in the United States. Admired in England, Crane thought himself attacked back home: "There seem so many of them in America who want to kill, bury and forget me purely out of unkindness and envy and—my unworthiness, if you choose", he wrote. Velestino the dog sickened and died soon after their arrival in England, on August 1. Crane, who had a great love for dogs, wrote an emotional letter to a friend an hour after the dog's death, stating that "for eleven days we fought death for him, thinking nothing of anything but his life." The Limpsfield-Oxted area was home to members of the socialist Fabian

Society and a magnet for writers such as Edmund Gosse, Ford Madox Ford and Edward Garnett. Crane also met the Polish-born novelist Joseph Conrad in October 1897, with whom he would have what Crane called a "warm and endless friendship".

Although Crane was confident among peers, strong negative reviews of the recently published The Third Violet were causing his literary reputation to dwindle. Reviewers were also highly critical of Crane's war letters, deeming them self-centered. Although The Red Badge of Courage had by this time gone through fourteen printings in the United States and six in England, Crane was running out of money. To survive financially, he worked at a feverish pitch, writing prolifically for both the English and the American markets. He wrote in quick succession stories such as The Monster, "The Bride Comes to Yellow Sky", "Death and the Child" and "The Blue Hotel". Crane began to attach price tags to his new works of fiction, hoping that "The Bride", for example, would fetch $175.

As 1897 ended, Crane's money crisis worsened. Amy Leslie, a reporter from Chicago and a former lover, sued him for $550. The New York Times reported that Leslie gave him $800 in November 1896 but that he'd repaid only a quarter of the sum. In February he was summoned to answer Leslie's claim. The claim was apparently settled out of court, because no record of adjudication exists. Meanwhile, Crane felt "heavy with troubles" and "chased to the wall" by expenses. He confided to his agent that he was $2,000 in debt but that he would "beat it" with more literary output.

Soon after the USS Maine exploded in Havana Harbor on February 15, 1898, under suspicious circumstances, Crane was offered a £60 advance by Blackwood's Magazine for articles "from the seat of war in the event of a war breaking out" between the United States and Spain. His health was failing, and it is believed that signs of his pulmonary tuberculosis, which he may have contracted in childhood, became apparent. With almost no money coming in from his finished stories, Crane accepted the assignment and left Oxted for New York. Taylor and the rest of the household stayed behind to fend off local creditors. Crane applied for a passport and left New York for Key West two days before Congress declared war. While the war idled, he interviewed people and produced occasional copy.

In early June, he observed the establishment of an American base in Cuba when Marines seized Guantánamo Bay. He went ashore with the Marines, planning "to gather impressions and write them as the spirit moved." Although he wrote honestly about his fear in battle, others observed his calmness and composure. He would later recall "this prolonged tragedy of the night" in the war tale "Marines Signaling Under Fire at Guantanamo". After showing a willingness to serve during fighting at Cuzco, Cuba, by carrying messages to company commanders, Crane was officially cited for his "material aid during the action".

He continued to report upon various battles and the worsening military conditions and praised Theodore Roosevelt's Rough Riders, despite past tensions with the Commissioner. In early July, Crane was sent to the United States for medical treatment for a high fever. He was diagnosed with yellow fever, then malaria. Upon arrival in Old Point Comfort, Virginia, he spent a few weeks resting in a hotel. Although Crane had filed more than twenty dispatches in the three months he had covered the war, the World's business manager believed that the paper had not received its money's worth and fired him. In retaliation, Crane signed with Hearst's New York Journal with the wish to return to Cuba. He traveled first to Puerto Rico and then to Havana. In September, rumors began to spread that Crane, who was working anonymously, had either been killed or disappeared. He sporadically sent out dispatches and stories; he wrote about the mood in Havana, the crowded city sidewalks, and other topics, but he was soon desperate for money again. Taylor, left alone in England, was also penniless. She became frantic with worry over her lover's whereabouts; they were not in direct communication until the end of the year. Crane left Havana and arrived in England on January 11, 1899.

Death

Rent on Ravensbrook had not been paid for a year. Upon returning to England, Crane secured a solicitor to act as guarantor for their debts, after which Crane and Taylor relocated to Brede Place. This manor in Sussex, which dated to the 14th century and had neither electricity nor indoor plumbing, was offered to them by friends at a modest rent. The relocation appeared to give hope to Crane, but his money problems continued. Deciding that he could no longer afford to write for American publications, he concentrated on publishing in English magazines.

Crane pushed himself to write feverishly during the first months at Brede; he told his publisher that he was "doing more work now than I have at any other period in my life". His health worsened, and by late 1899 he was asking friends about health resorts. The Monster and Other Stories was in production and War Is Kind, his second collection of poems, was published in the United States in May. None of his books after The Red Badge of Courage had sold well, and he bought a typewriter to spur output. Active Service, a novella based on Crane's correspondence experience, was published in October. The New York Times reviewer questioned "whether the author of 'Active Service' himself really sees anything remarkable in his newspapery hero."

In December, the couple held an elaborate Christmas party at Brede, attended by Conrad, Henry James, H. G. Wells and other friends; it lasted several days. On December 29 Crane suffered a severe pulmonary hemorrhage. In January 1900 he'd recovered sufficiently to work on a new novel, The O'Ruddy, completing 25 of the 33 chapters. Plans were made for him to travel as a correspondent to Gibraltar to write sketches from Saint Helena, the site of a Boer prison, but at the end of March and in early April he suffered two more hemorrhages. Taylor took over most of Crane's correspondence while he was ill, writing to friends for monetary aid. The couple planned to travel on the continent, but Conrad, upon visiting Crane for the last time, remarked that his friend's "wasted face was enough to tell me that it was the most forlorn of all hopes."

On May 28, the couple arrived at Badenweiler, Germany, a health spa on the edge of the Black Forest. Despite his weakened condition, Crane continued to dictate fragmentary episodes for the completion of The O'Ruddy. He died on June 5, 1900, at the age of 28. In his will he left everything to Taylor, who took his body to New Jersey for burial. Crane was interred in Evergreen Cemetery in what is now Hillside, New Jersey.

Fiction and poetry

Style and technique

Stephen Crane's fiction is typically categorized as representative of Naturalism, American realism, Impressionism or a mixture of the three. Critic Sergio Perosa, for example, wrote in his essay, "Stephen Crane fra naturalismo e impressionismo," that the work presents a "symbiosis" of Naturalistic ideals and Impressionistic methods. When asked whether or not he would write an autobiography in 1896, Crane responded that he "dare not say that I am honest. I merely say that I am as nearly honest as a weak mental machinery will allow." Similarities between the stylistic techniques in Crane's writing and Impressionist painting—including the use of color and chiaroscuro—are often cited to support the theory that Crane was not only an Impressionist but also influenced by the movement. H. G. Wells remarked upon "the great influence of the studio" on Crane's work, quoting a passage from The Red Badge of Courage as an example: "At nightfall the column broke into regimental pieces, and the fragments went into the fields to camp. Tents sprang up like strange plants. Camp fires, like red, peculiar blossoms, dotted the night.... From this little distance the many fires, with the black forms of men passing to and fro before the crimson rays, made weird and satanic effects." Although no direct evidence exists that Crane formulated a precise theory of his craft, he vehemently rejected sentimentality, asserting that "a story should be logical in its action and faithful to character. Truth to life itself was the only test, the greatest artists were the simplest, and simple because they were true."

Poet and biographer John Berryman suggested that there were three basic variations, or "norms", of Crane's narrative style. The first, being "flexible, swift, abrupt and nervous", is best exemplified in The Red Badge of Courage, while the second ("supple majesty") is believed to relate to "The Open Boat", and the third ("much more closed, circumstantial and 'normal' in feeling and syntax") to later works such as The Monster. Crane's work, however, cannot be determined by style solely on chronology. Not only does his fiction not take place in any particular region with similar characters, but it varies from serious in tone to reportorial writing and light fiction. Crane's writing, both fiction and nonfiction, is consistently driven by immediacy and is at once concentrated, vivid and intense. The novels and short stories contain poetic characteristics such as shorthand prose, suggestibility, shifts in perspective and ellipses between and within sentences. Similarly, omission plays a large part in Crane's work; the names of his protagonists are not commonly used and sometimes they are not named at all.

Crane was often criticized by early reviewers for his frequent incorporation of everyday speech into dialogue, mimicking the regional accents of his characters with colloquial stylization. This is apparent in his first novel, in which Crane ignored the romantic, sentimental approach of slum fiction; he instead concentrated on the cruelty and sordid aspects of poverty, expressed by the brashness of the Bowery's crude dialect and profanity, which he used lavishly. The distinct dialect of his Bowery characters is apparent at the beginning of the text; the title character admonishes her brother saying: "Yeh knows it puts mudder out when yes comes home half dead, an' it's like we'll all get a poundin'."

Major themes

Crane's work is often thematically driven by Naturalistic and Realistic concerns, including ideals versus realities, spiritual crises and fear. These themes are particularly evident in Crane's first three novels, Maggie: A Girl of the Streets, The Red Badge of Courage and George's Mother. The three main characters search for a way to make their dreams come true, but ultimately suffer from crises of identity. Crane was fascinated by war and death, as well as fire, disfigurement, fear and courage, all of which inspired him to write many works based on these concepts. In The Red Badge of Courage, the main character both longs for the heroics of battle but ultimately fears it, demonstrating the dichotomy of courage and cowardice. He experiences the threat of death, misery and a loss of self.

Extreme isolation from society and community is also apparent in Crane's work. During the most intense battle scenes in The Red Badge of Courage, for example, the story's focus is mainly "on the inner responses of

262

a self unaware of others". In "The Open Boat", "An Experiment in Misery" and other stories, Crane uses light, motion and color to express degrees of epistemological uncertainty. Similar to other Naturalistic writers, Crane scrutinizes the position of man, who has been isolated not only from society, but also from God and nature. "The Open Boat", for example, distances itself from Romantic optimism and affirmation of man's place in the world by concentrating on the characters' isolation.

While he lived, Stephen Crane was denominated by critical readers a realist, a naturalist, an impressionist, symbolist, Symboliste, expressionist and ironist; his posthumous life was enriched by critics who read him as nihilistic, existentialist, a neo-Romantic, a sentimentalist, protomodernist, pointilliste, visionist, imagist and, by his most recent biographer, a "bleak naturalist." At midcentury he was a "predisciple of the New Criticism"; by its end he was "a proto-deconstructionist anti-artist hero" who had "leapfrogged modernism, landing on postmodernist ground." Or, as Sergio Perosa wrote in 1964, "The critic wanders in a labyrinth of possibilities, which every new turn taken by Crane's fiction seems to explode or deny."

One undeniable fact about Crane's work, as Anthony Splendora noted in 2015, is that Death haunts it; like a threatening eclipse it overshadows his best efforts, each of which features the signal demise of a main character. Allegorically, "The Blue Hotel," at the pinnacle of the short story form, may even be an autothanatography, the author's intentional exteriorization or objectification, in this case for the purpose of purgation, of his own impending death. Crane's "Swede" in that story can be taken, following current psychoanalytical theory, as a surrogative, sacrificial victim, ritually to be purged.

Transcending this "dark circumstance of composition," Crane had a particular telos and impetus for his creation: beyond the tautologies that all art is alterity and to some formal extent mimesis, Crane sought and obviously found "a form of catharsis" in writing. This view accounts for his uniqueness, especially as operative through his notorious "disgust" with his family's religion, their "vacuous, futile psalm-singing". His favorite book, for example, was Mark Twain's Life on the Mississippi, in which God is mentioned only twice—once as irony and once as "a swindle." Not only did Crane call out God specifically with the lines "Well then I hate thee / righteous image" in "The Black Riders" (1895), but even his most hopeful tropes, such as the "comradeship" of his "Open Boat" survivors, make no mention of deity, specifying only "indifferent nature." His antitheism is most evident in his characterization of the human race as "lice clinging to a space-lost bulb," a climax-nearing speech in "The Blue Hotel," Ch. VI. It is possible that Crane utilized religion's formal psychic space, now suddenly available resulting from the recent "Death of God", as a milieu for his compensative art.

Novels

Beginning with the publication of Maggie: A Girl of the Streets in 1893, Crane was recognized by critics mainly as a novelist. Maggie was initially rejected by numerous publishers because of its atypical and true-to-life depictions of class warfare, which clashed with the sentimental tales of that time. Rather than focusing on the very rich or middle class, the novel's characters are lower-class denizens of New York's Bowery. The main character, Maggie, descends into prostitution after being led astray by her lover. Although the novel's plot is simple, its dramatic mood, quick pace and portrayal of Bowery life have made it memorable. Maggie is not merely an account of slum life, but also represents eternal symbols. In his first draft, Crane did not give his characters proper names. Instead, they were identified by epithets: Maggie, for example, was the girl who "blossomed in a mud-puddle" and Pete, her seducer, was a "knight". The novel is dominated by bitter irony and anger, as well as destructive morality and treacherous sentiment. Critics would later call the novel "the first dark flower of American Naturalism" for its distinctive elements of naturalistic fiction.

Written thirty years after the end of the Civil War and before Crane had any experience of battle, The Red Badge of Courage was innovative stylistically as well as psychologically. Often described as a war novel, it focuses less on battle and more on the main character's psyche and his reactions and responses in war. It is believed that Crane based the fictional battle in the novel on that of Chancellorsville; he may also have interviewed veterans of the 124th New York Volunteer Infantry Regiment, commonly known as the Orange Blossoms, in Port Jervis, New York. Told in a third-person limited point of view, it reflects the private experience of Henry Fleming, a young soldier who flees from combat. The Red Badge of Courage is notable in its vivid descriptions and well-cadenced prose, both of which help create suspense within the story. Similarly, by substituting epithets for characters' names ("the youth", "the tattered soldier"), Crane injects an allegorical quality into his work, making his characters point to a specific characteristic of man. Like Crane's first novel, The Red Badge of Courage has a deeply ironic tone which increases in severity as the novel progresses. The title of the work is ironic; Henry wishes "that he, too, had a wound, a red badge of courage", echoing a wish to have been wounded in battle. The wound he does receive (from the rifle butt of a fleeing Union soldier) is not a badge of courage but a badge of shame.

The novel expresses a strong connection between humankind and nature, a frequent and prominent concern in Crane's fiction and poetry throughout his career. Whereas contemporary writers (Ralph Waldo Emerson, Nathaniel Hawthorne, Henry David Thoreau) focused on a sympathetic bond on the two elements, Crane wrote from the perspective that human consciousness distanced humans from nature. In The Red Badge of Courage, this distance is paired with a great number of references to animals, and men with animalistic characteristics: people "howl", "squawk", "growl", or "snarl".

Since the resurgence of Crane's popularity in the 1920s, The Red Badge of Courage has been deemed a major American text. The novel has been anthologized numerous times, including in the 1942 collection Men at War: The Best War Stories of All Time, edited by Ernest Hemingway. In the introduction, Hemingway wrote that the novel "is one of the finest books of our literature, and I include it entire because it is all as much of a piece as a great poem is."

Crane's later novels have not received as much critical praise. After the success of The Red Badge of Courage, Crane wrote another tale set in the Bowery. George's Mother is less allegorical and more personal than his two previous novels, and it focuses on the conflict between a church-going, temperance-adhering woman (thought to be based on Crane's mother) and her single remaining offspring, who is a naive dreamer. Critical response to the novel was mixed. The Third Violet, a romance that he wrote quickly after publishing The Red Badge of Courage, is typically considered as Crane's attempt to appeal to popular audiences. Crane considered it a "quiet little story." Although it contained autobiographical details, the characters have been deemed inauthentic and stereotypical. Crane's second to last novel, Active Service, revolves around the Greco-Turkish War of 1897, with which the author was familiar. Although noted for its satirical take on the melodramatic and highly passionate works that were popular of the nineteenth century, the novel was not successful. It is generally accepted by critics that Crane's work suffered at this point due to the speed which he wrote in order to meet his high expenses. His last novel, a suspenseful and picaresque work entitled The O'Ruddy, was finished posthumously by Robert Barr and published in 1903.

Short fiction

Crane wrote many different types of fictional pieces while indiscriminately applying to them terms such as "story", "tale" and "sketch". For this reason, critics have found clear-cut classification of Crane's work problematic. While "The Open Boat" and "The Bride Comes to Yellow Sky" are often considered short stories, others are variously identified.

In an 1896 interview with Herbert P. Williams, a reporter for the Boston Herald, Crane said that he did "not find that short stories are utterly different in character from other fiction. It seems to me that short stories are the easiest things we write." During his brief literary career, he wrote more than a hundred short stories and fictional sketches. Crane's early fiction was based in camping expeditions in his teen years; these stories eventually became known as The Sullivan County Tales and Sketches. He considered these "sketches", which are mostly humorous and not of the same caliber of work as his later fiction, to be "articles of many kinds," in that they are part fiction and part journalism.

The subject matter for his stories varied extensively. His early New York City sketches and Bowery tales accurately described the results of industrialization, immigration and the growth of cities and their slums. His collection of six short stories, The Little Regiment, covered familiar ground with the American Civil War, a subject for which he became famous with The Red Badge of Courage. Although similar to Crane's noted novel, The Little Regiment was believed to lack vigor and originality. Realizing the limitations of these tales, Crane wrote: "I have invented the sum of my invention with regard to war and this story keeps me in internal despair."

The Open Boat and Other Tales of Adventure (1898) contains thirteen short stories that deal with three periods in Crane's life: his Asbury Park boyhood, his trip to the West and Mexico in 1895, and his Cuban adventure in 1897. This collection was well received and included several of his most critically successful works. His 1899 collection, The Monster and Other Stories, was similarly well received.

Two posthumously published collections were not as successful. In August 1900 The Whilomville Stories were published, a collection of thirteen stories that Crane wrote during the last year of his life. The work deals almost exclusively with boyhood, and the stories are drawn from events occurring in Port Jervis, where Crane lived from the age of six to eleven. Focusing on small-town America, the stories tend toward sentimentality, but remain perceptive of the lives of children. Wounds in the Rain, published in September 1900, contains fictional tales based on Crane's reports for the World and the Journal during the Spanish–American War. These stories, which Crane wrote while desperately ill, include "The Price of the Harness" and "The Lone Charge of William B. Perkins" and are dramatic, ironic and sometimes humorous.

Despite Crane's prolific output, only four stories--"The Open Boat", "The Blue Hotel", "The Bride Comes to Yellow Sky", and The Monster— have received extensive attention from scholars. H. G. Wells considered "The Open Boat" to be "beyond all question, the crown of all his work", and it is one of the most frequently discussed of Crane's works.

Poetry

Many red devils ran from my heart

And out upon the page.

They were so tiny

The pen could mash them.

And many struggled in the ink.

It was strange

To write in this red muck

Of things from my heart.

— Stephen Crane

Crane's poems, which he preferred to call "lines", are typically not given as much scholarly attention as his fiction; no anthology contained Crane's verse until 1926. Although it is not certain when Crane began to write poetry seriously, he once said that his overall poetic aim was "to give my ideas of life as a whole, so far as I know it". The poetic style used in both of his books of poetry, The Black Riders and Other Lines and War is Kind, was unconventional for the time in that it was written in free verse without rhyme, meter, or even titles for individual works. They are typically short in length; although several poems, such as "Do not weep, maiden, for war is kind", use stanzas and refrains, most do not. Crane also differed from his peers and poets of later generations in that his work contains allegory, dialectic and narrative situations.

Critic Ruth Miller claimed that Crane wrote "an intellectual poetry rather than a poetry that evokes feeling, a poetry that stimulates the mind rather than arouses the heart". In the most complexly organized poems, the significance of the states of mind or feelings is ambiguous, but Crane's poems tend to affirm certain elemental attitudes, beliefs, opinions and stances toward God, man and the universe. The Black Riders in particular is essentially a dramatic concept and the poems provide continuity within the dramatic structure. There is also a dramatic interplay in which there is frequently a major voice reporting an incident seen ("In the desert / I saw a creature, naked, bestial") or experienced ("A learned man came to me once"). The second voice or additional voices represent a point of view which is revealed to be inferior; when these clash, a dominant attitude emerges.

Legacy

In four years, Crane published five novels, two volumes of poetry, three short story collections, two books of war stories, and numerous works of short fiction and reporting. Today he is mainly remembered for The Red Badge of Courage, which is regarded as an American classic. The novel has been adapted several times for the screen, including John Huston's 1951 version. By the time of his death, Crane had become one of the best known writers of his generation. His eccentric lifestyle, frequent newspaper reporting, association with other famous authors, and expatriate status made him somewhat of an international celebrity. Although most stories about his life tended toward the romantic, rumors about his alleged drug use and alcoholism persisted long after his death.

By the early 1920s, Crane and his work were nearly forgotten. It was not until Thomas Beer published his biography in 1923, which was followed by editor Wilson Follett's The Work of Stephen Crane (1925–1927), that Crane's writing came to the attention of a scholarly audience. Crane's reputation was then enhanced by faithful support from writer friends such as Joseph Conrad, H. G. Wells and Ford Madox Ford, all of whom either published recollections or commented upon their time with Crane. John Berryman's 1950 biography of Crane further established him as an important American author. Since 1951 there has been a steady outpouring of articles, monographs and reprints in Crane scholarship.

Today, Crane is considered one of the most innovative writers of the 1890s. His peers, including Conrad and James, as well as later writers such as Robert Frost, Ezra Pound and Willa Cather, hailed Crane as one of the finest creative spirits of his time. His work was described by Wells as "the first expression of the opening mind of a new period, or, at least, the early emphatic phase of a new initiative." Wells said that "beyond dispute", Crane was "the best writer of our generation, and his untimely death was an irreparable loss to our literature." Conrad wrote that Crane was an "artist" and "a seer with a gift for rendering the significant on the surface of things and with an incomparable insight into primitive emotions". Crane's work has proved inspirational for future writers; not only have scholars drawn similarities between Hemingway's A Farewell to Arms and The Red Badge of Courage, but Crane's fiction is thought to have been an important inspiration for Hemingway and his fellow Modernists. In 1936, Hemingway wrote in The Green Hills of Africa that "The good writers are Henry James, Stephen Crane, and Mark Twain. That's not the order they're good in. There is no order for good writers." Crane's poetry is thought to have been a precursor to the Imagist movement, and his short fiction has also influenced American literature. "The Open Boat", "The Blue Hotel", The Monster and "The Bride Comes to Yellow Sky" are generally considered by critics to be examples of Crane's best work.

Several institutions and places have endeavored to keep Crane's legacy alive. Badenweiler and the house where he died became something of a tourist attraction for its fleeting association with the American author; Alexander Woollcott attested to the fact that, long after Crane's death, tourists would be directed to the room where he died. Columbia University Rare Book and Manuscript Library has a collection of Crane and Taylor's personal correspondence dating from 1895 to 1908. Near his brother Edmund's Sullivan County home in New York, where Crane stayed for a short time, a pond is named after him. The Stephen Crane House in Asbury Park, New Jersey, where the author lived with his siblings for nine years, is operated as a museum dedicated to his life and work. Syracuse University has an annual Stephen Crane Lecture Series which is sponsored by the Dikaia Foundation.

Columbia University purchased much of the Stephen Crane materials held by Cora Crane at her death. The Crane Collection is one of the largest in the nation of his materials. Columbia University had an exhibit: 'The Tall Swift Shadow of a Ship at Night': Stephen and Cora Crane, November 2, 1995 through February 16, 1996, about the lives of the couple, featuring letters and other documents and memorabilia. (Source : Wikipedia)

NOTABLE WORKS

NOVELS

Maggie: A Girl of the Streets, 1893.

The Red Badge of Courage, 1895.

George's Mother, 1896.

The Third Violet, 1897.

Active Service, 1899.

Crane, Stephen and Robert Barr. The O'Ruddy, 1903.

The Black Riders and Other Lines, 1895.

The Open Boat and Other Tales of Adventure, 1898

War is Kind, 1899

The Monster and Other Stories, 1899

Wounds in the Rain, 1900

Great Battles of the World, 1901

The O'Ruddy, 1903

SHORT STORY COLLECTIONS

The Little Regiment and Other Episodes from the American Civil War, 1896.

The Open Boat and Other Tales of Adventure, 1898.

The Monster and Other Stories, 1899.

Whilomville Stories, 1900.

Wounds in the Rain: War Stories, 1900.

Great Battles of the World, 1901.

The Monster,1901.

Last Words, 1902.

POETRY COLLECTIONS

The Black Riders and Other Lines, 1895.

War is Kind, 1899.

UNFINISHED WORKS

Sources report that following an encounter with a male prostitute in the spring of 1894, Crane began a novel on the subject entitled Flowers of Asphalt. He reportedly abandoned the project and the manuscript has never been recovered.

CPSIA information can be obtained
at www.ICGtesting.com
Printed in the USA
LVHW052053261020
669863LV00017B/312